'Not so fast, M...

'How dare you put h... before I summon serv...

'I would not advise t... mistress. The fuss would alert your father and I would be loth to explain to him the reason for my concern that you are leaving the house so late.'

Isabel spluttered in her rising anger against Adam. 'Do you dare suggest that I go to meet some paramour? How dare you impugn my honour, sir?'

Dear Reader

Two of your favourite authors this month! After her 'faction', Paula Marshall has returned to the Regency period with MY LADY LOVE. Shad is horrendously insulting to Nell, and from then on nothing goes according to plan! Joanna Makepeace makes a very welcome reappearance with RELUCTANT REBEL, when all Isabel wants to do is settle down, but Adam still supports the deposed Plantagenets — and that results in adventures she could do without! Absorbing books, both — do enjoy them!

The Editor

Joanna Makepeace taught as head of English in a comprehensive, before leaving full-time work to write. She lives in Leicester with her mother and Jack Russell terrier called Dickon, and has written over thirty books under different pseudonyms. She loves the old romantic historical films, which she finds more exciting and relaxing than the newer ones.

Recent titles by the same author:

BATTLEFIELD OF HEARTS
THE SPANISH PRIZE

RELUCTANT REBEL

Joanna Makepeace

CHAPTER ONE

ISABEL felt the intense heat from the bread ovens as she paused in the entrance to the kitchen. Ralf Padgett, their cook, was wielding his long wooden paddle skilfully as he drew out the round, crusty loaves. Isabel revelled in the hot yeasty smell and reached, childlike, to break off a portion of one of them.

'Now, Mistress Isabel, you know you'll burn your fingers,' the old man warned, smiling.

He crossed to the long, scrubbed chopping table, cut off a corner from one of the cooling manchet loaves, and brought it to her, pushing nearer the pot of clear honey.

Isabel picked up a knife, smeared the delectable golden substance over the new bread, and chewed contentedly.

It was nearly Easter. Through the open door behind her the watery sun was streaming into the kitchen and causing the floury dust motes to dance and gleam in its path. Winter had been long and hard and now it seemed that the longed-for relief of this spring of 1486 was here at last.

The old cook watched her affectionately. He had served her father, Sir Edwin Hatfield, for many years before she was born. Now she must be almost seventeen, he mused, and as lovely a young woman as she had been a sprightly, mischievous and pretty child. He sighed. But for the terrible events on Redmoor, near Bosworth, Mistress Isabel would have been wed by now and gone from the manor. Young Sir John Heyward had perished at that battle fighting for his king. Sir Edwin had returned to the manor with the dread news, himself suffering the result of a pike wound which had sliced through his vambrace and torn into the flesh of his upper arm. The wound had not been grievous, but Sir Edwin had, ever since, appeared to feel the effect of it.

Constantly he sat by the smoky fire in the solar, rubbing continuously at the injured limb.

Isabel perched, boyishly, on the corner of the chopping table, swinging her legs. She was without hennin or veil this morning and her bright auburn hair streamed unrestrained to her waist. Her eyes, golden hazel, were staring dreamily out through the door to the courtyard and stables facing, and the stone mounting block beyond. Her gown of finely woven brown wool clung to her youthful curves. Ralf mused that the gown was sore rubbed and would soon be far too tight for her budding womanliness, but still it suited her vivid colouring well.

As if aware of the old man's scrutiny she turned her golden brown eyes full on him and there was no mistaking that direct stare down the small, straight nose with the aristocratic flaring nostrils inherited from her lovely dead mother, Mistress Alice, and the slight petulant curl of the finely sculptured lips. Since the disaster at Redmoor, Mistress Isabel had been the true mistress of this manor and none was in doubt of it.

'That was lovely, Ralf,' she said as she rose in one graceful, fluid movement, 'but I must go and chivvy the house servants. We must have new rushes strewn for the holy season.'

'I shall need fresh spices for the Easter feasting, Mistress Isabel,' Ralf reminded her. 'We have had little fresh meat this winter and the salted flesh has taken its toll of my supplies.'

Isabel nodded as she turned to leave him. She needed no reminding that her father had spent the hunting season in his great chair by the fire when he could have been providing them all with fresh meat — boar or even hare or rabbit — as a welcome change from the monotony of salted meat and fish from the casks in the undercroft.

She paused in the doorway, looking beyond the low slate roof of the stable to the gentle sloping hills of the pasture and the beginning of the tall woods in the distance. Swithland was so beautiful, and richly endowed, too, with its fertile soil and slate quarries. Hatfield Manor lay some three miles from the village, square in the gentle heartland of England's Midlands, those Midlands which had so recently endured the depredations of Henry Tudor's victorious armies. Now the conquering Welshman was crowned England's King as Henry VII and the news had nigh broken her father's heart. Isabel bit her lip thoughtfully as she considered why it had not done the same for her. She had known John Heyward since childhood. They had been betrothed when she had been scarcely out of her cradle and she had liked him well, had expected to rule over the neighbouring manor. Her father had ridden off with John at his side so confidently. How could King Richard, experienced in warfare both here in England and on the Scottish Borders, and the realm's rightful king, with all the might of the royal army behind him, possibly be defeated by this upstart Welshman whose claim, even to the Lancastrian lineage, was dubious in the extreme? Yet it had happened. Those two great Stanley lords, Thomas and William, had treacherously turned on their lord on the battlefield, and great Northumberland had remained aloof from the battle so the standard of the White Boar had fallen and King Richard, despite that gallant charge down Ambien hill, slain and ignominiously buried within the Grey friary in nearby Leicester Town.

First her father had returned, wounded and dispirited, then came the news of John's death, then, in only a few short weeks, Isabel's lovely mother had died of the sweating sickness brought to the county by the Tudor's French mercenaries — the sweepings of the brothels and jails, her father had said bitterly. Sir Edwin had failed to recover from this last terrible loss. His hurts had healed, but his spirit had not. He had remained unmoved when he'd heard of the crippling fine levied on the manor by the new monarch, not even commenting on the seizure of John's lands by the Crown and the gift of them to Sir Gilbert Tarvin, who had accompanied Henry Tudor from the Welsh Marches to his jubilant victory. Isabel's heart fluttered a little as she thought of James Tarvin, Sir Gilbert's son, who also had fought at Redmoor. She could not bring herself to hate James, who was brown-haired and big and comely and whom she saw often, whenever she could, without the knowledge of her father.

She hastened up to her chamber, fumbling with the keys on her girdle. It still seemed strange to her that she, Isabel, was wearing those keys. It should have been Alice Hatfield who had the ordering of this house. Her mother might well have brought her father from this strange apathy which had fallen upon him since Redmoor. Yet it had been left to Isabel alone to deal with the autumn slaughter and salting down of the meat. Now the doling out of the rare spices was in her hands, another tacit reminder that her dear mother had gone forever.

Isabel sighed as she undid the padlock which held fast the carved chest beneath her window, threw back the lid, and lifted out the sandalwood box. She opened the exquisitely carved lid and drew in the pungent scents of ginger, cinnamon and nutmeg. Their supplies were getting low. She must see to it that they were replenished. She would ask her father if he would ride into Leicester to the market or allow her to go in his place.

Bess Swinton put her tousled head round the door.

'Is anything missing, Mistress Isabel?' she asked anxiously.

'No, Bess, I'm just checking on the spices.'

Bess always looked as if she had been pulled through a hedge backwards, but she was willing enough and even-tempered. Her mother's maid had left the manor to return to Isabel's maternal grandmother's household and Bess had been promoted to her duties as lady's maid. Her cheerful, ruddy cheeks were grease-streaked and her hair straggled free from her linen coif. Isabel said briskly, 'Now, Bess, I'm going to the church, so you can help me change now you're here.'

Since they had received no visitors over the last months she had taken to wearing her old gowns about the house, but she needed to be decently clad in mourning black when she rode into the village.

Ruefully she noted that this gown in fine wool trimmed with fur fitted her better than anything else she possessed and was probably the most fashionable too. She surveyed herself critically in her mother's glass mirror while Bess turned to find her winter cloak. It was just as well the gown became her. She flushed darkly. It was likely James Tarvin would be in the village as she emerged from church. He had been for the last few days and it had tacitly been understood between them that each would visit the village when the other planned to be there. Her brows drew together in a doubtful frown. Was it a sin that she gave the excuse of praying by her mother's tomb in order to leave the manor? Her father took little note of what she did, but she knew, only too well, that his complacence would erupt into furious anger if he were to discover her interest in their neighbour's son. Bess would not accompany her. She could not be trusted to hold her tongue as Wat Jessop, their groom, would do.

'Go and ask Wat to saddle my palfrey, Bess.'

Bess did not argue. Isabel could hear her racing down the stair and smiled a little wryly. She took her own way downstairs at a more decorous pace and was surprised to hear her father's voice from the hall.

'Isabel, is that you, my lass?'

She went at once to his chair by the fire.

'Yes, Father.'

He was a big man, sprawled inelegantly, his doublet open, his shirt unlaced. Times past he would have taken great pains with his appearance; now he cared nothing about that. Only Isabel's watchfulness made sure there were no food stains on his linen. He was drinking malmsey and put the cup down to look at her curiously.

'You are going out?'

'Yes, Father, to church, to burn a candle for Mother.'

His dark eyes grew misty and he instantly looked away from her into the depths of the fire.

'Aye, lass, do that, and burn one for me too.'

She hesitated.

'Why don't you come with me, Father? It's weeks

since you went to mass and even longer than that since you inspected the manor desmesne.'

He nodded absently. 'Aye, I know I've been remiss lately. Thank the Virgin we have a good steward, aye, and I'm blessed with a good daughter. You have been a tower of strength to me lately, my lass. I won't go today. My arm pains me more when the wind's still chill. Tell Father John I'll ride over soon to give instructions for the memorial brass. Ask him what news he has of affairs about the shire.'

It was her father's usual request. Though he appeared to have little interest in matters which should most concern him he never tired of enquiring what news there was of noted men in the shire, particularly those who had fought at his side at Redmoor. Most had returned to their manors chastened, anxious to lie low, unwilling to have the eyes of the new King's followers turned towards them and their doings. One or two had fled the country and some, she knew, kept in traitorous communication with the King's enemies, the most notable among them being the late King's sister, Margaret, dowager Duchess of Burgundy. That their vicar, Father John, was an admirer of the late King Isabel knew well. Somehow the wily priest got wind of affairs abroad and was more than willing to keep his old comrade in touch with events.

Isabel kissed her father and hid her sigh of exasperation. Much better for Sir Edwin to put behind him his old life and concentrate on rebuilding his health and his fortunes.

Wat Jessop had led her palfrey to the mounting block by the time she emerged from the house. She blew gently into the mare's nostrils and patted her shiny nose, then Wat lifted her expertly into the saddle. He was a tall, spare, dour man, but Isabel knew he had great affection for her. Wat had taught her to ride and comforted her through the minor spills and injuries she'd suffered learning. He knew well enough what happened in the village and could be trusted to keep his own counsel.

The sun was shining quite brightly by the time they rode into the village, and the church interior seemed dim by comparison. Isabel knelt by her mother's tomb in the chancel while Wat waited watchfully at the rear near the bell tower. She rose at last and went to the small Lady chapel to light the candles she had promised. Father John came briskly into the church and to her side.

'Greetings, my daughter,' he said gravely. 'How is your father this fine day? It is some time since I was able to speak with him. If I didn't understand the source of his great grief I would feel it necessary to send a sharp rebuke for his want of piety.' His smile softened the sternness of his words and Isabel smiled back in answer.

'I think his general health is improving, Father. I tried to persuade him to come with me today, but the wind is still cold and his wound aches badly in such conditions. Now Easter is near I'm sure he will soon be about the village and manor again.'

'I see I have no need to ask after your health, Isabel. In spite of your mourning, you look radiant this morning.'

Isabel felt herself flushing hotly. Father John had such sharp eyes. Had he guessed at the reason for her repeated visits to the village recently?

She walked with him towards the west door. 'I cannot help but be cheered by the nearness of the Holy Season. It does teach us to hope,' she said softly.

He nodded and glanced back to the as yet unadorned tomb.

'Be comforted, Isabel. Your father will get over his loss. It will take time, but release will come from his suffering.'

His bushy eyebrows were drawn together in concentration and she waited, knowing instinctively that he had something on his mind which he was not sure if he should impart to her. At last he turned in the doorway and took both her hands in his.

'Tell your father some close friends are said to be free

of church restraints at last and may be in touch with
him. Urge him to take heart.'

Isabel was by no means sure that she wished to carry
such news. Certainly it would bring a flush of colour to
her father's sallow cheeks, but the hope Father John
hinted at did not make for her peace of mind. Obviously
rebels in the late King's cause had decided to take the
dangerous decision to leave sanctuary, and that could
only be because they were plotting further moves in the
game to overthrow King Henry. Isabel would be grateful
for anything which would rouse her father from his
apathy, but not if it threatened his safety.

She took her leave of the priest, turning at the lich-
gate to see his tall, wiry figure make for the priest's
house. Wat held her mare's reins with those of his own
mount when she professed a desire to walk for a while
in the small village street.

As they neared the one small inn the village boasted
Isabel was hailed pleasantly by the young man taking a
jack of ale outside.

'Good morrow, Mistress Hatfield. How good it is to
ride out on such a fine spring day.'

He slammed down the leather ale jack on to the rough
bench and came towards her, his hat doffed in greeting.

Isabel flushed rosily and allowed him to bow over her
slender fingers. As ever, she was charmed by the slight
Welsh intonation of his voice.

'Master Tarvin, it is indeed. I have been in the church
but the sun is shining so well I. . . I thought I would
linger awhile before riding home.'

'Will you come inside with me and take a cup of
spiced wine?'

'I think not, sir, though the offer was kindly meant. I
should not be gone from the manor for too long.'

He was a half a head taller than her, well made, a
pleasant-featured, round-faced young man of twenty or
so, with a mop of curling brown hair that was touched
now with gold in the sunlight. His doublet of fine-spun
green wool was trimmed with marten fur, as was his
close-fitting hat of the same colour. She could not help

but notice that his limbs were sturdy but shapely in the brown hose. He was wearing no cloak despite the wind's chill edge and she thought he had most probably left the garment inside the inn where he had hoped to lure her. He was still holding her hand, but she did not try too hard to withdraw from the gentle but intimate clasp.

'Back to your duties as chatelaine. Your father expects too much of one so young. There should be time for you to sit back at your embroidery or ride out more often, Mistress Hatfield,' he chided.

Instantly her spine stiffened at the implied criticism of her father.

'There is much to do at Hatfield, Master Tarvin,' she retorted, a trifle sharply. 'There are fewer hands to do the work since the sickness of the autumn and — the battle from which several of our men did not return.'

His brows drew together in a frown of concern that he had angered her.

'I meant no harm, Mistress Isabel. I merely wish to see you more often.' The last words were uttered more softly so that Wat was unable to hear them, and the pressure on her gloved hand increased.

She withdrew her fingers from his hold gently but firmly, but her expression showed she was not still annoyed with him.

'I imagine we shall see one another at the Easter mass,' she said quietly.

He shrugged wryly. 'Indeed, but I had no wish to share my good fortune with most of the villagers.'

Her lips broke into a smile again. 'With that you will have to be content for the moment, sir.'

'Have you spoken to your father of —— ' he hesitated meaningly ' — of my interest in you?'

'No.' Her reply was very soft and he was forced to bend lower to try to read her expression again.

'He does not still hold a grudge against my family, surely?'

'Master Tarvin, it is not a year since the last occupant of your house was killed. My father cannot forget how your family came by the land.'

'He cannot hold me responsible for that.'

She shook her head. 'Reason is not uppermost in the mind when the heart grieves.'

He looked troubled again. 'And do you still grieve for your betrothed?'

He had never asked her outright before and she turned from him, biting her nether lip.

'I was deeply fond of John Heyward. We had known each other since we were babies and expected to wed for almost that length of time. Naturally I cannot put the sorrow of his loss entirely to the back of my mind, but. . .' She hesitated.

'You were not in love with him?' he pressed determinedly.

'I. . . I do not know. I'm sure I would have come to love him — as you mean — in time, but. . .' She shrugged expressively again.

His slight sigh showed her that he was satisfied with her reply, and his brown eyes grew warm again.

'Then I must wait patiently until our fathers meet and come to terms with their circumstances. Mistress Isabel, you must know by now that my feelings for you go deep.'

'You have known me for so short a time, James.' She spoke his name wonderingly. It was the first time she had done so. Always she had kept the formality between them. Now, gazing into the depths of his adoring brown eyes, she was forced to acknowledge her own very real attraction to this man.

'I know you to be honest and gentle, and am struck by your very great beauty. Isabel, you must let me put my feelings into words at last. I have spoken to my own father —'

'You should not have done that,' she interrupted, flustered. 'I have given you no leave to believe —'

'I demand nothing, yet I pray and hope for — everything.'

His tone was truly intimate now and she turned a little huntedly in case they had been overheard by some passing villager.

'We must — see,' she said doubtfully.

'My father is anxious to see you. He will make no objections if. . .'

She was truly alarmed now. Things were going altogether too fast. It had been pleasant to bask in this young man's admiration, but there had never been any intention to allow him to believe that she would receive his suit. There could not be. Her father would never be brought to give his consent.

She turned anxiously to search for Wat, give him instruction to bring up her mare.

It was then that the unexpected happened. A man emerged suddenly from the door of the inn. He was muffled in a great frieze cloak, his face shielded by the wide brim of a shapeless, old felt hat. His head was lowered to a heavy leather pack he was manhandling on to the step, so that he did not see the two by the door until he had cannoned into James Tarvin's back. The impetus thrust James forward so that he stumbled and fell sprawling at Isabel's feet. She gave a startled cry.

James rose and, with a roar of fury, turned on the pedlar, who uttered a murmur of apology and made to come towards James and help him to stand. James felt himself humiliated and was in no conciliatory mood. He let out an oath and aimed a vicious blow at the man's chin. Taken by surprise, the pedlar fell backwards on to the step and the pack tumbled into the dirt of the road and disgorged its motley content of ribbons, laces, pins and tawdry pieces of cheap jewellery.

'God's teeth, you wandering scum,' James roared, 'I'll teach you to be more careful and keep a wide berth of your betters.' To Isabel's utter astonishment he drew his sword on the helpless man.

'James,' she called sharply, 'what are you doing? The poor fellow meant no harm.' She was mortally afraid that he was going to murder the pedlar right there before her eyes. Never had she seen a man in such a temper and for so paltry a cause.

James ignored her protest as if he had not heard her and, as the pedlar attempted to rise, he began to belabour the man's bowed shoulders with the flat of his blade.

Isabel rushed up to the two and tried to catch James's arm as it rose and fell, dealing out punishment without hint of tiring or sign of mercy. He brushed her aside with a twist of one shoulder as if she had been a troublesome gnat.

Angry now, in her turn, she shouted at him, her voice rising in pitch to match her growing indignation.

'James, for love of the Virgin, stop it. You'll kill the man.'

To her surprise the pedlar suddenly rose to his feet, revealing himself to be much taller and younger than she had first supposed. He was still staggering back from the force of the repeated rain of blows, but he straightened and, without warning, reached out and seized James Tarvin's wrist in a grip of steel. James let out a shrill scream, half in anger, half of pain, and the sword went skimming away from them some yards along the road. Panting with exertion, the two men stood and glared at each other. The pedlar's hat had fallen off during the struggle and Isabel saw that his long, thin face was comely enough, tanned and weathered from walking the roads throughout the seasons, but relatively unlined. He might be perhaps thirty years old or a little more, though his life of hardship might well have appeared to age him prematurely and he might have been considerably younger. His dark hair fell untidily on to his shoulders and his black eyes were fixed belligerently upon his tormentor. Isabel gave a little shiver of unease when those eyes were turned on her as she made some movement of alarm. Almost instantly they were hooded as the man bowed his head and again muttered some unintelligible words of explanation or apology. It was as if, in one second of time, the whole personality had changed and the pedlar, recollecting himself and his position as a stranger and vagabond in this village, reverted to his former servile role.

James Tarvin also seemed at last to remember that he was in Isabel's presence and had shown himself in no good light. He swallowed and gave a half ashamed laugh, turning away from the pedlar and towards Isabel, his expression revealing his embarrassment.

'Mistress Isabel, you must forgive me. When this stupid oaf took me by surprise I reacted without consideration for your more tender feelings.'

Isabel felt bewildered. The encounter had shown her a side to James Tarvin that she had not realised existed. His irritation was, to some extent, understandable. He had not wished their meeting to be overseen and chapmen were notorious for their tendency to gossip. Indeed, they were welcomed into many remote homes and inns for the news they had to tell. It would be embarrassing for both of them if this fellow were to remark on what he had seen to some interested villager, but the unleashed violence Isabel had witnessed had quite unnerved her. She turned her attention to the injured man, who was scrambling about in the dirt, trying to recover his soiled items of stock.

Her gaze went uneasily back to James Tarvin.

'It would be a pity, sir, if so pleasant a day were to end in tragedy,' she said quietly, and he had the grace to flush and lower his head a little.

'Yet you will forgive me so uncharacteristic a display of temper?' he pleaded, his voice lowered so that the man would not overhear.

She nodded, but she was by no means sure that his behaviour had been so uncharacteristic, and he could not fail to note that the set of her chin remained somewhat stiff. He sighed and turned to summon Wat Jessop to bring up the horses.

Isabel stooped and picked up two of the crumpled ribbons, holding them out to the pedlar.

'I trust the rest of your stock is not too badly damaged, Master Chapman. If you call at Hatfield Manor just a mile or so from here, my maids will be glad to see your wares, I'm sure.'

He rose to his full height and she saw again that he would tower over James Tarvin. Lowering the pack, he made her a low, servile bow she felt was quite foreign to his nature. He approached cautiously, his eyes watching James Tarvin warily. The hand which reached out to take the tawdry ribbons from her grasp was unexpectedly strong and lean, dusty from the dirt of the road, but not so soiled that she recoiled from his touch.

Again she was discomfited by the direct, clear gaze from those gypsy-dark eyes which was at variance with the servility of his tone.

His voice was low-pitched, a trifle hoarse.

'Thank you kindly, mistress, there's no great 'arm done to me or me wares.' His hand went to pull his forelock and she nodded curtly.

'Good. I should go about your business quickly, man. The village constable has no easy way with vagabonds.'

She thought she saw a flicker of animosity in those dark eyes, then he pulled his forelock again and, reaching down, lifted and shouldered his pack. He half turned to James Tarvin and gave a slight bow of acknowledgement which was half subservient and half mocking, then he trudged off towards the church.

Wat Jessop was at her elbow now.

'Forgive me, mistress, but the morning is almost gone.'

She nodded as he cupped his two hands to lift her into the saddle.

'Good day, Master Tarvin.' Her tone was still somewhat cold and he bowed low, coming close up to peer into her face.

'I shall see you again?'

'Doubtless I shall be at early mass on Easter Day.'

With that he was forced to be content. The groom mounted and the two cantered off towards the manor house. Tarvin stood for a moment, watching them, then turned into the inn, thrusting open the warped door with more force than was necessary.

CHAPTER TWO

ISABEL was aware that she had been away from the manor far longer than she had intended. When Wat lifted her down in the courtyard she cast him an imploring look. He nodded gravely and she knew that nothing would be said about the incident in the village. Grateful, she gathered up her skirts and hastened into the house. As she entered the hall the servants were already setting up the trestles for the midday meal. Her father peered anxiously round the back of his great chair as she hurried up to him, a little breathless.

'Isabel, my lass, I was beginning to wonder what had happened to you.'

'I'm sorry, Father. I lingered, talking to Father John.'

'He is well?'

'Yes, indeed. He sends his greetings, and hopes he will see you at the Easter mass.'

She drew close a faldstool and seated herself very close to him, glancing back at the servants to be sure they were out of earshot.

'He had some news for you, though, as usual, he was very guarded in what he actually said. It would seem that Sir Humphrey and Thomas Stafford have left sanctuary. Were they not at Colchester?'

He nodded thoughtfully. 'So I heard. The brothers must have had some cheering news which made them risk such a thing.'

'So I thought. Tidings from Burgundy, I imagine.'

Sir Edwin grinned. 'This must have cheered Father John.'

Isabel said quietly, 'Don't you think he should forget all this intrigue and remember he is a man of God?'

'When the late King's rightful heir has his own again,' her father replied curtly.

He had sat upright in the chair and, as Isabel had

19

feared, his eyes gleamed with enthusiasm for the first time in months. She sighed. She had her wish. Her father would bestir himself at last, but for what — to conspire with the priest in dangerous matters which could only bring them all to disaster?

She rose. 'I must see to it that everything is ready for the meal, Father.'

'Did you see anyone else we knew?'

She had her back to him now and was glad of it, for she could feel her face flaming.

'I saw Sir Gilbert Tarvin's son at the inn,' she said in what she hoped was a casual tone.

Sir Edwin sniffed audibly but he made no comment.

Bess waited for her in her chamber and Isabel divested herself of her fine wool gown and put on her plain homespun one. There was much to do about the manor and she would be more comfortable so. She should oversee work in the dairy, visit the kitchen again to confer with old Ralf about the Easter preparations, and there was still plenty to occupy her in the still-room.

She was about to descend to the hall and order the midday meal served when Bess, coming hastily from the kitchens, told her that there was a man at the kitchen door asking to see the master of the house.

'Looks like a travelling man, mistress, and in rare state, all dust-bespattered and ——'

'You told him that the master did not receive visitors without prior warning, I trust?' Isabel stemmed Bess's excited chatter sharply.

'Oh, yes, mistress, then he asked to speak to you.'

'To me?'

'Oh, not by name.' Bess giggled. 'I 'spect he doesn't know that; just for the mistress of the house.'

'You say he looks like a travelling man. Has he a large, shabby pack?'

'Yes, mistress, I thought he be a chapman and I asks him to open it up so's we can see what — but he insists on seeing you first.'

'But this is quite ridiculous. We are about to dine. Tell him to be about his business. I *did* see a pedlar in the village and gave him permission to show his wares here, but I have no need to see him. Oh, Bess, he may well be hungry. See he gets fed in the kitchen, then you girls buy what you want and get rid of him.'

'Yes, mistress.' Bess was off at her usual run and Isabel sighed in exasperation. What call had the fellow to bother her? Surely he had no intention of forcing unwanted wares upon her by an implied threat to talk too freely of her affairs? Two hectic spots burned in her cheeks when she thought of it and she stood, hands on hips, waiting for Bess to return with the information that the man would not leave, and prepared to do battle on her own account.

Her father's voice bellowed from the hall.

'Isabel, what's keeping the servants? Dinner should have been served long ago.'

Isabel hurried downstairs and paused in the hall doorway.

'I know, Father. I'm dealing with it. A pedlar arrived suddenly, and you know what the girls are.'

'Well, let's dine first, then the girls can choose what they like. It'll soon be Easter and they'll want ribbons and falldidols for the feasting, I suppose. I'll see the fellow myself afterwards. He may have some news from the South.'

Isabel signalled for the kitchen maid, poised, round-eyed, near the trestle, to bring in the meat.

A voice, low pitched, faintly husky, but without the servile tone she had heard in the village, reached them from the hall door.

'Can you not see me before dinner, Sir Edwin, and perhaps stretch that invitation to include a place at table for a hungry and weary friend?'

Isabel swung round, startled, to find the tall pedlar advancing up the length of the hall, pulling off his shapeless hat as he approached her father's chair.

Sir Edwin turned abruptly and stared at the shabby vagabond coming close without permission and without apparent fear of rebuff. His jaw dropped in astonishment and his eyes widened, then he rose and hurried towards the pedlar, hands outstretched in welcome.

'By the Saints, Adam, Adam Westlake! I can hardly believe it. I thought you dead, lad.'

To Isabel's horrified amazement, her father flung his arms round the pedlar's dusty shoulders and the two men embraced. She found the presence of mind to dismiss the kitchen girl hastily.

'Tell Ralf to keep the meat hot for a while till I call and — and tell him we have a guest.' She halted the girl as she made to run from the hall. 'Tell Ralf also that — that no one is to leave the house until after we have eaten; no one at all, you understand?'

The girl's eyes were saucer-huge by now, but she nodded and scuttled out.

Sir Edwin stood back from his companion at last and turned to the dumbfounded Isabel.

'Allow me to present Sir Adam Westlake. He fought beside me at Redmoor, lass, and was with me when we were forced to retreat. The last I saw of him was near Leicester gate. I thought he was lost. Make him welcome, lass. You'll stay with us some days, Adam?'

Their visitor turned towards Isabel and bowed low. There was no vestige of recognition in those dark eyes and she swallowed hurriedly any words that might betray that they had already met. She was grateful for his discretion. Apparently he had concluded that until he was sure of her motives in behaving as she had in the village he would not blab to her father of anything she might find embarrassing. She held out her hand in greeting and he came closer and bent to kiss her fingers. It was a gesture as courtly as any she might have been afforded at Westminster and she curtsied low in acknowledgement.

'Forgive my disgraceful appearance and arrival without due warning, Mistress Hatfield. I'm sure you must be aware of my reason for appearing in this ridiculous guise. I can assure you I'll not remain long enough at your manor to place your father or yourself in any danger, but it was imperative that I speak with him.'

'You are my father's friend and welcome here for as long as you wish to stay, sir,' she replied, and his black eyes danced as if he noted her cool tone and restrained manner.

He stripped off his cloak and went close to the fire. Sir Edwin was already busied in pouring wine, and the visitor took the cup gratefully and drained it.

'Can your servants be trusted not to gossip, Edwin?' he queried crisply.

'Aye, Adam, if I give the orders, they'll obey me.' Sir Edwin was eyeing his friend shrewdly. 'Have you King's men after you?'

'Not to my knowledge. I've been in England for close on two weeks now and in this guise it's proved simple enough to visit the manors I needed to, but —' he hesitated and looked towards the hall door '— I'm not alone. If you feel you could offer a safe haven for just a night, no more, I'd be grateful.'

'You know you have only to ask,' Sir Edwin said gruffly.

'My companion might well be more easily recognised than I.'

The two men exchanged meaningful glances and Isabel stirred warily.

'I thought the Staffords still in the south.'

The erstwhile pedlar shook his head deliberately. 'Edwin, my travelling companion is even more markedly recognisable than either Humphrey or Tom Stafford, and one whom the King's men would be most anxious to apprehend.'

Incredulously Sir Edwin's eyes, hazel like Isabel's, widened again, then his mouth split in a huge, delighted grin.

'My Lord Lovell, here, in the Midlands?'

'Aye, Frank Lovell, but he's not well, Edwin, like to cough his lungs up. He developed the chill soon after we began our journey north and it's got gradually worse. Most of the time he's lain low in barns and under hedges and let me take the risks of approaching the houses, but I'd feel easier in my mind if he could lie warm and well

fed tonight. Will you risk it for——' he hesitated and
the slightly harsh voice softened '—for our late King's
sake?'

'For his sake and memory of it, I'd risk far more than
that, Adam. You know that well enough. Is my lord safe
where he bides for the present?'

'Yes, well hid.'

'Right, then you stay and eat with us and between us
we'll devise a plan to bring him here without undue
comment and see him safe bestowed.'

Isabel took the opportunity of hastening into the
kitchen to give her orders. Ralf looked at her quizzically.

'It seems our Joan is more curious than she ought to
be concerning Sir Edwin's visitor.'

A frown creased Isabel's brow. 'I'm worried, Ralf.
Will you see to it that the girls and all the men are too
busy to leave the manor for any reason whatever today?'

'You can leave it with me, mistress. There'll be no
loose talk, I promise you. I'll see to it.'

Dinner was served quickly then and Isabel saw that,
though their visitor's manners were faultless, he ate with
haste and decided concentration. Seeing her eyes on
him, he grinned wryly. It was the first time she had seen
his lean, serious face light up in this way, and he looked
much younger than she had first thought.

'Forgive me, mistress, if I eat like a hungry wolf, but
food such as this has been denied me since I left the
Duchess Margaret's Court at Malines.'

'How is the Lady Margaret?' Sir Edwin queried.

'Well enough and thoroughly elated by the progress
of our cause.'

'There is to be a rising, and soon?' Sir Edwin had
lowered his voice, though by this time Isabel had given
the nod to the serving girls to leave the hall at the
conclusion of the meal.

'Aye. The Staffords have it well in hand, but it will
be local, merely a ruse to keep the Tudor's eyes off
Lovell's doings and Lincoln's intentions. You must stay
quiet on your manor for the present, Edwin. There are

more serious matters afoot and you will receive word when you are needed.'

Isabel's father drained his wine cup and nodded, frowning. Clearly he was disappointed that his services would not be required immediately to aid the rebels, but he was prepared to obey orders willingly enough.

Whose orders? Isabel wondered. Viscount Lovell she knew to have been the late King's chamberlain and one of his closest friends. He had managed to survive the rout at Redmoor and escape into sanctuary, but why was he now in the Midlands and, apparently, sick enough to need a refuge here? If word of his presence leaked out, Sir Edwin could be in grave danger of an accusation of treason. King Richard had left no child, his only son having died a boy of eleven at Middleham Castle in 1484. Queen Anne had followed her child to the grave the following year. It had been supposed that if the King did not remarry and sire a son to inherit he might well be succeeded by his nephew, John, Earl of Lincoln, his sister's son. Lincoln had been imprisoned briefly with other nobles in the Tower of London following the Yorkist defeat, but had been released and had seemingly offered his allegiance to the new King, despite the knowledge that he himself had a greater right to the throne. Necessity had forced his hand, and his cousin, Elizabeth, the eldest daughter of King Edward IV, had been for months the wife of Henry Tudor and was about to bear his heir. If most of England had been prepared to accept the new King through his alliance with the Yorkist heiress, it was plain that many of the late King's adherents had no such intentions. Was Lovell here to meet with Lincoln, a hazardous venture indeed, since surely the Earl would be closely watched? These two men most near in blood and loyalty to the dead King were the likeliest leaders to appeal to the sympathies of those men fretting after the lost cause.

Again she found their visitor's black eyes scrutinising her closely and she toyed nervously with her fork, a new-fangled invention from the Continent that her

mother had proudly brought to Hatfield among her
other treasures.

'You look pale, Mistress Isabel. I trust you are not
alarmed for your father's safety. I promise to take all
precautions. He shall not be placed in peril for our
sakes.'

'I do not see how you could guarantee that, sir,' she
replied curtly.

'Isabel.' Her father's tone was unwontedly sharp.
Rarely did he publicly rebuke her, and she winced
inwardly. 'Sir Adam is our honoured guest. I expect you
to treat him with special courtesy.'

She lowered her head to conceal her rising anger. Did
he mean to treat her as a refractory child before this
man? She would not be treated so, she who had been
mistress here for months now.

Her temper was not improved by the stranger's next
incautious words.

'I take it your lady is away from the manor, Edwin. I
hope she is not unwell.'

There was a silence, and Sir Adam looked up quickly
at his host, sensing he had said what he should not.

'My Alice died in October, of the sweating sickness,
Adam, lad. Nay,' he said gravely, a hand raised to check
Sir Adam's intended apology for his clumsy words, 'you
were not to know.'

'Sweet Jesus receive her soul,' the other breathed
softly. 'I had not realised just how deeply you had
suffered following the battle, my friend. We have all
been too intent about our own sorrows to heed the
misfortunes of others. She took ill of the sweat, you
say?'

'Aye, more than likely brought by those mongrels in
Henry's train, one more reason I have to hate him and
one that gnaws away at me to find some way of thwarting
him.'

'Your hopes will come to fruition, Edwin, that I
promise you, but it will be wiser for you to remain
patient for just a little longer.' Sir Adam glanced quickly
at the tense form of Isabel. 'For the sake of your lovely

daughter you must appear to be remote from these coils for the present.'

'Lovell goes to meet Lincoln?'

'Aye, we are making for the north and would be nearer our destination now if my lord had not insisted on going into Leicester.'

'Surely that was to risk much?'

'Indeed, but he had not seen where they had laid Richard and nothing would content him until he had satisfied himself that all was decent and seemly.'

Sir Edwin sighed gustily. 'It is now. The Grey Friars saw to it that our late lord was laid to rest with all due reverence, but his body was treated shamefully when he was brought from the field.'

'We heard—naked and with a halter round his neck like a common criminal. May Henry rot in hell for his vicious spite towards a gallant defeated enemy.'

'The man is of ignoble stock. What can we expect from such?'

Sir Adam's dark eyes gleamed in sympathy. 'I am well fed and warmed, Edwin. I should be off about my business. If you are sure you can trust your household, I will return later with your second guest.'

'Isabel will see to it that a chamber is prepared.'

'Is there a trustworthy apothecary in the neighbourhood?'

'No need of that. Isabel has learned all the still-room skills from her mother. She will do her best for my lord. You can rest easy. He'll be in good hands. Is he mounted?'

'No, we felt it safer to proceed on foot.'

Sir Edwin turned towards Isabel. 'Which of our men is to be most trusted if he goes with Sir Adam and takes a suitable mount to fetch our guest?'

'Wat Jessop would allow his tongue to be torn out before he betrayed us.'

'Good. Isabel, you go down and speak with him. You are more likely to go down to the stables these days than I am.' Her father grimaced. 'We'll not do anything that is likely to arouse suspicion.'

Isabel rose and excused herself. The two men remained at table, their heads very close together in conference. Again she felt a stab of exasperation that she was so ignored in their decision-making.

She found Wat peering anxiously down over the wooden partition of one of the stalls.

'What is it? Something wrong?'

'No, mistress, I'm just trying to decide if Cass is about to whelp today and whether I should stay with her. It is her first litter.'

Isabel stared down at the brown-haired brachet bitch who was moving restlessly about in the straw.

'I thought she wasn't due for some days yet.'

Wat shrugged. 'By my reckoning, she ain't, but Nature's not always to be trusted. Apt to play funny tricks 'specially the first time.'

Isabel had a special fondness for Cassandra. The bitch had paid her marked attention, insisting on being petted as a puppy and following her everywhere since.

'You think she might have a bad time, Wat?'

'Nay, mistress, she's a strong enough bitch; it's just that I'd like to keep my eyes on her till she's safely delivered.'

'Yes, we must do that. Wat, Father wants you to go on a special errand.' She hesitated. 'One that is not to be discussed in the hall, you understand?'

The dour, serious face turned to her immediately. 'Of course, mistress, anything you say will go no further; you know that.'

She bit her lip uncertainly. 'That pedlar, the one we saw in the village, he — he's no true travelling man.'

Wat's stolid gaze did not falter. 'I guessed as much, mistress.'

'You did?' Her eyes widened.

'He knew too well how to handle himself with young Master James.'

'Yes, well — he is to stay here tonight as our special guest and he brings with him another man who is not well. I want you to accompany him. Take three horses and guide them back here after dark.'

'Aye, mistress.'

'If—if the second man were to be found here it could go hard with all of us.'

Wat gave a simple nod. 'I understand, mistress. Trust me.'

'I do, Wat.' She gave a little premonitory shiver. 'I wish—oh, I wish the day had not turned out so—so uncertainly. It began so well,' she added sadly.

'Your father knows what he is about, mistress. He'd not put you in any danger.'

'I'm not so sure of that. He is—obsessed with the desire to. . .' She broke off uncertainly. 'Where shall I tell our pedlar friend to meet you?'

'In the wood. I'll take all three horses and wait in the copse by the stream. You can give him clear directions, mistress? Best if he's seen to leave the manor the way he came, in his pedlar's garb.'

'Yes, much the best.' Isabel leaned down once more to look at the bitch busily trampling down the straw for a bed. 'I'll come down from time to time and watch her.'

'Aye, she'll be happier if you are close.' Wat pushed open the partition and bent to stroke the bitch's silky ears. 'You'll do all right, old girl. Just trust us.'

Cass turned at his well loved voice and wagged her tail. Isabel smiled. Here was one at least who knew whom she could trust.

She hastened back into the house to give instructions for the preparation of the guest chamber, then she must check the still-room for her remedies for colds and coughs. If Lord Lovell were to proceed on his mission safely it were best that he recover speedily.

CHAPTER THREE

ISABEL had expected their noble visitor to be a much older man, then she remembered that her father had told her that Lord Francis Lovell and the late King had been close friends, brought up together in the northern castle of Middleham. King Richard had been hardly thirty-three years old when he had been killed at Redmoor, so Lord Francis could be little more than thirty now. She was quite dazzled by his good looks, and exceptional charm of manner. Despite his pallor and that dreadful cough he thanked his host most gratefully when Sir Edwin met him at the hall door and instantly escorted him to the chair near the roaring fire.

'My lord, how good it is to receive you under my roof. Please seat yourself and my daughter will see to it that all is provided for your comfort.'

Lord Lovell stretched out blue-tinged hands to the welcome blaze.

'Edwin, old friend, it is good of you to risk yourself.' He coughed, and Isabel winced at the harsh, dry sound. 'We have slept out two nights and it has sorely tried my bones, not to say increased the discomfort of this damned cough.'

'No one in this house would betray you, my lord, or anyone I chose to shelter. Isabel has already prepared your room and supper will be served almost instantly.'

Isabel said quietly, as if afraid of being contradicted, 'It is my opinion, Father, that my lord would be better to go instantly to bed and have his meal there. I have already prepared a soothing compound of horehound and honey. The cough must be loosened, or my lord will indeed become too severely ill to travel.'

Lord Lovell turned to regard her. She stood hesitantly in the doorway, her head held high, her manner deferential but authoritative. She was going to be a beauty and a force to be reckoned with. Young she might be, but she had already established herself as the chatelaine of this house, and woe betide those who attempted to thwart her. He smiled, the corners of his lips twitching at sight of Adam's frown of discomfiture.

'Mistress Isabel is the skilled nurse here, I see. I would be churlish indeed to gainsay her. Edwin, we can talk more freely in the privacy of your chamber.'

'After my ministrations, my lord,' Isabel pressed inexorably.

Lord Lovell rose and bowed in courtly fashion.

'I am your servant, Mistress Isabel, and will obey with good grace. Lead me to my chamber, mistress.'

Isabel led the way upstairs, stopping to give a flustered Bess instructions as the girl passed her on the stair.

At the entrance to the room Adam Westlake moved by her with a muttered apology and looked quickly round as if to assure himself that there could be no other means of entry or possibility of their private talk being overheard. Isabel was angered by the suggestion that either man had anything to fear beneath the roof of an avowed friend.

Westlake's dark eyes met her clear hazel ones and he smiled faintly as if he read her mind. He said brusquely, 'There will be no need to send up a servant. *I* will wait upon his lordship.'

She curtsied and withdrew, seething at his ungracious tone.

In the still-room she stirred her potion where it was kept warming on the low trivet before the fire, then, holding the handle of the small iron pan carefully by a padded cloth, lifted it clear of the flames and poured it into a warmed waiting earthern cup. She had sent Bess to hurry the serving men into providing the evening meal. Lord Lovell looked both pale and hungry. She doubted if the men had taken much hot food over the last days.

Lord Lovell was undressed and in bed, propped high on the pillows, a woollen shawl round his shoulders, when she entered the guest chamber. Adam Westlake was busily engaged in stirring the logs in the grate to a blaze. The Viscount was in a paroxysm of coughing and fighting for breath. Clearly the effort of making the journey then mounting the stair and undressing had worsened his condition. Once over the worst he looked up to smile gamely in her direction.

'Here comes my good nurse with some noxious potion, I imagine.' His merry brown eyes screwed up like a child refusing to take unpleasant medicine, then he grinned at her and reached for the cup.

'You should not find it too bitter, my lord. It is compounded with plenty of honey.'

'I do but tease you, Mistress Isabel. I have endured greater hardships over the last months than taking foul-tasting medicines.'

'I know, my lord. May I feel your brow? I fear a fever developing. If so we must sweat it out of you tonight.'

He lifted her small hand to his forehead. His skin felt hot and dry as she feared, and she frowned.

'Does your chest hurt? That cough is so harsh and dry.'

'Aye, mistress, I am certainly sore here and it hurts abominably when I cough again.'

'You must take more of this potion later and I'll bring you feverfew and other herbs for the fever, also a healing salve to rub on your chest.'

His brown eyes twinkled again. 'Faith, mistress, you remind me of my old nurse who rubbed me with goose grease till I stank to high heaven. Not,' he amended hastily, 'that you in any way resemble that dame, for, dear as she was to me, she was four times your width and boasted a distinct moustache.'

Isabel smiled in answer. 'I fear you may find the ointment somewhat strong to the nose, but that must be endured, my lord. Now you should rest. Supper will soon be served and my father will join you.' She turned to Sir Adam. 'Will you please see to it that my lord does not talk too much? It will merely exacerbate the cough and weaken him further.'

Sir Adam nodded. '*I* will do the talking. I am totally in my lord's confidence.'

He *would* be, she thought irritably as she excused herself, curtsied and withdrew.

Her father was waiting anxiously in the hall as she descended the stair. 'Lord Lovell is not seriously ill, is he? Do you think we should summon a physician?'

'No, no, Father. He will be well enough after a few days. We must ease the cough and break the fever so that he has a restful night. I think Sir Adam would not welcome the suggestion that we call in any other person while Lord Lovell is here.'

'Aye, likely you are right. I pray God you are, my lass, for we need him sorely to lead us. I'd not have any further ill overtake him.'

Isabel thought, hastily, that it would be a stunning blow indeed if a noted traitor were to die in their house. She told herself consolingly that she was sure she was right in her diagnosis. Lord Lovell was a comparatively young man, strong and formerly well fed. He would recover quickly and leave the manor. Everything then would return to normal again.

She ordered her own supper to be served in the solar and sat hunched before the fire afterwards while the candles flickered and the shadows appeared suddenly threatening in the erstwhile pleasant and cosy room. She was being fanciful, needed to take her mind from worrying about what the men upstairs were planning. Then she remembered her promise to Wat concerning Cass. She would put on a warm cloak and go over to the stable to assure herself that all was well with her favourite.

She was about to push back the heavy door to the courtyard when her arm was suddenly seized in a grip of steel and she was dragged summarily back towards the wooden screens which partitioned this entrance way to the hall from the rest.

'Not so fast, Mistress Hatfield. Might I ask first where you're bound?'

She turned furiously to face Sir Adam Westlake and

struggled vainly to free herself. Her hazel eyes blazed
with golden lights which someone who knew her well
would recognise as signs of impending storm.

'How dare you put hands on me? Let me go at once
before I summon servants. . .'

'I would not advise that, mistress. The fuss would
alert your father and I would be loth to have to explain
to him the reason for my concern that you are leaving
the house so late.'

She was struck dumb for vital seconds while she
considered his words, and he smiled grimly.

'I think I guessed rightly and that Sir Edwin is not
aware that you meet with his enemy's son in the village.'

She spluttered in her rising anger. 'Do you dare
suggest that I go to meet some paramour at this hour?
How dare you impugn my honour, sir?'

'If I misjudge you, I am sorry, mistress, but it is my
only concern to see that Lord Lovell remains safe in this
house.'

Her face flamed. 'Do you think I would betray him—
or any creature in need of help?'

'I trust you would not, knowingly, but women are
prone to chatter and——'

'I am no more prone to that weakness than many men
I know,' she retorted hotly.

'And you are acquainted with so many,' he gibed
softly.

With an effort she withdrew her arm from his grasp
and dealt him a stinging blow across the face which
momentarily sent him staggering backwards, blundering
into the carved wooden screen.

'Forgive me, Mistress Isabel.' He regained his balance
and came towards her, one hand upraised. 'Pax, I beg
you. That sally was unworthy of a knight and given only
in the spirit of jest often employed at Court. I meant
you no insult.'

She was breathing hard and two spots of hectic colour
stained her cheeks.

'I think you despicable to believe so much ill of me
without true knowledge of my nature. I am not going to

visit James——' she bit off the name quickly '—the man you saw talking with me in the village. I certainly would meet no man unescorted and certainly not at this hour.'

'James Tarvin?' he enquired coolly.

'How did you know?' she countered stiffly.

'I guessed it would be he. He had a slight intonation of the Welsh Marches and I know his father is now established on John Heyward's lands.'

'He cannot now be considered an enemy.'

'Your father would consider him so, I am sure.'

She said, defensively, 'There is nothing between us. I—I have seen him once or twice in the village. He has gone out of his way to be pleasant with me. Our groom has always been near in attendance. There are so few men left now; so many died on Redmoor.'

'I know,' he said drily. 'I was there.'

Her eyes dropped away from the intentness of his gaze. He made no further criticism of her conduct, but she felt suddenly wanton and was ashamed, as if the knowledge that the Tarvins had profited by John Heyward's death had made it distasteful that she had allowed any dalliance between herself and James Tarvin. She gave the ghost of a sigh.

'If you must know, I was about to visit the stable. One of our brachets is about to whelp. It is her first litter. I was worried about her. She seemed restless this afternoon.'

'A sure sign.' He nodded. 'Will you allow me to accompany you?'

She looked at him suspiciously. 'Do you still not trust me?'

He shrugged. 'I cannot afford to trust anybody. If I prove mistaken it could mean my head, and, far more catastrophic than that, the loss of Lord Lovell's, to say nothing of those others who may be found to be implicated.'

'You mean you would betray them—if you were caught?'

He shrugged again. 'Who knows what I would do and

say in extremity? Some carelessly dropped word or, worse, an outright betrayal to save myself pain.'

'You would be tortured?'

His lips curled derisively. 'Oh, certainly; it is the way of the Tudor's creatures.'

'And King Richard was so forgiving? What of Lord Hasting's sudden execution and those of Sir Richard Grey and others?'

He was silent and she bit her lip under his scrutiny.

'I see you listen to scurrilous gossip, mistress. Were those thoughts bred in you or were they placed there by Master Tarvin?'

'Certainly not. I would never discuss Court affairs or allegiances with Master Tarvin. The thoughts are my own. Can you deny those men died and by the late King's orders?'

'No, I cannot deny that.'

'The realm is settled now. There has been enough blood spilt. We must have peace. The King wed a Yorkist princess; can not that satisfy you all?'

'A bastard princess,' he said softly, 'accepted as such by Parliament, who passed an act approving King Richard as his brother's rightful successor. Those men you spoke of were traitors. Can you deny that?'

'And suppose they believed otherwise, that the alleged illegitimacy of King Edward's children was a declared ruse to simplify King Richard's pathway to the throne he had always desired?'

He caught her wrist again and twisted it cruelly. 'Never say that again in my hearing. You know nothing of the man.'

'And you did?' she said wonderingly.

'Aye, knew him, and loved him.' He released her wrist after examining it as if he was sorry that he had caused her pain and was fearful that a dark bruise would form. 'Forgive me; I had no wish to hurt you. Come——' almost roughly '—it is pointless and foolish for us to stand here talking of matters that have gone beyond redemption. Let us see how your bitch is faring.'

She slipped on pattens before crossing the yard, her

mind in turmoil. How could she have been so foolish as
to engage in argument with this man? He considered
her a child, a rustic, knowing nothing of affairs of the
realm. Yet she was entitled to an opinion, certainly so
when it affected her future. She had no grudge against
the dead king, had merely used her attacks on his
honour as means of establishing her points. Sir Adam
Westlake had, apparently, been closely acquainted with
King Richard. He had no title, so he must have been
one of the household knights. How loyal they all
appeared to be to him, true to that motto of his which
had floated free on the boar banner, 'Loyalty Binds Me'.
Loyal he had been to his elder brother, yet he had so
soon usurped the throne from his young nephew, as this
Welshman had usurped the throne from those her father
thought to be the true descendants. She thrust the
thoughts angrily from her mind. Let these warring
nobles fight for their place in the King's counsels. How
did any of this matter to the people who worked and
struggled to force a living from the land here in
Swithland?

In the stable Isabel kindled one of the lanterns with
the tinder and flint laid ready and, pushing back the
wooden partition to the stall, called her favourite to her.
It was immediately clear that Cass was in labour. The
bitch whined and moved uneasily. She was panting
hard, obviously in severe pain. Isabel gave an exclamation of pity and slipped to her knees by the suffering
dog, gently reaching out to stroke the silky coat reassuringly. Sir Adam Westlake stooped to lift the lantern
high, his lips pursed, his brow creased in concern. She
looked up at him anxiously.

'There is something wrong, you think?'

He nodded, then pulled off his rough woollen jerkin
and rolled up the sleeves of his frieze shirt. 'Get me
some water and then come back and hold the lantern
high for me.'

She hastened to do his bidding. 'Should I summon
Wat? She is used to him and he is skilled with the dogs.'

'Not unless you don't trust me. I'm good with dogs as

well. In all events, we must waste no time. One of the
pups is placed wrongly, unless I'm mistaken, and must
be released before she can give birth.'

She looked beyond him anxiously to where the frightened bitch was already weakening. 'Of course I trust
you. What do you want me to do?'

'Are you squeamish, liable to faint?'

'Of course not,' she snapped.

'Then simply stand by, hold the lantern steady for
me, and keep talking to her, reassure her; she's used to
the sound of your voice.'

She obeyed him, watching, fascinated, as he worked
with gentle, sure fingers. All the time he made soothing
noises with his tongue and Isabel supplemented them
with reassurances to Cass.

'There, there, girl. You're a clever old thing. It'll
soon be over.'

It was only moments later before the first of the litter
was lying in the straw beside its mother, bloody and
slick with mucus, but mewling loudly and clearly alive
and apparently healthy. Adam Westlake stepped back,
thrust his bloodied hands into the water bucket, and
turned to Isabel.

'She should do well enough now. Poor old girl. She
was very distressed.'

Padding her voluminous skirts beneath her, Isabel sat
on the straw and watched as, one by one, six healthy
pups were delivered and the mother, allowing her brood
to suckle, turned contented eyes on them both. Isabel
rose stiffly and gave a last caress to the bitch's ears.

'I think she's finished now.'

Adam Westlake had been seated cross-legged some
feet away and sprang easily to his feet. 'It's been some
time since the last one. It seems the contractions are
over. I think we can safely leave her now.'

'Father will be very proud. He's very fond of Cass.
We all are. Wat will be sorry he wasn't here, but he has
a great deal to do these days.' She said awkwardly, 'As I
said before, we lost many good men from the village.'

His dark eyes were inscrutable in the lantern light, but he made no sardonic comment this time.

She said, a little embarrassed by the fact that she had spent the last hour in his company without chaperon, 'I have to thank you most sincerely, sir. I think we would have lost Cass if you had not been here and so skilful.'

He gave that little shrug which was already becoming familiar to her.

'I was glad to be of service, Mistress Isabel.' Those unfathomable black eyes regarded her dishevelled state. There were wisps of straw clinging to her gown and her hair straggled loose from her cap. She had sweated in her fear for her favourite and there were beads of it on her upper lip, despite the chill of the stable. 'You will take cold. Let us get you back to the house so that you can get back to your chamber to wash and refresh yourself. Then, I suggest, you try to get some sleep.'

Her gaze followed his and she flushed hotly. 'I look a sight. My father would be furious if—if. . .'

'I do not think so, Mistress Isabel,' he said gravely. 'Your father knows you well and trusts you. He would not readily think ill of you. You would need only to explain your presence here and he would understand and be grateful.'

She considered his remark carefully, then looked up to him, a slight frown creasing her smooth brow.

'Yes, he does trust me. I take your point, sir. I realise, only too clearly, how necessary it is to have complete trust in those we know and love and be utterly trustworthy to their interest in return.'

He inclined his head then stooped to reach his discarded jerkin.

'We shall be gone from here very soon. I promise you, Mistress Isabel, that if it lies in my power I shall strive very hard to keep your father from all harm.'

Their eyes met and held. At last she said softly, 'I know where his heart lies. Whatever he decides I shall accept, but he is very dear to me, sir, and——' her voice trembled a little '—he is all I have left.'

He stooped and, taking her grubby little hand, he turned it to the palm and kissed it.

'You have my word. I shall try to prevent him from any foolhardy acts of courageous loyalty.'

'I think you have summed up my father's character very well, Sir Adam.'

'I know him and have the greatest respect for his courage and sense of honour.' He gave a wry little smile. 'Lately, I have discovered how dangerous it can be to disregard a healthy esteem for one's own skin.'

She gave a little chuckle of approval for his frankness. All the hostility she had felt for this man was beginning to dissipate, to be replaced by a wondering approval. She had watched him handle James Tarvin's aggression without servility yet with enough discretion to guard the safety of his mission. She felt that he no longer regarded her with the contempt for her youth and rusticity that she had thought earlier. In their shared concern for the little dog they had come to understand each other better. Together they walked back to the house as comrades. In the hall she whispered a quick word of gratitude before hastening up the stair to her own chamber.

Bess was snoring loudly, still fully dressed, across her own truckle-bed in Isabel's chamber. Isabel pulled off her gown and undershift, washed in the cold water left in the ewer on her dressing chest, shivered at the shock of it on her shrinking flesh, then climbed into bed and snuggled under the covers.

She thought there was so much on her mind she would be unable to sleep, but exhaustion took its toll and sunbeams were tickling her lashes to wakefulness before Bess was able to rouse her. Isabel sprang up, startled, knowing the day was already well advanced.

Bess's cheerful face looked decidedly worried. 'Are you not well, mistress? You seemed so fast off. When I tells your father you seemed that 'ard to wake, he tells me to let you sleep.'

'He did?' Isabel thrust back her dishevelled hair impatiently. 'Has he breakfasted? What of our guests?'

'The one as is sick 'as 'ad 'is in his chamber, mistress.

'E seems a might better, t'other; 'e's bin eating with your father in the 'all.'

So Sir Adam must have given some explanation to her father about their doings in the stable last night, and that was why he had instructed Bess to allow her to sleep. She thrust her legs clear of the bed and ordered Bess to bring a clean shift and gown.

'I must hurry. I should not be remiss when we have guests here.'

She was soon washed and dressed and about to go downstairs when she heard the sounds of arrival from the courtyard. Quickly she ran to the casement and peered down. She craned her neck but could not see the visitors. Isabel's heart raced. Would her father have some warning and be able to keep Lord Lovell well hidden? Bess was hesitating uneasily in the doorway.

'Tell my father I shall be down presently, and Bess?'

'Yes, mistress?'

'Do not gossip about our other guests. You understand?'

Bess's eyes widened, but she nodded her head decisively and Isabel knew she would be obeyed. She waited till Bess had gone down to the hall and then hastened to Lord Lovell's chamber.

He was propped up, completing a hearty breakfast, and his eyes met hers enquiringly as she quietly closed the door and put down the catch.

'Something wrong?' His voice was still a trifle husky, but he looked much better this morning.

'My lord, we have visitors. I don't know yet who they are, but you must remain here until I can send you word all is well.'

He nodded.

'Where is Sir Adam?'

'He went down to breakfast with your father.'

She bit her lip uneasily. 'It is to be hoped he manages to get clear of the hall.'

Lord Lovell's handsome face looked grave. 'Is there any way I could leave the house before your father could be implicated?'

She shook her head. 'No, far better to remain here. There is no reason why anyone should demand to search the house.'

'But the servants. . .'

'Will keep close mouths, I promise you. I must hurry down to my father now. You will keep well clear of the windows?'

He grimaced. 'Naturally.'

Concerned for Adam Westlake's safety, Isabel hastened into the hall. She stopped dead in her tracks at sight of James Tarvin near her father's chair with another, older man who turned at her approach.

Sir Edwin's expression revealed his relief at her arrival. She gave an imperceptible nod of her chin and hoped he would understand that Lord Lovell had been well warned.

'Our neighbours have, at last, come to call on us, Isabel. Sir Gilbert Tarvin, my dear, and his son. Allow me to present my daughter, Isabel, sir.'

Isabel sank into a curtsy, only managing a brief impression of James's father's appearance. The man looked smaller than his son, stocky, brown-haired like James, and, as she looked up when he took her hand, she saw that hair was thick and curly and his brows were bushy and almost met over the bridge of his nose. The eyes beneath were shrewd and grey, and, though they were smiling now, Isabel felt, with a slight shiver, that they could become clear as glass and just as expressionless.

Sir Gilbert's voice was decidedly more accented than that of his son.

'A pleasure to see you, Mistress Hatfield. My son James, here, has glimpsed you once or twice in the village and was impressed by your beauty. I see he did not exaggerate your charms.'

Isabel blushed hotly. Sir Gilbert continued to keep hold of her hand and she felt herself under close scrutiny, as if she were a heifer brought to market.

'Thank you, sir,' she replied dutifully, deliberately not looking in James's direction. How much had he told his father?

'Yes, Sir Edwin,' Sir Gilbert continued, in his soft singsong voice, 'so much was James taken with this lovely young daughter of yours that he has been pressing me for some time to make your acquaintance. I had hoped to meet you by chance at mass or in the village, but, since I was informed that you have not been well, and kept to your own manor, I felt it necessary to call and hope I would be welcome as your nearest neighbour.'

Her father was making some polite rejoinder and Isabel's thoughts were still chasing each other within her brain. Did James know Adam Westlake was here? No, how could he? Yet why had the Tarvins chosen today, of all days, to make a courtesy call? Sir Gilbert, she knew, was in the Tudor King's counsels, so it was imperative he had no knowledge of Lord Lovell's presence in the vicinity.

The screen door behind her jerked suddenly open and she swung round, startled, to find Adam Westlake stop abruptly.

Her heart seemed to leap into her throat. He was in terrible danger. How dared he live like this, visiting men who must, by their previous allegiance, be suspect? Suppose Sir Gilbert was to order his arrest as a possible malcontent? He could be dragged off, tortured. . . She pictured this tall, lean body ruined after hours on the rack. She had known him so short a time, yet her whole being ached to do something—anything—to ensure his continued freedom.

Immediately his authoritative stance altered and, before her amazed eyes, he became the subservient pedlar she had believed him to be on their first meeting.

Her eyes silently implored her father to come to their rescue, and he understood at once.

'What do you want, man?' he snapped testily. 'Can you not see I've no time for you now?'

Westlake knuckled his forehead and bowed. 'Sorry, sir,' he said, 'I've just come to say I'm leaving and to thank you kindly.'

James Tarvin regarded the man frostily. 'What is this

fellow still doing in the neighbourhood? I thought him
long gone. This is the impudent fellow I told you about,
Father,' he explained. 'I told him to take himself off my
land before I set the constable on him.'

Sir Edwin said quietly, 'He is on my land at present,
Master Tarvin. The fellow was not well and I allowed
him to stay the night snug in my barn. My serving
wenches are always partial to the gewgaws these fellows
sell. There's no harm to be had in letting him stay for a
while.'

Sir Gilbert shot a warning glance in his son's direction. 'No, no, of course not. It seems this fellow had the
impudence to waylay my son, and he feels strongly
about the matter. No harm done, of course, especially
as the man appears to be about to leave the county.' He
stared coldly at the seemingly obsequious pedlar.

'I'll be off then, sir,' Adam addressed Sir Edwin
direct. 'It will be a long time before I forget your
charity. My friends shall know of it; be sure of that.
You'll not be troubled by any man of our fraternity and
if you need our help at any time you only have to call on
one of us.'

He bowed again and, as Sir Edwin acknowledged his
flowery farewell with a cool nod, he turned and left the
hall.

Isabel let out a pent breath and James looked at her
sharply. She smiled with a warmth she was not feeling.
What would Adam do now? Would he take the pack
and leave? Certainly he must appear to be taking the
road. The Tarvins would no doubt make enquiries. But
how was Lord Lovell to be smuggled from the house to
meet up with his travelling companion? She could only
hope that Adam would leave some instructions with Wat
Jessop. Meanwhile it was imperative that their visitors
be made to feel welcome.

Sir Gilbert said jovially, 'Would it be too forward of
the boy to be allowed to walk in your pleasance with
your daughter, Sir Edwin, just for a moment? With her
maid present, of course.'

Isabel saw an imperceptible shudder pass over her

father's frame and his lips tightened ominously. She could give him no warning and could only hope that he would give a conciliatory answer. Sir Gilbert Tarvin must not be antagonised. Lord Lovell's safety must be their first consideration now. However distasteful it would be for her father to be pleasant to his neighbour or to accept that man's son as a possible suitor for his daughter, his own feelings must be cast aside in the name of the cause. He looked smilingly in Isabel's direction and she nodded in answer.

'Bess,' he said sharply to the girl who was hovering uncertainly near the screen door, 'accompany your mistress into the pleasance with Master Tarvin. Fetch warm cloaks for you both. Do not stay too long in the cold air, my dear,' he admonished Isabel.

James came delightedly to her side and Isabel placed cold little fingers on his arm as he led her towards the door, impatient to be out of the presence of both their parents.

Bess returned with the cloaks, looking obviously unhappy, uncertain what was expected of her, and Isabel instructed her to sit on a wooden bench sheltered by the pleasance wall. Here Bess would not get too cold, and Isabel would see to it that she and James remained clearly within the girl's sight but just out of hearing.

James said impulsively, 'You are not angry with me, are you?'

'Why should I be angry?'

'I thought you might chide me for insisting that my father and I come here.'

'You both know my father's former sympathies. It was just that I was uncertain about his reactions. He has been very low-spirited since my mother's death. I am glad to see that he greeted you warmly.'

'When I saw that pedlar fellow in your house I thought you would censure me for my treatment of him. Did you tell your father what happened — that I hit the man?'

'No mention was made of it. I doubt if the pedlar has exchanged more than a word or two with my father, and those only of a grateful nature for his forbearance in allowing him to stay on our property.'

'He was not really hurt?'

'His leg pained him and the pack is so heavy. I asked Father to let him stay. It was so cold last night and our girls were delighted to buy his wares, Easter being so near.'

He sighed heavily. 'I shall not be in Leicestershire during the Holy Season.'

'Oh?' Isabel was astonished and somewhat disappointed.

'I have been summoned to wait upon the Queen until the birth of the royal heir.'

'But that is a great honour, James. Your father must be very proud.'

'He is,' James agreed grimly, 'and will not hear of my refusal.'

'But you couldn't refuse. It would be an insult to the King himself and damn all your hopes of preferment.'

'It would. Father thinks I may well be appointed to the prince's household.'

'Oh,' Isabel laughed, 'I see the king is very sure it will be a son.'

'He hopes and prays it will be. That would be the seal of God's approval and the people would all accept him at last and with great rejoicing.'

Isabel did not think that very likely but she forbore to say so.

'I shall miss you,' she said a little wistfully. She meant it, and the remark was totally without coquetry. Her meetings with James Tarvin had added spice to her dull life over these last weeks, and the Queen was not expected to give birth until the autumn. James would be away from Leicestershire for long months.

'I shall insist on returning as soon as I can,' James said fervently. 'I have made it clear to my father that I want to ask for your hand. He has no objections to a possible match. Say you have none, Isabel. If I can take that hope with me, I can bear the long parting.'

She deferred giving a decisive answer. 'There will be

ladies at Court wealthier and more beautiful than I. There will be time for you to make such a declaration and——' she hesitated '—if you are to enter the royal household it will be for the King to approve any match you make. I doubt he would look on my family with favour.'

'Nonsense,' James said stoutly. 'Your father served the then king dutifully. That could in no sense be termed treasonable.'

'But, if you will recall, the King dated his accession the day before the battle so that loyal men like my father could be held culpable,' Isabel said with a trace of asperity. 'We have been fined heavily for that grievous sin.'

He looked at her wonderingly, as if he were not aware of the cynicism of that last remark, and she felt a stab of irritation. Was he insensitive or merely stupid? She was forced to keep back a wry twist of the lips as she thought how quickly Adam Westlake would have taken up such a challenge.

James said stoutly, 'I'm sure His Grace can be made to understand my desire for you. Perhaps, when things are settled, and the Queen safely delivered, he will be in an expansive mood and will graciously accede to my request.'

'Perhaps,' Isabel agreed, cautiously. 'I am grateful for the honour you do me, James, but I can make no promises without my father's approval; you know that.'

'Of course. It is just that I could not leave without making clear my intentions. I can hope, Isabel?' He lifted her hands to his lips, turning her directly to face him.

Isabel glanced uncomfortably to where Bess waited by the wall. If this had happened two days ago James's avowed love for her would have set her heart aglow. Now she could think only of the Tarvins' speedy departure. Every moment they were in the manor spelt deadly danger to them all. Had Adam Westlake got clear? She hoped and prayed that he had done so and, irrationally, she wished they could have had some

moments together to make their farewells. She wanted
him to understand that her coldness towards him had
only been because of her fears for her father. She wished
him well and, though she longed only for the realm to
remain at peace, she would pray earnestly for his safety
and that of Lord Lovell.

The pressure of James's fingers increased and she
turned anxious eyes to his.

'You know I have your interests at heart, James. I
cannot say more than that.'

He bent and kissed her fingers and his mouth was hot
and eager. 'With those words I must be content. At least
now your father is aware of my interest and I will be
able to send you messages from Winchester.'

She withdrew her fingers firmly and moved back
towards the nervously wriggling Bess.

'Your father will be waiting.'

'He will,' he agreed reluctantly. 'There is much to do
before I ride south in the morning.'

Sir Gilbert was tapping his riding whip impatiently
against his boot when they re-entered the hall.

'I have informed Sir Edwin of your singular good
fortune, lad,' he said. 'Mistress, I can well understand
why my son is reluctant to leave Swithland, but there
can be no delay when one is on the King's business.'

'Of course not, Sir Gilbert.' Isabel curtsied low. 'I
wish you all Godspeed on your journey.'

They took their leave then and her father moved to
his chair and sank down heavily. 'The Virgin be praised;
they have gone at last. All the time the man was braying
about the usurper's marks of favour, I was fearful that
he would become aware that Lord Lovell was above
stairs or he would come into the hall at any moment.'

'I was able to warn him of their arrival,' Isabel
soothed, 'but unable to convey that message to you.'

Sir Edwin was immediately on his feet again.

'We must see to it that my lord is got away from here
as soon as possible.'

'I'll go down to the stables myself and see Wat Jessop.
Probably he and Sir Adam have made some plan.'

Sir Edwin made for the stair while Isabel hurried to the stable. She found Wat admiring Cass, who was contentedly suckling her litter.

'She's doing very well, mistress — thanks to you, so I hear.'

'Thanks to Sir Adam, if the truth is known. Wat, have you seen him?' Her heart thudded with renewed alarm for him.

'Aye, mistress, he's safe away. I've arranged to get my lord to the place where I picked him up yesterday — as soon as it's dark, that is.'

'Thank the Virgin. I'll see he has provisions and medicines for the journey. He seemed much improved this morning, which is a mercy as we cannot keep him here in safety for another night.'

Wat nodded his agreement. He spoke as she was about to turn away.

'Sir Adam, he gave me something for you, mistress — a sample of his wares, so he said.'

She turned back, puzzled, as Wat fumbled in the fastening of his jerkin and handed her a morsel of silk ribbon. It was pure white and fashioned, cunningly, into the shape of a single white rose. She touched the silken petals fleetingly and placed it carefully within the vest of her gown, close to her heart. He had understood. This was his message to her. As she turned back towards the house she was glad that Wat was unable to see the bright tears spark into her eyes. This strange man, whose arrival she had resented and feared, had touched her heart. She would pray for him, for the Saints knew he was going willingly into great danger. One part of her wished fervently that they would not see him again, for his coming would bring more danger to her beloved father, yet she hoped with the other, inner part of herself that he would survive the coming hazards and that they would meet again and rejoice together in the new-made peace and prosperity of the realm.

CHAPTER FOUR

ISABEL was busied in the still-room drying herbs. It was late July and very hot. She pushed a hand through the sweat-streaked hair escaping from her cap. The window was opened wide and she could hear the steady hum of the bees as they settled on the last of the lavender.

Her father was engaged on manor business. Lord Lovell's visit had brought him from the state of deadly despair. Isabel had been afraid that the disappointing news from Worcester and the north would have set him back. He had been savagely angered by the tidings filtered through Father John, but those black days following Redmoor were over at last, and Isabel was greatly relieved.

The rising in Worcestershire led by the two brothers, Humphrey and Thomas Stafford, had petered out miserably, and most of the peasant following just melted away. The King had proclaimed that all rebels who laid down their arms would be pardoned, and that had spelt the end. The Staffords had fled into sanctuary again, this time with the Abbot of Culham near Oxford, but even here they were not safe for long. On May the thirteenth the King had defied the ancient law of sanctuary and seized the brothers, together with many others of their followers. The Abbot had pleaded in vain for sanctuary rights, but though the Exchequer chamber had had qualms the council had decreed that treason was a common-law offence over which no spiritual agency, not even the Pope himself, had jurisdiction, and the brothers now lay imprisoned at Henry's mercy. Sir Edwin had raged against this decision, calling the men of Parliament and council 'arrant cowards'.

Even worse came ill news concerning Lord Lovell. There had been an attempt to raise the city of York, well known to have been fiercely loyal to the dead King

Richard. Yorkist supporters, attainted since Redmoor, had demanded entry to the city, brandishing letters patent pardoning them, though later it was alleged that these had been forged, but the city fathers had been fearful of reprisals, and when King Henry entered York on April the twenty-second he had been greeted loyally by the mayor on Tadcaster Bridge and a pageant had been given in his honour at Micklegate Bar. Again Henry's offer of unconditional pardon had caused Lovell's supporters to disperse, and he had been forced to flee into Lancashire.

Father John and Isabel's father had speculated endlessly on where Lovell had taken refuge and Isabel's heart had pounded uncomfortably at thought of Sir Adam Westlake in the same danger. They had heard nothing more. Isabel had comforted herself with the thought that at least she had not heard the two men had been taken. Adam was resourceful and would manage to get them clear of the King's men, she was sure. By now they were most likely out of the country. She hoped and prayed that that were so.

It was some time also since she had heard from James Tarvin in Winchester. She had received several messages soon after his departure, full of awed tales of Court life peppered with anecdotes regarding his own importance in the Queen's train. Isabel wondered if some of them were exaggerated, yet she missed him sorely and, now that the Queen's deliverance was near, hoped he would soon be back in Leicestershire.

She was abstracted, her mind intent on the careful drying of the rose petals, when a soft whisper from the window failed, at first, to gain her attention. The words had to be repeated louder — 'Mistress, it's Wat; please look up,' — before she lifted her head and saw the groom's sturdy form limned against the casement window-frame.

She wiped her hand hastily and went to him.

He lowered his voice conspiratorially. 'I've seen someone who would like to see you.'

'Master Tarvin; he's home?'

'Not that I know so, mistress. That weren't who I meant.'

She stared back at him wonderingly and her lips formed the words almost silently. 'Sir Adam?'

'Aye, mistress.'

'He is unhurt?'

'He looks well enough, mistress.'

'Can you take me to him?'

'Aye, mistress, best if you hurry. He shouldn't be staying around for long.'

'I'll come at once. Is he well hidden?'

'That place we both knew where I collected him and my lord.'

She was already moving towards the door and joined him in the courtyard.

'I have the horse ready, mistress.'

She was not dressed for riding but allowed him to lift her up into the saddle, bunching her skirts beneath her for comfort and modesty. Fortunately the village was deserted as they passed through.

In the clearing near a ruined barn they drew rein. Wat dismounted and was about to lift his mistress down when Adam Westlake forestalled him. He kissed her soundly in greeting as she laughed up at him, his face more tanned than ever after trudging the roads through this hot summer, his dark eyes for once alight with laughter.

Once he'd set her down on the grass and led her by the hand into the shade of the crumbling wall, she felt shy suddenly, and drew back a little to where Wat was securing the reins of their mounts to a nearby low bush.

Adam grinned at her. 'Does it concern you that you might be found with me — a wanted traitor?'

'You know it does not.'

'Then is it that we are here alone? What, Mistress Isabel, in full daylight and you at ease almost all of one long night with me!'

'That was quite different,' she retorted, 'and you know it. I was only concerned then about Cass. There were no other thoughts in my mind.'

'And no fears for my safety fill your mind now?' he mocked.

'You know only too well that we have been frantic for news of you, both of you,' she added lamely. 'Do stop teasing me and tell me of Lord Lovell. He has not been captured?'

'No, praise the Saints; he is safe and snug at the Duchess Margaret's Court in Burgundy by now. After the rout at York we took refuge in Sir Thomas Broughton's house in Furness Fells. The man is absolutely loyal, had been a friend and retainer of our late lord since his days as a squire at Middleham. We were totally safe in his hands. Later, when the hue and cry had quietened, we were able to take the road again, first to friends in Ely, and then he was able to take ship for Hainaut. I saw him last on the quay at Bishops Lynn.'

'Then why did you not go with him?'

He shook his head. 'I'll follow later. There is still work for me to do.'

'Every moment you stay in England you are in terrible danger. There must be others who could carry on the work, and surely it is over now.'

'No, Mistress Isabel, by no means over, and I have the means and the wish to complete my part of it.' He pointed towards the battered pack which had been discarded by the wall. 'Besides, it has given me the opportunity to renew our acquaintance.'

She was annoyed by the continued teasing note in his voice. Matters were too grave to be dismissed so lightly. 'You will really wish to see my father, though. . .'

'You would rather I did not.'

'I did not say as much. You know how afraid I am for him.'

'He is not a child, Isabel. He is your father and you should credit him with the ability to make decisions. Anyway, it was you I asked Wat to find for me.'

She felt herself reddening under his scrutiny.

'That fellow, Tarvin, is he still hanging about Hatfield?'

She was really rattled now. 'No,' she said sharply,

'though that is not your business. Master Tarvin is in
attendance on Her Grace the Queen at Winchester.'

'And what of his father?'

'He has been only twice to Hatfield. I think he senses
my father's hostility, though, for discretion's sake, I
have pleaded with him to be civil to the man. It would
be unwise to make an enemy of him. At the moment he
is away in Winchester visiting his son.'

Adam shot her a searching glance. 'You have a liking
for the younger Tarvin?'

'And if I have?' she queried stiffly.

'That is none of my business, I know,' he completed
hastily, 'but, Isabel, it is. For your father's safety it
would be wiser if you saw no more of Tarvin, at least
for the present.'

'Because of some new stupid plot?'

'A determination to unseat this usurper cannot be
termed stupid by any loyal countryman.'

She sighed. 'We shall never be as one on this point,
Adam. This latest ploy failed and many good men are
like to lose their lives——'

'One good man has already done so,' he said harshly.
'Sir Humphrey Stafford has been executed at Tyburn.'

She caught her breath, pity welling up within her for
the brave man who had been torn so cruelly from
sanctuary. 'Oh, I am so sorry to hear that. My father
will be very distressed. What of his brother?'

'He is still imprisoned. It's being rumoured that
Henry will pardon Thomas in a bid to appeal to the
hearts of the commons by a show of exceptional clemency. It would be that viper's way to attempt to divide
and rule.'

'He can do no good in your eyes, can he?' she said
softly. 'Can't you see that it would be better for all
Englishmen to accept his rule and allow the realm to
become prosperous again?'

He grinned mirthlessly. 'As you said before, Isabel,
we shall never be as one on this matter. Henry is a
usurper; he has no right to the crown. Until he is

unseated, I shall continue to work for his downfall. I believe your father is with us in this.'

She sighed. 'He is, I know it. You have a message for him?'

'Yes. Tell him the Earl of Warwick is in our hands and will soon come into his own again. He must hold himself in readiness but the call will come, if not this year, very soon after.'

'But the young Earl is a prisoner in the Tower still.'

'Tell him what I said, nothing more.'

His black eyes had become hard again and were boring into her. She was aware that he looked older, more tired than she had first thought. His healthy tan and cheerful manner had misled her, but now she saw there were lines of stress round his eyes and mouth and he looked round huntedly as if suddenly realising he had stayed too long in one place. How terrible it must be to be constantly hunted; yet he had chosen this way. He could, even now, be safe in Burgundy and apparently living a life of comfort, even one of luxury. Despite her irritation at his stubbornness, her admiration for his courage and loyalty grew, and she looked back at him steadily.

'You can rely on me to relay your words exactly, Sir Adam. Though I have no sympathy with your cause, I would do nothing to harm it, nor would I bring any added danger to any one of its adherents. You can be sure no incautious words will be spoken before Sir Gilbert Tarvin either by my father or me or any member of our household.'

He nodded, satisfied.

'Take very great care of yourself, Isabel. I hold you in high regard, despite our differences, and — do not sell yourself short.'

Her head jerked at this last remark and she felt herself reddening again. Obviously he had no good opinion of James Tarvin, and her lips set mutinously. Clearly he could not be expected to have. The two men had nothing in common and truly James had treated him shamefully, even supposing him to be the pedlar he appeared. She

could not deny that, yet her feelings for James Tarvin
were no concern of Adam. He had no right to give her
advice on a subject so patently outside his control.

Her manner was cool when she rose from the grass
where they had been sitting together in the shelter of
the wall and dusted down the skirt of her gown.

'You should be gone from here quickly, Sir Adam,
since you have so definite a distrust of Sir Gilbert. Here
the Tarvins hold sway and you could be suspected if you
are seen too often in the village.'

'I know it. I stayed only to see you.'

'I — I should get back to the house. One of the maids
will be missing me. . .' She dropped her icy tone and
said huskily, 'God guard you, and, Adam, thank you for
your gift. I — I treasure it.'

He shrugged lightly. 'It is all I have to offer anyone at
the moment — the badge of my loyalty. How is Cass?'

'Very well, and the pups are almost grown now and
roistering round the stables and courtyards.'

She knew he would have kissed her in parting. They
were friends, comrades, almost to be regarded as kissing
kin, but she drew away uncertainly. She had longed to
see him, to be assured of his safety, but now, in his
presence, she felt gauche, childish, a foolish chit unable
to understand and acknowledge the rightness of his
cause, and she was angered by her reaction. She turned
quickly to where Wat waited with the horse, ran across
the grass, and, after she was settled in the saddle again,
turned and lifted her hand in farewell.

He stood tall and straight, his black hair blowing in
the breeze which had freshened with the approach of
evening, and lifted his hand in salute. Her eyes filled
irrationally with sudden tears and, abruptly, she urged
her mount forward. A shiver ran through her as she
thought of the butchery perpetrated on Sir Humphrey
Stafford. The Virgin guard Adam Westlake from a like
fate.

She turned back, panic welling up in her at the
thought of his terrible danger, anxious to see him again,

warn him more urgently, but already he had disappeared, melted into the undergrowth.

As her mount moved forward again she dashed away angry tears. She had not meant to part from him so coldly. Always he angered her. She feared the hold he had over her father — yet after that night in the stable she knew she would never be able to dismiss him from her mind. She told herself angrily that she would feel so for any man so hunted, that it was a natural pity she had for all downtrodden, disgraced men who followed her father's allegiance, but understood in her own heart that it was more than that. She had been angry with James for his shabby treatment of Adam, but it was not concern for the humble vagabond who trod the highways in the heat of summer and bitterly cold winds of winter. In her first exchange of glances with Adam she had recognised his standing, had realised he was no common chapman, and had known that her feelings for James had undergone a change, subtle at first, now deepening into doubt. Irrationally she hoped to see Adam Westlake again, yet feared another meeting, knowing the dangers it posed for them all.

They were almost in the village when Wat pulled up short and cautioned her to rein in. A little knot of men-at-arms was gathered outside the inn, drinking and ogling two pretty village girls. Isabel's mouth went suddenly dry. She saw by their livery that they were Sir Gilbert Tarvin's men, and she had hoped the man safely away from Leicestershire visiting his son in Winchester. It was possible that these men were not those who had ridden south escorting Sir Gilbert, but it was very likely. She glanced hurriedly at Wat, who nodded, his eyes wary. If Adam was to be seen trudging the road he could be stopped and questioned. James Tarvin had made it plain he had a grudge against this particular pedlar, and he might well be seized and imprisoned at the Tarvin manor until Sir Gilbert's return. Tarvin had served in the Tudor's train at Redmoor. Now, while the last remnants of the rebels were being rounded up, it was especially unhealthy for Adam to be in this area.

One of the men straightened and put down his ale jack, calling the small company to attention, and, with a sinking heart, Isabel saw Sir Gilbert emerge from the inn. To her utter amazement, she saw the man who followed, pulling on his riding gauntlets, was James.

She had longed for sight of him and now he appeared at the very moment she could wish him far away. She also recalled the untidiness of her appearance and swallowed hard. It could not be helped. A meeting between them could not now be avoided. Even were she and Wat to turn back they were bound to have been noticed, and such conduct could only cause speculation in the minds of the two men she had most need to placate.

She urged her mount forward, forcing her most happy smile. She must try to see to it that James's attention was fixed wholly on her. It might be possible to draw the two men to Hatfield manor, so allowing Adam to pass through the village unchallenged.

Her welcoming smile became fixed when Sir Gilbert acknowledged her presence with the merest of nods. James, in the act of mounting, stopped short and stared at her. She waited for his greeting, but he touched his hat briefly, then uncomfortably looked first at the ground, then away. His father's curt word of command caused him to pull himself into the saddle and move to ride off after him. His eyes met the puzzled, hurt ones of Isabel and she saw him swallow hard, and shake his head very slightly, then he was spurring his mount to catch up his father's escort.

Isabel reined in her own mount and pricked back angry tears. Never had she been so humiliated. He had deliberately ignored her. Instinct told her his disgraceful behaviour had been due to his father's instructions, but she could not forgive him for that. Any man worth his salt would have disregarded such strictures. Furiously she dug in her heel against her mount's smooth flank so that the surprised animal gave a whinny of fear and displeasure and plunged forward so energetically that Isabel was forced to lean forward and cling tightly to the saddle with one hand to save herself from losing her seat. Once out on the open road she slackened rein and allowed a breathless Wat to catch up.

They rode on in silence. Isabel's head ached with the thoughts that spun round in it. Had James met some more noble lady at the Queen's Court and been ordered by his father to cease his attentions to her? That would certainly explain matters. He might very well have come to truly love some other lady. His letters had fallen off recently.

In her own chamber she dismissed Bess, who was anxious to help her change, and sat down on her bed. She had wrenched off her linen cap and now sat pulling it restlessly through her fingers. Then distress took the place of anger and she allowed herself the solace of tears.

She had mastered herself when Bess arrived to tell her that her father had returned and was asking for her. When she presented herself in the hall she had changed her gown and was completely presentable. There was no trace of redness about her eyes to betray the fact that she had been weeping.

'Well, my lass, what have you been up to?' Sir Edwin regarded her genially as he stretched out his legs indolently in his favourite chair. 'I put my head round the door of the still-room, where I expected to find you, but Ralf told me you'd ridden out hurriedly with Wat. Is anything wrong?'

'No,' she said quietly, glancing back towards the door to see if they were alone. 'Wat had met Sir Adam Westlake in the wood and took me to meet him.'

Sir Edwin started. 'Adam, back here? He's not wounded? Does he need to lie up here for a while?'

'No, he was anxious to get off on his travels, which is just as well as the Tarvins are back from Winchester.'

Sir Edwin's bushy brows met across the bridge of his nose. 'That's soon. I wonder why. Aye, best if they don't run across Adam. What had he to tell you?'

'Lord Lovell is safe in Burgundy, but Sir Humphrey Stafford suffered a traitor's death at Tyburn.'

'I feared that. His brother?'

'Still imprisoned, but Adam thinks the King will make a show of clemency.'

Sir Edwin nodded thoughtfully. 'Adam should be out of the country too if he knows what's good for him. If he's taken in his present guise they'll hang him for sure, worse if they suspect he has been acting as a spy for Lincoln and Lovell.'

A spasm of increased terror turned her body to ice. Now the Tarvins were back in Leicestershire their presence could mean disaster for the Yorkist agent.

'Please, sweet Virgin,' she prayed inwardly, 'see him safe out of the county.'

She swallowed, forcing her voice to become calm so her father would not realise the depth of her feelings.

'I think he's still here to drum up support for a second attempt to wrest the throne from Henry.'

Sir Edwin's eyes lit up at this and Isabel's spirits sank again. Now she would never be able to extricate her father from these plots.

'He said you were to know that the Earl of Warwick was well and in their hands. Father, that cannot be; didn't the King parade the Earl through the London streets? I put that to Adam, but he would tell me no more.'

Her father's eyes were narrowed and clearly he was thinking hard.

'If the boy Henry *is* the Earl of Warwick.'

'But surely there can be no doubt of that. . .'

'There have always been doubts. King Richard himself was troubled by the boy's apparent simpleness. But there, I cannot speculate as to why. . . When the Earl's father, Clarence, was killed in the Tower back in 1478, there was wild talk that the child had been smuggled out of the country to Ireland. The Duke's accusations against the King, his brother, were concerned with alleged plots against Clarence's heirs. I always considered these rumours to be entirely false, yet now. . .'

'You really think it possible that my Lord Lovell has charge of the true heir?' Isabel looked incredulous.

'If it is a sufficiently weighted stick to beat Henry

with, I welcome it,' her father retorted drily. 'Now what of the Tarvins? Had Sir Gilbert any news from Court?'

'He had nothing to say at all,' she said coldly.

'Nothing to say? What do you mean, Isabel? I thought you said you met them in the village.'

'We did, but they hardly acknowledged my presence. Sir Gilbert bowed in the saddle as they rode past, that was all. James. . .well, James looked merely uncomfortable.'

Sir Edwin's expression was thunderous. 'That man dared to insult you! By God, he'll answer to me for it. . .' he blustered, but Isabel placed a restraining hand on his arm.

'You will do no such thing, Father. Remember your commitment to Lord Lovell. Adam asks you to hold yourself in readiness for a new assault. You cannot afford to make a show of enmity now.'

Sir Edwin's mouth tightened and she thought he would expostulate, then he nodded and patted her hand comfortingly. 'Right as always, Daughter. There, forget the fellow; he was never good enough for you. There will be other men more well born, more suitable.'

Isabel could not restrain a wry smile. 'More suitable' meant committed to the right cause. Her own hurt feelings for James could not be so simply dismissed.

She busied herself about the house, thrusting aside her unhappiness and her anxiety about Adam Westlake. She was crossing the courtyard to make her daily call on Cass and her thriving litter when a man withdrew himself from the shadows round the stable wall and slid nervously over to her. She opened her mouth to call to Wat or one of the other stable hands, for the man was not one of their servants or workers on the desmesne, when he said softly, 'Master Tarvin sent me to you, Mistress Hatfield. He begs you to meet him in the church tomorrow just before noon, says you must not speak to anyone about it except your groom.'

Before she could give an indignant reply the fellow was off and had melted into the lengthening shadows as quickly as he had materialised from them. She stood, biting her lip uncertainly. Her first thought was to ignore the request, or, more pointedly, send back a cold-worded message to James Tarvin, then she reconsidered. Obviously James had gone to some inconvenience, not to say possible stricture, to send this man to her. She owed him the opportunity to explain his outrageous conduct of this morning. She drew a deep breath and determined to get Wat to ride into the village with her next day.

Sir Edwin was so busy nowadays that he rarely noticed where she was, and Isabel had no difficulty in making the tryst in the church next morning. Wat, as usual, kept his wary watch near the doorway. James Tarvin was already inside. He rose from his kneeling position near the altar rail when she entered.

'Isabel, thank the Virgin you came. I had feared you would not.' He drew her to the bench which lay down the whole length of the north side of the church wall for the convenience of those too frail or ill to remain standing or kneeling throughout the services.

Isabel moved slightly from him when he made to place his arm too familiarly around her waist.

He sucked in his breath sharply. 'You are angry. Of course you are. I knew I must see you and explain——'

'I think you made yourself very plain yesterday, Master Tarvin. You wanted no more of my acquaintance. Well, so be it; I was never so dull-witted that I could not take so pointed a hint.'

'Surely you saw how it was with my father?'

'I saw plainly enough that he no longer considers me a fit mate for his son and that he had every intention of preventing us from meeting in the future.'

James's comely face reddened. 'That may well be *his* intention. It is not mine, Isabel. *My* feelings have not changed. I want you to be my wife and have every intention of pressing for a marriage settlement between us.'

She stared at him wonderingly. 'James, how can that be if your father is so strongly against it?'

'Tell me *you* are not against it.'

'I. . .' She looked away, confused. Now that James was close to her again, she wanted everything to be as it had been between them before he had left for Winchester. She had missed him sorely, looked anxiously for his return, and now he was here and as ardent as ever. 'James,' she began again, 'I don't know if——'

'Tell me *you* have not changed.'

'I have not, but——'

'The King is hot against all former adherents of the late tyrant. Since your father was one of their number he fears that the King could not be brought to look kindly on a match between us. He has ordered me to forget you.' James gave a harsh little laugh, half a sob. 'As if I *could* forget you. I have thought of nothing but you since I left for Winchester—of your glorious hair, of your golden eyes, even more beautiful when you are angered. Isabel, Isabel, tell me you will be patient and wait until this blows over and I can bring my father to my own point of view again.'

He was bending towards her, desperation making him bolder than he had ever been before.

'Kiss me, Isabel, just once, a token that you do believe me and will do what I ask. Do not let your father betroth you to another while I am away. Promise me, Isabel.' He was leaning so close now that his breath fanned her cheek, then, suddenly, before she could draw back or prevent him, he drew her into his arms and kissed her hard on the lips.

She panicked and began to struggle. Understanding her fear, he kept control over himself and withdrew a little.

'Forgive me, Isabel, I presume too much, but I am so desperate to hear you say you will remain true to me.'

She said gently, 'All is as it was. When—when you come home again from Winchester, after the Queen's child is born, we. . .we must hope that the kingdom is quiet again, that our fathers will not be enemies. But, James, if you should meet someone at Court that your father and the King favour——'

'Do not speak of such a thing, Isabel.'

'Our fathers control our destinies; you know that as well as I do, James. You may find it impossible to disobey his command, especially if that command is at the behest of the King's Grace.' She put one finger lightly on his lip as he made to interrupt. 'No, listen to me, James. If — if that should happen, then know that I will not reproach you. We have not plighted our troth, must not. If the Virgin wills it, things will come right. We must hope and pray.'

'We could plight our troth here and now, before God's altar, then you could never be another's and my father could never force me to choose ——'

'I will not harm you so, James. It might be that you would come to regret such a vow, yet feel helpless to repudiate it.'

She saw he was struggling with his own longings, yet she saw also by his very expression that he was coming to accept the logic of her words. He bowed his head and kissed her palms passionately.

'As you wish, Isabel, but know, whatever happens, there will never be anyone I could love as I love you.'

She stroked his bent head gently. 'I must go. We must not be seen here together, not now.'

She signalled for him to remain where he was, then moved to genuflect before the altar. Afterwards she rose and went to her mother's tomb.

This illicit meeting had left her trembling violently and she needed the solace of prayer, seeking some guidance from the dear remembrance of the woman who had loved and cherished her always.

Why had she held herself off from the total commitment to James? She *did* love him. That kiss had affected her strangely. She sensed he had been controlling himself only with effort. Had she promised herself there, before the altar, surely her future would have been assured, despite the hostility of Sir Gilbert towards the match. Her marriage to James Tarvin would ensure some protection for her father, should he be unwise enough to commit himself too rashly to the rebel cause.

Yet she doubted her own feelings and she could not dismiss from her mind the sight of the tall, lean knight, dark hair blowing wildly in the wind, black eyes flashing with the intensity of his cause. She sighed. She knew so little about him, save that he posed a threat to her father's security and her own content.

She rose quickly and left the church with Wat. It would never do for Father John to find her here, possibly to pass James Tarvin on the path from the lich-gate.

CHAPTER FIVE

ISABEL was, in fact, chagrined to find herself away from Leicestershire when at last James Tarvin did return. The Queen was delivered of a son on September the twentieth, but it was not until the following March that James was released from service in her household and rode home again. The little prince had been received with great rejoicing and named Arthur, in honour of the legendary king who had established the court of chivalry and about whom Sir Thomas Malory had written so gloriously. Henry had recognised the need to focus attention on the symbolism of the child's name and had purposely arranged for his birth to be at the ancient capital of England. This royal prince would ensure the succession in his new dynasty. The occasion of the christening was marked by splendid festivities attended by the greatest nobles of the land.

Isabel had found the long months of separation tedious, and matters were not helped by the fact that the few messages James *was* able to send her had to be dispatched and received in utmost secrecy. Sir Gilbert did not call again at Hatfield Manor and whenever he met Sir Edwin in church or in the village the two men barely acknowledged each other's presence.

Christmas was celebrated quietly. James managed to write that the King had honoured him by appointing him to the household of the baby prince. In November rumours had swept the country that the Dowager Duchess of Burgundy was plotting another coup against the Tudor King and that a young man calling himself the Earl of Warwick had landed and been received joyfully in Ireland. Isabel remembered Adam Westlake's words and the strange conversation she had had with her own father concerning the Duke of Clarence's heir and could only wonder about the true identity of the

declared impostor. Naturally, during this period of
uncertainty, it would be unlikely that James would leave
the Queen's service. Henry would wish to assure himself
that his Queen and heir were surrounded by men he
could most trust.

In early March a messenger arrived at the manor with
a letter from Isabel's aunt Cecily in Newark.

'Cecily writes that she would be comforted if you
could be with her during the last weeks of her preg-
nancy,' Sir Edwin announced. 'As you know, she lost
her other two children and is so anxious that she should
carry this one to full term. The weather is sufficiently
improved for you to make the journey, and, frankly, I
think it would be a good thing for you to be away from
Leicestershire during these next critical months.'

'Why?' Isabel demanded suspiciously. 'Father, you
promised me you would do nothing rash. This boy in
Ireland cannot be the true son of the Duke of Clarence.
To implicate yourself in these coils can only bring you
into terrible danger, and with Sir Gilbert Tarvin living
so near——'

'Exactly, Isabel. I shall be under close scrutiny and I
shall feel happier if you are safe in Newark. You will
take Bess, of course.'

Isabel was fond of her mother's youngest sister, who
had married a successful gold and silversmith. Cecily
had always been delicate, and had not only had difficult
confinements but, of the two children she had con-
ceived, one had not survived more than three days and
the other she had miscarried. Now she was longing for
this new baby and Isabel understood her need to have
her favourite niece with her during these trying and
uncomfortable weeks of waiting. At any other time she
would have been pleased to go. Now she was not sure.
James might contact her at any time and she could not
trust her father to distance himself from the conspira-
tors. Already they had heard that even the dowager
Queen Elizabeth, the Queen's mother, had allowed
herself to be involved, or, at least, the King had
considered her so guilty. In February that beautiful

intriguing woman had been forced to enter a nunnery in
Bermondsey, under the King's extreme displeasure, it
was said, for the grievous sin of having allowed the late
King to receive her and her daughters at Court. Since
he had known that from the beginning when he had
been betrothed to the Princess Elizabeth, it seemed very
strange indeed that he should now turn so savagely upon
his mother-in-law. Isabel's father had yelped with
laughter.

'And to add insult to injury he has stripped her of her
estates and granted her an annuity of only four hundred
marks. How will she survive such an existence? It will
be true purgatory.' Like many Yorkists he had never
liked the Woodville woman whom King Edward had
married so secretly and whose machinations had caused
so many problems for King Richard.

'Why do you think he should imprison her now? After
all, she is the Queen's mother. This is bound to cause a
scandal,' Isabel said, shocked.

'She may know more about the fate of her sons than
Henry would wish to be divulged.' Sir Edwin shrugged
expressively.

Isabel had never mentioned the possible fate of King
Edward's sons. Following King Richard's accession the
two princes had been seen no more and it was publicly
believed they had been quietly murdered. Isabel had
been puzzled that no outcry had been made when King
Henry had acceded. Now that the Tower and all the
castles of the realm were in his hands the fate of the two
boys should have been discovered and made public, but
though the late King had been accused of many crimes,
including a vague accusation of the murder of innocents,
no information regarding the two princes, Edward and
Richard, had been forthcoming. Isabel's father had
never made known his own opinion on the matter and,
knowing his fanatical loyalty to the late King, Isabel had
been dubious about questioning the accusation of
murder which had besmirched his memory. It seemed
more than likely that either her father was right in his
assumption or the Dowager Queen had been unwise

enough to have been discovered communicating with
the plotters. Since her son the Marquis of Dorset was
also being kept under virtual house arrest, it was more
probable that the latter reason was the cause of the
King's anger. None of these scraps of information gave
Isabel comfort. Soon this treasonable venture would
come to a head and her father would become embroiled.

In the privacy of her chamber she took out the white
silk rose Adam Westlake had given her and recalled his
promise that he would do everything in his power to
protect her father. She had worn it always, hidden
beneath the embroidered vest of her gown, close to her
heart. Once she had thought to discard it — its presence
seemed a betrayal of James — but she had not been able
to do so and it continued to nestle there, a reminder of
her concern for Adam's safety. They had had no further
news of him. Surely now he was with Lord Lovell in
Burgundy, or perhaps he had accompanied this young
impostor to Ireland.

Since the winter had not been too hard the roads
proved passable and the journey to Newark was not too
uncomfortable. Wat Jessop accompanied them and was
to remain with Isabel throughout her stay.

Cecily Skelton was overjoyed to see her. Already she
was big with the child, but she informed Isabel that her
discomfort had not been as great this time as formerly.

'I was sick at first, but that was not prolonged, and
the woman Tom called in assures me that is a good sign.
She has an excellent reputation in the town and is going
to oversee my progress right up to the birth.'

Tom Skelton bustled in soon after Isabel's arrival, his
good-natured face beaming with pleasure.

'Eh, Isabel, you're looking rosy. It's a wonder to me
you're not carrying a child yourself by now. Some fellow
will be proud to have you take his name. Still, his loss is
our gain; it will be a great help to have you here with
your aunt. Welcome to Newark, my dear.' He gave her
a great smacking kiss and drew her into the luxuriously
appointed solar.

'Tom.' Cecily grimaced at him over her niece's head,

reminding him of the loss of Isabel's betrothed and the tactlessness of his remark, 'You are embarrassing Isabel. You get back to the shop and let me see her settled into her chamber.'

Tom Skelton shook his head, though, smiling. He was used to being reproved. His Cecily was bred from the gentry and had more fancy manners than he possessed. He had a shrewdness for business and was highly profitable, but left all matters of hospitality and the dealings with his more noble customers to her. He was a small, plump man who was already balding, some ten years older than his wife, but his pleasant features exuded good humour and Cecily was more than contented with her lot.

Isabel did appreciate the decided splendour of the rooms situated behind and above Tom's shop and workroom. The solar had glass windows, there were Eastern carpets and tapestries to enhance walls and floor, and the court cupboards boasted an array of fine pewter and silver. The small chamber she was to share with Bess was also extremely comfortable, though noisier than her own room at the manor. It overlooked the main road to the north and the great Norman castle, and was always filled with the sounds of iron wheels on cobbles and the cries of apprentices selling their wares and the voices of ostlers and grooms from the nearby castle stables and inn.

Leaving Bess to unpack their saddle-bags, Isabel went to the solar to exchange family gossip with her aunt.

'I haven't seen you since your mother's funeral,' Cecily sighed. 'How is your father now? He spoke hardly a word to me then and I could see it would take him long weeks to conquer his grief.'

'I think he would be still downcast if events had not given him other interests,' Isabel replied laconically. She knew well enough that she could trust her aunt and Tom to be discreet regarding her father's doings.

'Ah, then Edwin *was* involved in all that excitement last year. We feared as much. He was in no great danger?'

Isabel shook her head. 'Thank the Virgin, he was not directly implicated, never left the manor, but he was contacted and became more animated than he had been since Redmoor.'

Cecily nodded sympathetically. 'All this must have been gravely worrying for you. How are things with you, Isabel? It was a great shock to us to hear of John Heyward's death. He was a good man.'

'I revere his memory.' Isabel crossed herself. 'But life must go on.'

'There has been no other young man to touch your heart?'

Isabel hesitated. She loved Cecily dearly; she was more like an older sister to her than an aunt. 'There is one who. . .has paid me some attention — James Tarvin, our neighbour's son — but neither my father nor his approve the match.'

'But you are still fond of him?' Cecily eyed her shrewdly. 'And are still communicating with him, I suppose.'

Isabel blushed hotly. 'He has been appointed to the household of the young Prince Arthur, so has been away from Leicestershire. He has sent me several messages. We can but hope that matters will resolve themselves so that we may meet openly.'

'In the Prince's household?' Cecily mused. 'So this young man has a bright future, but I can understand why your father would disapprove of him.'

'His father is most hot against the match. He fears to lose the King's favour.'

'Do you love this James so much, Isabel?'

'I — I don't know, Aunt Cecily. He is handsome and attentive. He swears he loves me, but —— '

'Is there someone else, less suitable even than he?' Cecily queried smiling.

'No, certainly not; I. . .' Isabel broke off indignantly. 'I have scarcely set eyes on young men of my father's persusasion except. . .'

'Except?' Cecily pressed mischievously.

Isabel's eyes rounded in wonder as she thought of the

errant Sir Adam Westlake. 'I—I merely meant that I *had* seen one man, but he showed no interest in me whatever.'

'Then he must be blind,' Cecily said drily. 'Was he as handsome as your James?'

'Handsome?' Isabel considered the word and her mind conjured up a picture of Adam, his long, clever face, straggling black hair and his tall, slender form in that ridiculous disguise. 'No, I think not, but. . .distinctive, yes, I think I could say that—distinctive—but he has no amorous intentions towards me. His mind is bent on other, more pressing matters; in all events I do not know even if he is wed.' She reflected suddenly that the thought had not occurred to her before, and it upset her.

'And you did not think to enquire?' Cecily laughed. 'It seems that this James Tarvin holds all of your heart.'

'I think we should talk about something else,' she said hastily. 'Is Uncle Tom as prosperous as ever?'

'Indeed, yes. We have no Court patronage, of course, but his clients are wealthy and buy from him on a regular basis. He did get some of the silverwork ordered for the King's triumphant entry into York, though it did seem for days then that he might never enter the city and that the rebels would prevail.'

Isabel sighed. 'The trouble in the north was near to you. That must have been disturbing. And matters are not settled now. This young man in Ireland. . .'

'They say his real name is Lambert Simnel, and that he has been trained for the imposture by some foolish priest.' Cecily nodded. 'It is an unusual name. Tom wonders if it has been invented especially for the boy.'

'You mean he thinks the King is not sure——'

'Hush,' Cecily said gently. 'We cannot always know who lingers in the shop and can overhear us.'

She chattered on about affairs in the little market town and Isabel was relieved she asked no direct questions about her father's sympathies concerning this particular young man. At length she declared that Isabel was looking decidedly tired and she should go to her chamber and rest until it was time for supper.

Isabel found her stay in Newark comfortable but uneventful. Cecily continued to keep well, but she was too heavy now to accompany Isabel in rides about the countryside so, except for one or two sorties with Wat, Isabel remained largely in the busy little market town, most of the time in the pleasant solar, helping Cecily in the happy task of sewing the small embroidered garments for the much wanted child.

News from the south came to them more quickly than to the Leicestershire manor. Customers in the shop often stopped on their journeys north or were recent arrivals at the castle, so Tom Skelton was as well informed about Court affairs as any King's courtier.

'I hear that wily priest Stillington has been arrested at last,' he said as he sat with them in the gathering dusk one day towards the end of March. 'The King sent an armed band to Oxford to take him. He is being questioned and held at Windsor.' He chuckled. 'Henry would have hanged him long ago if he could have found a good enough excuse, but it's no simple matter to execute bishops with impunity.'

Cecily said mildly, 'Well, it was Stillington who declared Edward IV's children illegitimate. That cannot please the King, whose wife's honour is so besmirched. Do you think he has been plotting with Lovell, Tom?'

Tom Skelton chewed his nether lip reflectively. 'It's likely he will be accused of it, even if he is innocent. More grave tidings, I'm thinking, is that Lincoln has managed to evade the constant watch set on him and has sailed for Burgundy.'

Cecily put down her sewing with a little cry of distress as she observed the paleness of her niece's face. 'Oh, that makes these rumours of a possible invasion even more serious. The Earl of Lincoln was King Richard's heir. It seems strange, don't you think, that he should support this unknown young man in Ireland?'

Tom Skelton scratched his chin. 'The boy is a useful tool. Around him the disaffected will gather. Later, if

success is assured, Lincoln could then claim his own.'
He leaned forward to pat Isabel's knee comfortingly.
'There, child, don't distress yourself. This affair will
fizzle out as the last one did. You'll see.'

Isabel lowered her eyes to her stitching again to hide
the bleak despair she felt. If the Earl of Lincoln had
declared himself her father would be quick to follow.
Adam Westlake had promised he would guard Sir Edwin
from any rash behaviour. How could he keep his word
to her so far away, in Burgundy or Ireland?

Cecily's child was born on May the twentieth. The
confinement was comparatively easy and the child
seemed healthy, much to everyone's relief, but Cecily
developed puerperal fever two days later, and all Isabel's
herbal skills and devoted care were needed to bring her
aunt through the dreaded hazards which followed childbirth so frequently and took the lives of many young
mothers. She was therefore unable to send a satisfactory
reply to James when he sent her a message by a passing
carter that he had been released for a while from service
in the royal household and was back in Leicestershire.
He hoped she would soon return too. Cecily certainly
could not be left yet awhile. The fever had left her so
weak that the slightest exertion totally exhausted her.
Tom was frantic with worry and Isabel assured him she
would not leave Newark until Cecily was completely
recovered. Her little son continued to thrive and the
midwife had found a suitable wet-nurse for him, so at
least Isabel was not too concerned about the baby.
Scarlet with pride, Tom stood by the side of his wife's
carrying chair while his son was baptised William
Thomas, after his own father and himself. Isabel, as the
child's godmother, found her thoughts wandering as she
held her little cousin at the font of the parish church.
The following morning she sent the carter on his way
with a message to explain why she was delayed in her
aunt's house. The man assured her it would be less than
a week before he was back in Leicestershire and able to
deliver it for her.

Isabel's aching longing to be home again was com-

pounded when the most devastating news of all came.
The boy calling himself the Earl of Warwick had been
crowned as Edward VI of England in Christ Church
Cathedral in Dublin with a jewelled wreath borrowed
from a statue of the madonna. A sermon had been
preached by John Payne, the Bishop of Meath, and, it
seemed, most of the Irish nobility accepted him. The
boy had been hoisted on to the shoulders of Darcy of
Platten, recognised as the tallest Irishman alive, and in
this fashion carried through the streets of the city to be
greeted by a joyful crowd of well-wishers. The Earl of
Kildare was said to have taken the young prince under
his own wing and summoned a parliament to recognise,
publicly, his rights. A following council of war had laid
plans to invade England. Thomas Fitzgerald, the greatest of the Irish lords, resigned his seal of office to
accompany the invading army, but Kildare later made
the excuse of attending his own estates to avoid going
with them. Isabel's heart sank at the tidings. The die
was cast. Even more was she downcast when rumours
came that the Army was soon to set sail under the
command of a famous mercenary captain, Martin
Schwartz, the expedition largely paid for by Margaret of
Burgundy.

Tom Skelton could not hide his own disquiet.

'There's no mistake; the news is grave,' he said
quietly. 'The King will move north to meet the challenge, but have courage, lass; the worst of the fighting
will be in the north, since Lovell's and Lincoln's forces
will gather most support there and it's likely a landing
will be made on the Cumberland coast. Your father is
far from the area and should be safe enough.'

Isabel doubted that. She was racked with a gnawing
anxiety for him, and for Adam Westlake, who undoubtedly would be in Lord Lovell's train, and possibly, for
James, who was likely to be recalled into the King's
service immediately. Now that Cecily was recovering
she suggested, tentatively, that she should journey
home.

Tom shook his head doubtfully. 'I think your father

would strongly disapprove. Armies will be on the move
and an unprotected girl would be an easy prey. No,
Isabel, it is imperative you stay here with us until this
business is concluded.'

With this she was forced to rest content.

Adam Westlake sat with his back set against a hastily
erected canvas construction which gave temporary shelter from the force of the cutting wind. Foulney Island,
Cumbria, was surely the bleakest landscape he had ever
seen. The coastline was lashed by the biting gales and
merciless waves and he could see no trees or even bushes
to serve as shelter from the force of either. The square
pile of the dilapidated Piel Castle was to the east of him,
commanding the entrance to the harbour but long ago
left in a ruined, unmanned state. At least the invading
army of Irish peasants and Flemish mercenaries had not
been faced by an opposing force armed with ordnance.
Lincoln had been assured that the harbour was good,
even at low tide, and so it had proved to be.

The young Irish boy, Sean, who had attached himself
to Adam, grinned at him broadly as he polished Adam's
armour and sword. Adam's own squire had perished at
Redmoor and, though he had managed well enough
without an attendant, the boy had been persistent and
he had not the heart to turn him away. Adam looked
now towards the castle ruin where the commanders had
set up their control post and were even now planning
their next moves. Lord Lovell was of their number and
Adam must wait patiently for his captain to emerge from
the meeting before he could put to him his urgent
request.

A billowing silken tent sheltered the youngest
member of this expedition from the elements, and Adam
bared his teeth in a cynical smile as he noted the fact
that the lad had been excluded from the deliberations of
his captains. From time to time he had found himself
staring at the boy, slight and slim as a lath, with a grave
nobility of bearing. The boy was fair like most of the
Nevilles. The bright blue eyes had sometimes lingered

thoughtfully on Adam as if he doubted whether this tall, gypsy-looking knight accepted him as the true heir to England.

The meeting was breaking up and Adam rose and stretched himself. Lincoln came first, attended by the Abbot of Furness Convent. The man was whispering urgently into the Earl's ear and Lincoln was shaking his head impatiently. The other commanders followed and Adam saw that Schwartz was frowning. It was always the same. Noble lords rarely gave attention to the advice of seasoned commanders. Lovell came at last with his friend, Sir Thomas Broughton. The prominent Lancastrian landowner had been a retainer of Richard III from his days as Duke of Gloucester at Middleham. Broughton had never swayed in his loyalty and had fought determinedly against the Tudor from the remote fells of Furness. It was at his house, Broughton Tower, that Lovell had remained hidden before his desperate flight to Burgundy last year.

The two men came smilingly to Adam.

'All is decided, then. We move inland immediately and head first for Ulverston,' Lovell said. 'The Earl of Lincoln will inform the boy.'

Adam nodded. 'I waited to ask if I might ride out with one of the scouting parties.'

Lovell looked at him enquiringly. 'Where do you want to go, Adam?'

'Into the Midlands. I thought I would be the one best to convince our adherents there that they should march north to join us.'

'You are well known there. There could be risks, Adam.'

'Not if I travel in my customary disguise.' The white teeth shone in the swarthy, gypsy face.

'But to go on foot would take too long, surely?'

'Not if I ride my fastest horse till I reach Newark. Then I could travel more slowly. I want to go into Leicestershire and summon Edwin Hatfield. At the same time I'll have leisure to observe the King's force moving north.'

Lovell chewed his nether lip thoughtfully. 'You know the lie of the land there, certainly, and the King is said to be at Coventry. Undoubtedly he will proceed to Nottingham, and wait for news there, as Richard did in '85. Your information could prove invaluable to us.' He looked at Adam sharply. 'You hope to see Mistress Hatfield, I presume? She may be wed by now to that young coxcomb Tarvin.'

Again Adam grinned. 'I doubt that. At all events I promised her I would keep a close eye on her father. We owe her that, Frank.'

'Granted we do. All right, Adam. You get off about your business. I'll make your excuses to the King and to Lord Lincoln. We shall head into the Dales. Support is bound to come from Wensleydale near Middleham. Lincoln intends to waste no time in heading down the Great North Road to oppose Henry head-on. Meet us when you can with any of the Midlands contingent you can manage.'

They grasped each other's hand tightly.

Lovell said softly, 'God go with you.'

'And with you, Frank.'

Adam wasted no time in turning to order Sean to saddle his fastest hack and to look among his baggage for the familiar enveloping cloak and shapeless hat which were the symbols of his professed trade.

Isabel rejoiced in the fine May day as she and Wat rode home in leisurely manner to Newark. The May blossom was already budding in the hedgerows and she could hear a lark high overhead. Her father had a second cousin whose manor was close to the village of Fiskerton and, since Cecily had seemed so much improved this morning, Isabel had decided to take this opportunity to visit. She had been received gladly. Her cousins had last seen her when she had been just ten years old, and Mary Braithwaite had paid the blushing Isabel many compliments on her appearance. She carolled softly as her mare dawdled contentedly. Wat grinned at her, for once loosening his usual dour manner.

'You are thinking that now your aunt is improving we shall soon be able to go back to Leicestershire,' he commented, his eyes peering upwards to follow a hawk in its flight.

Isabel nodded happily. 'It has been an interesting experience in Newark, but I miss the people at home on the manor.'

They were about to pass through the archway which led to the stable and outbuildings behind Tom's shop when she was hailed delightedly.

'Isabel! Mistress Hatfield, thank the Virgin you are back so soon. They told me you were away from the shop visiting kinfolk. I thought you might stay overnight, and I have so little time. . .'

Isabel turned, open-mouthed with astonishment, as James Tarvin hastily dismounted from his own hack and came dashing towards her.

He had lifted her down from her mare before Wat could do so and stood holding tightly to her two hands. 'Oh, Isabel, it's been so long without sight of you.'

'James,' she gasped, 'whatever are you doing in Newark? I was thinking only this morning of writing that I should soon be home.'

'I'm on the King's business,' he said airily. 'Quartered at Newark Castle. Tomorrow I must be on my way to York. I could not believe my bad luck when they told me at the goldsmith's shop that you were away. I thought I might miss you yet again.'

'Yes,' she said, a little breathlessly, 'I can see how you might have feared that, but I do not leave my aunt for long. Does my uncle know who you are and — why you are here?'

'No, no, he doesn't know why I was determined to call.' He grinned, 'I told him it was your father I hoped to see, a neighbourly call only.'

'My father?' Isabel echoed, stupefied. 'Isn't he at Hatfield?'

James's eyebrows rose expressively. 'You did not know he was from home?'

'No.' Isabel's thoughts were racing wildly. He had

not come to Newark; then where was he? Alarm made
her cautious, and she hedged. 'We have cousins in this
part of Nottinghamshire. More than likely Father has
decided to stay awhile with some of them and then will
come on to Newark. Did they tell you at home he was
heading here to see me?'

James shook his head. 'No, I heard he was from home
and assumed he would be here with you.'

'Ah,' Isabel said, relieved. 'I did write and say Aunt
Cecily is so much better; he probably decided to come
personally to escort me home.'

'Most probably. It is as well I caught you alone even
for these few stolen moments.' His brown eyes were
shining with affection. 'My own father knows I have so
little time that he cannot fear that we shall meet.'

'He is still obdurate, then?' she said softly.

'More strongly so now that we know the rebels have
landed and everyone in the Midlands who is not heading
to join the King's defensive force is bound to come
under displeasure if not downright suspicion. It is as
well your father has a definite excuse to be from home
at this moment,' James said soberly. 'Knowing his
former sympathies, I doubt he would wish to support
the King with his retainers. Isabel,' he said hurriedly, 'I
bear him no ill will for that. I myself am committed. I
carry dispatches to York and must ride back quickly to
Nottingham with replies from the corporation.'

'The King is already moving north, then?'

'Aye. There will be fighting soon, and here, on the
main road to the north or nearabouts. It would be well,
Isabel, if you were soon away from here. It would be
safer for your aunt and uncle, too, to leave the town for
a while, especially as she is still weak from her ordeal.'
He looked at her longingly. 'It breaks my heart that I
must leave you so soon. I am bidden to sup at the castle
tonight. You will keep me in your prayers during these
dangerous times, my love?'

She put her gloved hand gently on his arm. 'You
know that I will, James. I will pray this will soon be
over and both of us safely back in Leicestershire.'

He turned away then and she watched him walk his horse towards the castle gatehouse.

Her thoughts were in turmoil as she entered the shop. Should she tell her aunt that her father had already left home on what Isabel was sure was the first step towards joining the rebel army? Cecily and Tom could be trusted, but other ears might catch what was said, and her father would be in grave danger of a traitor's death should King Henry succeed in routing the rebels. For the moment she must keep her fears to herself and hope that he would turn up in Newark, as she had told James Tarvin, to escort her home.

Cecily was cradling the baby and seemed well and cheerful when Isabel put her head round the solar door. She was about to go to her own room when one of the young apprentices came to the rear entrance to the shop and called up to her.

'Mistress Hatfield, would you be free to come into the shop for a moment? I know the mistress is busy with the child and the master is out. There is a young knight here and he requests that the lady of the house advise him about the purchase of a gift for his lady.' The boy pushed a hand through his tousled thatch of reddish hair and looked up at her appealingly. 'He is most insistent. I think he is from the castle.'

'I'll come down, Jem,' Isabel promised, 'the moment I have straightened my hair and brushed off the dust.'

She hurried into the shop some moments later to find that Jem had already laid out an assortment of gold rings, brooches and pendants for the appraisal of their demanding customer. The apprentice stepped back thankfully as she approached.

'Now, sir,' Isabel enquired cheerfully, 'how can I help you? I'm sure that your lady would appreciate any of these. The workmanship is particularly fine and——'

Her hands were seized and pulled across the counter. She gave a little angry gasp as the travelling hood their customer wore was partially put aside and she found herself staring into the hard black eyes of Sir Adam Westlake.

'What did you tell Tarvin, Isabel?' he hissed, his fingers biting cruelly into the soft flesh of her palms.

Isabel stared back at him defiantly. 'I don't know what you are talking about,' she snapped in a low voice, then added so that Jem could hear, 'I assure you, none of the brooches are overpriced, sir——'

'Get rid of the boy. I must talk to you alone.'

Angrily Isabel released herself and turned to the apprentice.

'Jem, I think this gentleman would like something particularly fine. The master has some reliquaries locked away in the solar. The mistress will give you the key. I take full responsibility,' she said firmly as the boy made to argue.

Jem nodded and left them, though somewhat reluctantly.

'Did you tell Tarvin where your father is?' Adam demanded sharply.

'That is hardly possible, since I don't know,' Isabel retaliated.

'I have just been to the manor and have ridden hard north when I heard he had left. He hasn't been here?'

'I haven't seen him. I presume he is. . .' she hesitated '. . .on his way to join the army.' She did not add which army.

She had not seen Adam Westlake out of his pedlar's clothes before. Today he was wearing well-cut riding clothes, woollen hose and a leathern jerkin. He had cut his hair since she had last seen him and wore it close to the scalp. She presumed with a heart-stopping breath, that it would be more comfortable worn so under the battle helmet. He had discarded leathern riding gauntlets and laid them down on the counter.

'I was watching outside and saw, through the open door, that the older lady had gone up to the solar. I guessed she was occupied with the child and thought it safe to request a woman's advice, hoping it would be you.'

Isabel acknowledged his explanation with a silent nod.

'Did Tarvin ask about your father's whereabouts? I saw you talking together on the street.'

'He told me he was not at home. That was the first I knew of his absence from the manor. I had to think very fast. I said he was probably with relatives of ours in the district — we have several — and that I believed he would come on here to fetch me home.'

'Good.' He wiped the sweat from his forehead. 'Are you to see Tarvin again?'

'No. He is commanded to supper at the castle. Tomorrow he rides with dispatches to York.'

'The devil he does,' Adam grated.

'Did you believe me foolish enough to betray my father? You must think me a lack-wit,' Isabel said tartly.

'I merely thought the man had caught you off guard.'

'He did, but I am perfectly aware of the gravity of my father's position should this ill planned and poorly equipped enterprise end as badly as it surely will.' Isabel's hazel eyes were blazing now with the scorn she felt for foolish, gallant men who would lead others to disaster. 'I blame you for putting him in this danger, Adam Westlake. My father would never have risked himself had you not come to summon him last year.'

'I think you know in your heart that is untrue, Isabel,' he said quietly. 'Sir Edwin was as anxious for the fray as any of us.'

Isabel was leaning helplessly against the counter now, the tears welling in her eyes. 'I'm sorry. I was so frightened. . . If this should go badly he could lose everything. . .and end horribly, as Sir Humphrey Stafford did, or perish miserably on the field.'

'That could happen to any of us,' he said softly. 'To James Tarvin too, if this goes the way we expect it to. You will weep for him, should he die; will you do the same for me?'

She stared back at him wonderingly. 'You know I will. Most of all I shall pray that hostilities do not begin at all, that the King will grant pardon to the rebels and they will all go home as they did last year. You cannot want another disaster such as Redmoor.'

'I want victory and my King in his rightful place,' he reminded her sternly.

She was about to expostulate that she could not believe the man he followed was the true heir when he came swiftly round the corner of the counter and took her by the shoulders.

'Listen to me, Isabel Hatfield; I might never see you again. For your sake I left my post by Lord Lovell and got his permission to scout out the positions and armoury of Henry's troops. I swear to you by all I hold holy that I will protect your father with my own life if it should prove necessary. Tell me that you wish me well and hold no grudge against me for my part in this.'

She drew a shuddering breath. He was very close to her and she could feel his heart thudding against her own, and the scent of horse sweat and leather came sharply to her nostrils. Fearful that someone would come into the shop or that Jem would return, she tried, unsuccessfully, to free herself from his hold.

'I—I hold no grudge, sir,' she said hoarsely. 'Sir Adam, you must let me go. You know I wish you well.'

'Do you grudge me one kiss in parting? I may never kiss another maid.' His tone was half teasing, but she sensed a great need in him and she nodded tremulously.

'Yes, yes, take your kiss, sir, but quickly; we might be observed and——'

He kissed her hard, so that she fought to get her breath. With mounting horror, she knew herself responding. Her mouth opened beneath his and her arms stole up around his neck, almost against her own will. They clung together desperately and she gave a little moan of panic. Almost immediately he released her and stooped to take her hand.

'You are a very gallant lady, Mistress Hatfield. These next days while you wait for news will be hard for you, harder even than those hours following Redmoor. I'll find your father, never fear. Meanwhile, should you see either of the Tarvins, make every effort to keep up the pretence that your father is innocent of any complicity in this rising. If things go badly wrong, and the Virgin grant they do not, he could then return to Leicestershire and take up life on the manor as if nothing untoward had happened.'

'And you, Adam, you could never do that—return to your own home?' she queried anxiously. For the first time it occurred to her that she knew so little about him. He came and went unexpectedly and left hurriedly, lived dangerously. There had been no time to talk of personal matters.

'I have no home—now,' he said harshly. 'Don't be afraid for me, Isabel. I have learned to live the life of the hunted, have had plenty of experience recently. If God wills it, I shall survive and either prosper or manage to escape.'

His kiss was warm on her palm as she heard Jem's feet thudding down the stair and his querulous voice raised in doubt. 'I can't think where those reliquaries were put, Mistress Hatfield. I've been looking every-where; that is why I've been so long. . .' His voice trailed off awkwardly as he entered the shop and saw that Isabel was alone, standing with one hand raised to her mouth as if she had been weeping.

'Has the young gentleman gone, Mistress Hatfield?' he asked incredulously.

She nodded, unable to find her voice.

'And didn't buy anything, and after all your trouble.'

Grumbling beneath his breath, Jem began to collect up the costly baubles and replace them carefully within the locked cupboard under the counter.

'It's a funny thing, but the people who cause you the most trouble either don't buy at all or keep you waiting weeks for your payment; that's what the master always says.'

Isabel swallowed hard and managed a tight little smile. For the moment she must not allow Cecily to guess how near the time was to open conflict. If James had been correct, they would be in the firing line here

in Newark, yet to venture on to the road would be
foolish in the extreme. Isabel had seen a little of what
plundering armies could do. No, they must wait
now and pray that no harm came to those they knew
and loved.

CHAPTER SIX

ADAM managed to rejoin his companions in the rebel army at Southwell by that same evening, June the fourteenth. Ordering young Sean to care for the horses, he went in search of Viscount Lovell. One of the mercenary sergeants informed him that the Viscount and the Earl of Lincoln had established themselves at the largest inn, the King's Arms, near the church.

Lovell was closeted with the other leaders in an upstairs chamber, but he kept Adam waiting only a short time before he descended to the tap-room to welcome him.

'Thank the Virgin you're back safe. I was beginning to fear you'd been taken.'

Adam grasped the other's hand, smiling. 'There was little chance of that. My identity was well hidden under that evil-smelling cloak and hat you hated so much on our last expedition. I only resumed my own clothes at Newark.'

'Have you news for the Earl?'

'Henry was heading for Radcliffe-on-Trent when last I heard. Our force appears to outnumber his but——' he hesitated '—as you and I are so well aware, our men are so poorly armed and equipped, especially the Irishmen.'

One hand on Adam's arm, Lovell guided him to one of the benches and called to the tap boy to bring wine. 'Now, did you accomplish your other purpose? Did you see the fair Mistress Hatfield?'

Adam reddened in annoyance at the Earl's teasing. 'Aye, I did. She's at Newark staying with an aunt. Her uncle's a noted goldsmith there. But what of her father? Has he joined us?'

'Yes, yesterday after noon he rode in and is lodged in

one of the houses in the church close. I'll escort you there shortly. He's in high spirits and raring for action.'

'Aye, he would be.' Adam stared moodily into the depths of his wine goblet. 'His enthusiasm is not shared by his daughter.'

'Ah, Mistress Isabel did not greet you kindly, I perceive.'

'She did not. Damn it, my lord, why should she hold me responsible for her father's doings?'

'Perhaps because you made yourself responsible. Did you not promise the lass you would guard her father from all hazards? A dangerous promise, since you are unlikely to be able to fulfil it.'

Adam was frowning, and Viscount Lovell prompted him gently.

'You did not find the lass wed, as I feared, Adam?'

'No.' The answer was short but forceful.

'Did she indicate that she still has a tenderness for the Tarvin cub?'

'I saw them together in Newark. Tarvin, it seems, is riding on Henry's business to York. She assured me she gave some excuse for her father's absence from home. I found he had already left when I arrived at the manor. I'm sure the girl is trustworthy enough, but discretion flies out through the window when love flies in at the door, and she still seems besotted with the fellow.'

Lovell smiled. 'That distresses you, Adam? I've never known you so taken with a lass before.'

'You mistake the situation. Nor am I now. My concern is that the Tarvins will gain information we would rather they did not.'

'I had not the feeling that Mistress Isabel would be loose-mouthed. She knows well enough what is at stake.'

'Aye, but she appears to dote on Tarvin.'

'Who is not fit to latch up her shoes.'

Adam turned angrily on his smiling persecutor. 'She is worthy of a better man. Anyone with half an eye to the situation could see that the fellow would be less than anxious to pursue the match if the Hatfield lands did not march so well with his own.'

'I think you do James Tarvin less than justice, Adam, if you think ambition his only motive in courting Mistress Isabel. From what I hear he has Henry's favour at Court and could do very well for himself in that quarter if he had a mind to do so. I think it likely that James Tarvin has truly fallen in love with our spirited redhead.' He rose and shrugged. 'At all events, matters will soon dispose themselves. Come, I will take you above stairs so that you can inform Lincoln and Schwartz of all you've managed to discover about the royal army and its present position.'

Adam woke to the sounds of frantic preparations outside the tent. It was still too dark to distinguish much, but as his eyes grew accustomed to the gloom he managed to see the thin greyish light of dawn limning the entrance flap. Sean stirred where he lay on guard across it and came quickly awake and to his side.

'You want me to help you arm, sorr?' The boy's voice was hoarse and unlike his usual cheerful pitch.

Adam grunted and thrust aside his rough blanket. 'Aye, lad, best to get to work at once. The chaplains will be busy this morning and will be hard put to it to hear all our confessions in time.'

The boy swallowed hard and Adam reached out and grasped the thin shoulder reassuringly. 'There'll be nothing to fear for you, boy. Your business will be concluded early and then I'll want you to stay with the baggage sumpters.' He looked round, rubbing his chin thoughtfully. 'Where is Sir Edwin?'

'He didn't seem to settle, sorr, went out very early. I saw him move over to talk to some of the men gathered round the watch fires.'

Adam nodded. Edwin Hatfield had been restless as a cat since he joined up with him at Southwell. There was not so much as one cowardly bone in the man's body. It was not so much fear of death in the coming battle which made him sleepless as a desire to bring this matter to a speedy conclusion. Adam sighed. He was going to have a hard job to keep his word to Mistress Isabel. Her

father would be eager to thrust himself into the heat of
the battle before there was need. His fierce, obsessive
hatred for the usurping Tudor who had stolen the throne
from his sovereign, and, worse, submitted that sovereign's body to infamous indignities, made him imper-
vious to all natural caution.

They had crossed the ford across the Trent at
Fiskerton last night and were now camped near the
church of East Stoke. Only a few miles away Isabel lay
in her bed at Newark. Did she know that her father
would commit himself to battle later today? Did she
spare a thought for him, Adam Westlake? He stretched
as Sean came to his side with the padded jerkin he
would wear beneath his breastplate. He must thrust all
thoughts of her from his mind. No woman had stirred
him as she had. He was irritated by the foolishness of it
all. There had been women in plenty in Burgundy,
yielding, submissive, some nobly born and of the
Duchess Margaret's court. He had satisfied his need
briefly, but always thoughts of the redheaded girl whose
anger was so fiercely directed against him intruded.
Curse the wench. Why should she hold him responsible
for her father's fate?

As if in answer to Adam's thoughts, Sir Edwin
Hatfield pushed back the tent flap and strode in.

'Ah, I see you are up. Can I call on the services of
your boy to help me arm?'

'Of course you can. Have you seen Lincoln and
Lovell? Are things moving already?'

'Aye. The chaplains have been busy all night. They'll
celebrate mass in the King's presence in an hour. We
can see the usurper's force clearly from the top of the
rise.' He snorted in grim amusement. 'Though I doubt
if our brave Harry will hazard himself. As ever, he'll
leave others to do his dirty work.'

Adam made no comment. He was not so sure of the
Welshman's cowardice as Edwin was, nor so ready to
condemn him for his tactics of allowing his captains to
counsel him wisely. He could wish that the young Earl
of Lincoln could be so guided. Richard's nephew he

might be, but his tendency to prevaricate and general lack of confidence in his own abilities made for problems in the war camp. Francis, Lord Lovell, though the man Adam most admired since the death of his King, was chivalrous and loyal to his friends but decidedly hot-headed. More than once Adam had seen him dispute hotly with Richard himself when there had been a question concerning the King's security. For all that, he could be relied upon more safely than Lincoln, who was prickly proud and liable to antagonise those who were most needed as supporters. The Earl had been so furiously angry with the Archbishop of Meath for refusing to take part in the coronation of the boy in Dublin that he had to be physically restrained from attacking the churchman. Both men would have been wiser to allow Schwartz with his greater experience to advise them. Both were too contemptuous of the man's lowly birth — he was the son of a shoemaker in Ausberg — to allow him free rein.

Adam waited while Sean finished buckling tight his right vambrace and nodded to the boy to fetch Sir Edwin's armour, which hung ready in the corner of the tent on its wooden stand.

He left the boy to do his work and went out to view the camp. All around him men were busy, giving last-minute adjustment to body armour and the protective leathern jackets worn by the men-at-arms. Fletchers accompanying the army were equipping bowmen, while smiths completed their final tasks of sharpening weapons. Grooms dealt with refractory stallions already excited by the commotion around them, scenting the sharp sweat of fear and anticipating the thrill of conflict. The Irishmen had no armour and precious few weapons. They carried rough-made pikes and billhooks for the most part. All had the rapt, withdrawn gaze of men who believed in the rightness of their cause. Small groups of men stood waiting to make their final confessions to the weary-looking, abstracted chaplains.

Lovell was standing near the royal tent and beckoned him over.

'Come and inspect the battle plans. Edwin has already seen them and approved.'

Adam lowered his head as they entered the silken tent near which the Clarence standard of the black bull floated in the breeze. He bowed respectfully to the boy who sat near the camp table, his priestly tutor, Richard Symonds, behind his folding stool. He acknowledged Adam's bow with a gracious nod of his head, and, as Adam moved towards the table, he saw that the boy's whole body was trembling violently. That wasn't surprising. Beneath his veneer of calm, Adam wasn't anticipating the coming hours with any sense of enjoyment. A man who did not feel fear before a battle was a rank fool. His own palms were sweating and his pulse racing. He bent to examine the parchment Lovell thrust beneath his nose.

'We shall take possession of the ridge overlooking the Trent, here.' Lovell sketched the line of the river with his finger. 'Adam, I want you and Edwin to stand to the right of the King. Those mercenaries haven't the same standards of loyalty as we have and the Irish are naturally less disciplined. I want men I can trust to guard His Grace.'

Adam smiled and quietly acknowledged the honour. The boy proffered his hand at Symond's prompting, and Adam touched the chilled fingers with his lips. He bowed again after hurriedly appraising the main points of the battle plans, and took his leave when the boy gave his faltering permission for him to do so.

Sir Edwin was fully armed when he emerged some minutes later from the tent they had shared. He was pulling on his mailed gauntlets as Adam approached.

'So we are to be royal nursemaids together,' Adam said, grinning. 'Mind you obey Lovell's orders and keep yourself out of the first shock of battle. I know you too well, Edwin Hatfield, and I've sworn to Isabel that I'll prevent you from committing stupid valorous acts of folly.'

Sir Edwin shaded his eyes from the glinting sun's rays. 'Ah, Adam, I was wanting to speak to you of

Isabel,' he said softly. 'You have seen her several times. You like my lass?'

Adam stared back at him intently. 'Like her? I have the greatest admiration for the courage and good sense of Mistress Hatfield.'

Sir Edwin hesitated and moved slightly from him, so that his back was turned. His voice came to Adam's ears a trifle hoarsely. 'If — if I should fall, Adam, will you swear to me that, before you even see to your own safety, you will look to Isabel's?' He turned back abruptly. 'I know I ask much, my friend, but I fear for her and the manor if things should go badly. I know nothing can be done about Hatfield. The manor will be lost to her, but I'd not see her harassed by Henry's underlings.'

Adam frowned. 'Her best plan, should the worst occur, might be to follow her heart's desire and marry Tarvin's heir. That way Hatfield might still remain hers.' His voice was deliberately flat and even.

'I can't believe she really loves that fellow,' Sir Edwin barked testily, 'nor do I think she will ever find happiness with him.'

'But what would you have me do, Edwin — snatch the lass off to a hazardous time in hiding while we made good our escape and then, at best, suffered a poverty-stricken, miserable exile in Burgundy?'

Again Sir Edwin stared back at him and his gaze did not falter.

'Aye, I'd rather see her live in penury than become that man's wife.'

Adam sighed heavily. 'Mistress Isabel has a mind of her own and is not one to be turned from her intentions. I swear I will do my best for her. You can trust me.' He clapped a hand heartily on his friend's shoulder. 'It's unlike you to be so pessimistic, Edwin. Let's make a good confession, check our weapons, and prepare for this business as thoroughly as our late King would have had us do.'

In obedience to Lovell's orders, Adam, with Sir Edwin Hatfield, took up his position near the Royal

Standard, on the rock escarpment overlooking the water-meadows. Before them the winding coils of the Trent glinted in the sun. The rebels were drawn up in a wedge formation and Adam, straining his eyes, could see the banners of the Earl of Oxford facing them, commanding the van of the Tudor's army.

In the battle centre there was soon fierce hand-to-hand fighting. It took all of Adam's persuasion to prevent Sir Edwin from deserting his post and hurling himself into the thickest of the mêlée. Symonds remained in attendance on his young charge and Adam saw the priest's lips moving constantly in prayer. The boy himself scarcely looked down at the battle raging in his name. His young face was white and strained and Adam knew his whole body was drenched in the cold sweat of terror. Once the battle had begun Adam felt no longer afraid. Like Edwin, he would have preferred to be in the van, but common sense told him he was more use to the commanders standing his ground here and guarding the youthful King.

At first it appeared that the rebels might prove successful, by dint of their greater numbers, for Oxford's force was seen to fall back as the rebel English and the Irish advanced, but Adam soon saw that the Earl of Oxford's command was reinforced by troops from Henry's main battle and the Royal force was equipped with superior weapons. Schwartz held the rear of the rebel army with his troop of mercenaries. Gradually the rebels found themselves being inexorably forced back and Adam felt a grim sense of satisfaction as he found himself at last engulfed by the tide of battle. He yelled an order to the priest, Symonds, and the boy's attendants to get the young King back towards the horse lines and baggage sumpters where he could be rushed to safety if the tide of battle turned completely against him.

Adam fought doggedly on foot, wielding his battleaxe as he had been trained to do all those years ago at Middleham. Soon he no longer felt the weariness of his right arm as it did its deadly work. Men fell before him screaming. To the rear he could hear the shrill, inhuman

cries of stricken horses. Once or twice the swirl of battle
brought Edwin Hatfield within his sight, then they were
parted again. Adam set his lips in a snarl and prayed
that his command had been obeyed and the lad had been
withdrawn out of the thick of the fighting. Sean, he
knew, was guarding his own equipment near the baggage sumpters. It was the least he could do for the Irish
lad, who had pleaded to fight at his side. Sean, like the
rest of his countrymen, was wildly enthusiastic for the
cause but lacked experience and was scarce strong
enough to handle a weapon.

Now he and Edwin were close again and his friend
called a warning as a man-at-arms aimed a pike in
Adam's direction. Off guard for a moment, Sir Edwin
failed to see the arrow which pierced his gorget and sent
him reeling to his knees, knocked almost flat by the
force of it. He gave a gurgling cry and Adam turned,
battleaxe poised high. He brought it smashing down in
a crushing blow on the shoulder of the Royalist knight
now facing him and dashed over to Hatfield's side to
stand, feet astride, over his friend's body.

For the next half-hour or so it seemed like a nightmare
of wearying struggle. Flying arrows and churned dust
made seeing almost impossible, and all Adam could do
was to remain over his fallen companion and fight off
blows which might have doomed them both. Soon he
realised the rebel army was in retreat. Men fell back
before the combined forces of the Earl of Oxford and
Sir William Stanley. He paused for a moment to wipe
the sweat of battle from his forehead, and viewed a pile
of fallen bodies before him. On all sides men were
abandoning weapons and fleeing towards the rocky
gulley behind them which separated them from the ford
at Fiskerton where they might have some hope of
crossing the river and finding some hedge or ditch where
they might lie hidden for some time and evade Henry's
triumphant pursuing army bent on exacting vengeance.

Adam cursed briefly and, bending, heaved Edwin
Hatfield's slack form over his shoulder and made
towards the only possible cover. Alone he might have

made the horse lines and ridden through the ford to
freedom, but he could not abandon his injured friend.
Every hope was lost now for the rebels; that was clear to
him. All that remained was to keep his pledge to Isabel
Hatfield and try to bring her wounded father safely back
to her.

He stumbled once under the weight of the unconscious man but managed to recover himself then stag-
gered on, his eyes set on the gulley ahead with its mass
of trees and scrub. He checked for a moment as a
youthful voice shouted to him from his right and Sean,
hoarse with fear and excitement, scrambled down a
grassy slope towards him, slipping and falling in his
haste.

'Sir Adam, sorr, wait for me, please, sorr, let me
help.'

Angrily Adam faced the boy, one arm steadying his
burden as Sir Edwin stirred and moaned.

'Sean, I told you to stay with the baggage. When you
saw how things were you should have got clear. . .'

Around them rebels streamed towards the ford. Some
yelled; most muttered prayers or grimly struggled
silently on. No one stopped to offer assistance except
the frightened boy.

'Where are you making for, sorr? Oi can help. Oi was
looking for you —'

'Some help you can be,' Adam raged. 'Look to
yourself, lad. Get away from here as quick as you can.
Get clear from the rest as soon as possible and lie low.
That's all you can do now.'

'But you, sorr, you won't leave Sir Edwin?'

Adam gritted his teeth in fury.

'No, damn you, I won't leave Sir Edwin.'

'The bushes beyond the ford, sorr, they're your best
hope,' the boy panted. 'The King's men'll be too busy
chasing the armed men. They'll want loot, sorr. Let me
show you. Oi wandered off while Oi was waiting, sorr,
for some summons from you. I think Oi know where we
can hide for a bit. You won't get far, sorr, burdened
like that.'

'No,' Adam agreed bitterly. 'Right, lad, show me where you think, then you must obey me and get yourself clear.'

The boy shook his head impatiently and set off, leading Adam through the dense bush and scrub of the gulley. Behind them they could hear now more screams and appeals for mercy and judged the royal cavalry was catching up with the fringes of the defeated rebel army. Soon they were splashing through shallow water and Edwin Hatfield was moving weakly against his rescuer's shoulder. Curtly Adam bade him lie quiet and set off again in pursuit of Sean's shaggy-headed figure as the boy turned left, setting himself against the path to Fiskerton village and into an area of scrubby gorse and low trees south of it. The going was bad; the ground rocky and deep-rutted, nettles and weeds choking the ground and dragging at Adam's unwary feet. Once into the depths of the spinney the boy turned and faced his master.

'Best to bide here, sorr, and let the worst of the pursuit pass.' His blue eyes were stretched wide in fear and he was panting with effort, but there was no sign of panic on his stolid young face.

Adam bent and lowered the injured man to the ground. Edwin Hatfield had fainted again during the jolting agony of the struggle over the rough ground and Adam knelt by his side, feeling for the pulse at his throat. He grunted his satisfaction at feeling it beat strong and true.

The boy squatted by his side and, for the space of some moments, neither spoke. The tree canopy sheltered them overhead and round them they could hear the stirring of animals and birds disturbed by their passage. In the distance could be heard the louder sounds of pursuit, the thundering of hoofs, frenzied yelling of men imbued with blood lust and desire for loot and the cries of men overtaken and summarily cut down.

Adam drew a hard breath and wiped a hand across his lips. Could it be possible that he and the others might

be overlooked here? Sean could be right. Pursuing
armies, he knew well, were driven to chase running men
like hounds a stag. Intent on slaughter and the desire to
strip the fallen of their harness, weapons and boots, they
might not step aside to find others wise enough to find
cover close at hand and yet not clearly within sight. Of
course he knew that their stay here could only be of a
temporary nature. Even should they evade capture
before dark, a thorough and ruthless search for rebels
would be set in motion tomorrow and on succeeding
days. He would have to get Edwin and the boy clear
before the Tudor's men cut off all roads and bridges in
the area.

'What happened to the horses?' he asked Sean.

'The first deserters took them, sorr. Some were
frenzied and took off on their own account. One of the
squires was struck down and killed trying to hold in one
of the destriers. Oi managed to keep a hold on your
bundle with your pedlar's clothes, sorr. Oi thought that
might be useful.'

Adam uttered a silent prayer to the Virgin for the
boy's forethought.

'Did you hear anything about the fate of our leaders?'

'The first men fleeing were shouting that the Earl of
Lincoln was dead, sorr. Someone else said he'd seen
milord Lovell trying to swim the river in full armour.
He might have made the other bank, sorr,' Sean said
hopefully, his eyes appealing for Adam's agreement.

Adam lifted one shoulder in a rueful shrug. In full
armour Frank Lovell would have a hard task to survive,
but there were worse deaths than drowning. He turned
his mind from fears of his friend's fate and tried to
review their situation competently.

Edwin needed medical aid but, obviously, the services
of a surgeon were denied them. He set himself to wait
until the worst signs of pursuit died down and he could
send Sean back to the river for water.

Edwin stirred again and came slowly to his senses.

'Adam?' He tried to struggle upright, but relentlessly
Adam pressed him down again to the ground.

'Where are we, Adam? Is the battle done? How went it?'

'Lie quiet, Edwin. Yes, it is over and things went badly for us. We must keep quiet for a while lest we be discovered. Are you in bad pain?'

'Aye, bad enough.' Edwin's voice was hoarse and weak. 'But I'll survive. What is it, an arrow?'

'Aye, through the gorget. When you can bear it I'll break off the shaft and try to knock it through. When we can get your harness off we'll be able to see the extent of the damage, but there's not too much bleeding for the moment.'

Edwin licked dry lips. 'I could do with a drink, Adam.'

'I know that,' was the snapped answer, 'but it's too dangerous to make the river for the present.'

Edwin nodded ruefully and sank back, his head resting against the bole of a sapling oak.

'You should not endanger your life staying with me, Adam. When you can, you and the boy must leave me here.'

Adam grinned mirthlessly. 'And what, pray, would I say to Mistress Hatfield when I next see her?'

'Isabel will understand.'

'I think not,' Adam rejoined softly. 'At all events, nothing can be decided at the moment. We are as safe here as anywhere. The pursuit will be through Fiskerton village and in the other direction into Newark over the bridge. Oxford and Stanley will have enough trouble reining in their hounds when the Tudor has need of them.'

'What of the Earl and Frank Lovell?'

Adam shook his head. 'I don't know. Sean here says it's rumoured that Lincoln is dead and Lovell was last seen swimming the Trent.'

Edwin Hatfield gave a low whistle. 'Then all is lost.'

'Aye,' Adam said bitterly. 'I notice you don't enquire about our young King.'

Edwin sighed. 'We knew the risks, Adam.'

'Aye, *we* did, but did the boy?'

Edwin made as if to speak, then abruptly changed his mind. The two men avoided each other's eyes as if their shared knowledge that the boy had been used solely as a pawn in the Yorkists' desire to defeat Henry Tudor weighed heavily on the conscience of both of them.

The noise of the savage hunt continued and the three settled themselves in silence to wait for some sign that it might be diminishing. Adam could see that Edwin's face was drawn with pain and his eyes closed in exhaustion. Sean sat a little withdrawn from them, chewing his nether lip. From time to time he looked towards Adam, seeking reassurance or further orders. The sun had been high overhead when they'd entered the copse, and, though the canopy showed only glimpses of light between the interweaving branches, it was possible to tell when it began to wester, and for some time it had seemed to the three breathless listeners that there was quiet around them save for the usual wood sounds. Adam sat bolt upright and signed to Sean to come closer.

'Boy, help me get Sir Edwin's harness off. I think he can stand the pain of it now and there appears less need for us to be fully armed.'

Hatfield sat up painfully and allowed Adam and the boy to work at the fastenings of his breastplate. Adam had already broken off the shaft and it was possible at last to draw off the body armour and lay bare the padded gambeson. The arrow had pierced the flesh beneath the gorget and breastplate and Adam now saw the shortened end protruding from Sir Edwin's left breast, surrounded by an ominous dark stain. He breathed a quick prayer to the Virgin and St Luke the physician that the deadly shaft had not damaged heart or lung. He had the soldier's knowledge of simple healing skills, could deal with an arrow as he planned to do now, pad a wound to check heavy bleeding, bind up a broken limb in the hope it would heal true, but he possessed no real expertise and could only trust that he did no further harm by his rough and ready surgery. Certainly there was no hope of calling in a barber-surgeon yet awhile. If

Edwin was to travel the shaft must be removed. He set his teeth for his grim task and looked enquiringly at his friend.

Edwin's face had gone ashen and his hazel eyes were dark with dread, but he nodded just once.

'Get behind Sir Edwin, Sean, and steady his shoulders. Try to hold him still for me.'

The Irish boy wriggled into position obediently.

Adam drew his dagger and cut through the padding of the gambeson. He'd no time for dealing with refractory buckles. Sean helped him remove the garment and tear the shirt beneath clear to reveal the wound.

It was not the first time Adam had peformed this service for a companion. Once, on the Scottish border, he had removed an arrow from a fellow knight's shoulder, but the shaft had lain higher, not so near to vulnerable organs, and he had had the services later of a skilled army surgeon. He cleaned his hands as best he could on a tuft of grass, wiping off the sweat of revulsion for the task in hand. He must get a firm grip. To probe the area round the broken-off shaft could give only further pain. The head must be knocked through as swiftly as possible. He bent to the work. Edwin Hatfield gave a strangled half-scream and Sean a gasp as the blood-stained arrow head emerged from between the wounded man's shoulder blades and Adam threw it aside and, tearing free a portion of Edwin Hatfield's ruined shirt, padded the wound to check the sudden rush of blood and bound it in place with a further strip of cloth. He watched anxiously for any sign that a vital organ had been damaged, but no blood issued from between his friend's lips. He had slumped back in Sean's arms and was unconscious again. Adam leaned back and wiped bloodied hands on the grass.

'So far, so good,' he grunted. 'The shaft is out; we can but wait now and hope for the best. Let him lie, Sean, better if he stays unconscious for a while.'

The boy lowered the knight's shoulders to the ground and looked enquiringly into his master's strained features.

'Is it safe to go to the river now, sorr?'

'I think so. Keep low when you emerge from the copse and if there are men in sight don't risk yourself. Obey me, now, boy.'

Sean rose to his feet and left the little clearing. Adam could hear the rustling as he crawled through the undergrowth. He turned his attention back to his friend. He'd managed to drape the remains of the torn shirt and gambeson round Edwin's shoulders. It was still very early summer and now that the sun was setting it was becoming already quite chill. Adam's thoughts went to Edwin's daughter waiting in tortured suspense for news of the battle. He hoped she and the goldsmith's family had taken his advice and remained within the house. They must know by now that the armies had engaged and the battle was lost. Isabel would be frantic for news. Possibly she would even now be praying earnestly for her father's safety and the life of her lover. Adam's teeth grated together in a sudden snarl as he thought of James Tarvin. They were natural enemies, but his contempt for the man was stronger than would have been usual in such a situation. A knight who treated his inferiors with such callousness was not to be trusted to care for Isabel's proud spirit. Once wed to the man, she would find herself trapped, and unless Edwin could be returned to his own manor without his neighbours being aware of his complicity in this débâcle he would not be near to help his daughter in her dire need. Adam sat back on his haunches, eyes narrowed, his thoughts churning around in an effort to think out what move would be most practical. Before morning Edwin must be moved. For that some conveyance was needed. The only people Adam could trust to help would be Isabel and Tom Skelton. He would rather a thousand times she be kept clear of this business, but their assistance was Edwin's only hope.

He froze into stillness, his fingers ready on his dagger hilt, as rustling told him of someone's stealthy approach. The noise stopped and Sean's voice called softly. The

lad was not fool enough to burst in on Adam without
prior warning.

'It's Sean, sorr; I've got the water.'

He moved slowly into the clearing, bearing muddied
water carried from the river in the discarded salet of one
of the dead men-at-arms.

Gratefully Adam took the helmet and gave a long pull
at the brackish liquid. Edwin's lashes began to flutter
open again and he proffered the helmet as his friend
struggled into a sitting position.

'Not too much, Edwin,' he warned, as Hatfield gulped
thirstily.

Sean shook his head as the helmet was offered. 'I
drank enough before Oi started back, sorr. It's quiet
back there now, but for the dead men.' He crossed
himself. 'Saint Brigid knows there's scores enough of
them and most of them ours.' He sank down on the
ground. 'What do we do now, sorr? Oi could see flaring
torches back along the river, down by the town, Oi
reckon. The chase 'as been called off for now, I'm
thinking. Do we rest here through the night?'

Adam smiled faintly with grim amusement at the
thought that the dead were not included in Sean's
assessment of what made for quiet. He moved slightly
out of earshot of the injured man and bent his head to
speak softly.

'You say you managed to bring my pedlar's clothes
and pack with you?'

'Yes, sorr, I thought you might have need of it.'

'I certainly have. Now listen, Sean, I want you to stay
here with Sir Edwin. Try to head him off from questioning where I'm going.'

'But what shall I say, sorr, when he asks?' The boy
scratched his head uncomfortably.

'If he sees you're reluctant to talk he'll know you've
been forbidden to say.'

The boy's eyes were troubled. 'Ye be going into town,
sorr? That be——'

'Very dangerous. I know that well enough, but we
have to have some means of getting Sir Edwin out of

here before the search for fugitives is renewed in the morning, as it surely will be.'

'Wouldn't it be safer if I go, sorr?'

'No,' Adam rejoined curtly. 'Your accent would give you away at once and you don't know Newark as well as I do. Now go and fetch the bundle.'

Sean opened his lips to argue, then, catching his master's fierce gaze full on him, went obediently to where he'd stowed the pitiful amount of gear he'd managed to get clear of the baggage train before the deserters had plundered it.

Adam went back to his friend.

'How are you feeling now, Edwin?'

'Deuced weak and sore, but I'll do well enough. You should be leaving now, Adam.'

'Aye, but I hope to come back with some horses.'

'The devil you will. . .' Sir Edwin tried weakly to pull himself up from the ground.

'Now lie quiet, Edwin, and keep your eye on the boy. He's like to panic and if he runs now he would be picked up easily by the Tudor's men as one of the Irish. There are horses running wild — must be. I'll see if I can round one or two of the beasts up. A sumpter would be better than nothing.'

'There'll be human ghouls among the dead.'

'Aye, I'll watch myself.' Adam was busy stripping off his armour with Sean's assistance, and pulled the pedlar's dark houppeland over his gambeson. 'With luck I'll be taken for one of them. Is there any food in that bundle, Sean?'

'Aye, sorr, just some black bread and cheese.'

'Then dole some out to each of us. It should be safe to go to the river for water, but there'll be looters stripping the dead soon, so mind how you go. Whatever you do, don't lead anyone back to Sir Edwin here.'

Before Edwin could question him further, he swallowed the stale dark bread and morsel of cheese hastily and donned the old, concealing felt hat. 'Right, I'll be off.'

He shouldered the heavy pack and, bending low,

pushed his way through the undergrowth towards the ford.

Dusk was shrouding the land as he made the path leading to Fiskerton village. As yet there were few living souls about. He splashed through the water and made for East Stoke church. From the rise he saw flaring torches again from the vicinity of the town and, even from this distance, could hear the yells and drunken laughter from the triumphant army. A man passed him near the churchyard gate, but merely glanced at his pedlar's garb and scuttled past. Adam had avoided the rocky gulley where he knew the greatest numbers of the dead lay, and, following the coils of the river, made for the town.

As he had expected, Newark was full to the brim with plundering soldiers. He trudged along determinedly and, like the man in East Stoke, no men challenged him once they had seen his clothing. Several men-at-arms actually called him over to inspect his wares and one bought ribbon for the woman who was screeching with drunken laughter and clinging to his arm.

Most of the householders had shown good sense and shuttered their windows and remained indoors. The goldsmith's shop was of their number, and Adam noted with gratification that the shutters were very soundly bolted. The standards of the Royalist nobles fluttered from the castle gatehouse, and no doubt many were feasting within its walls. Adam moved silently towards the archway which led to the rear of Tom Skelton's shop. As he feared, the gate there was securely locked. He lowered his pack and turned to see if he was being observed from the street. Again, no one heeded him. All were busy about their own amusements. With a grunt Adam heaved the pack high and heard it fall on the far side in Tom Skelton's yard, then jumped, catching with clawing fingers at the top of the gate itself. Fortunately no rough shards or obstacles tore at his questing finger-tips, and he was able to draw himself up and jump clear on the far side. The yard was dark and deserted. The rear windows, too, were shuttered and barred. Tom

Skelton was taking no chances that the army would be out of control and its men eager to break into the homes of peaceful and innocent citizens.

Adam padded over to the house and explored. He tried the door, but without hope of finding it unlocked. Glancing upwards, he saw the upper chamber windows were tightly shuttered, but, as no gleam of candle light showed there, he concluded all the household had remained below in the store-room behind the shop probably. As Tom Skelton kept his more valuable goods there it would be the strongest place, the least likely to be broken into easily. Adam took a long breath. He moved again to the door and knocked as loudly as he dared. He had little hope that anyone would be so incautious as to open for him, but drew back and waited. No one answered and he could hear no footsteps from inside. Patiently he tried again. At first he thought that knock, too, would be ignored, but this time his optimism was rewarded by the sounds of footsteps approaching the door, and a querulous voice called, 'Who's there? What be you wanting?'

Adam called, 'Just a pedlar. Tell your master that Mistress Hatfield asked me to call with some special ribbon she ordered.'

There was a pause and the voice retorted ungraciously, 'What a time to call. It's not likely the master'll deign to see you now.'

'Just give him my message, man.'

Grumbling loud enough to be heard outside, the servant or apprentice moved away and Adam went back to the gate where he'd abandoned his pack and returned to the door. Surely, if Isabel was still in the Skelton house, she would realise who the visitor was and know he had urgent news.

There was movement again on the far side of the stout door. Adam could hear a whispered argument, then a woman's voice. 'Tom, I'm sure it will be safe. Please open up.'

There was a noise of bolts being drawn back and the rattle of chain, then the door was pushed ajar, only sufficient for the owner to catch a glimpse of his unwelcome visitor.

Hurriedly Isabel Hatfield pushed by the goldsmith and peered anxiously out into the darkness. Her eyes focused on the dark shape of Adam Westlake and she gave a little frightened cry.

'Sir Adam, it is you?'

'Yes, Mistress Hatfield. Will you let me in?'

She reached out and drew him into the dim hall. Neither she nor Tom Skelton had carried a rushlight, and the only glimmer came from the store-room beyond.

'You'd better come in here, sir,' the goldsmith muttered gruffly. Adam moved into the lighted chamber and heard the door being secured behind him. Now he saw that the family and workforce were assembled, Mistress Skelton seated on a cushioned stool, clasping her child in her arms. Isabel's eyes were stretched wide with fear.

'We heard; the battle is lost. My father——'

'Is injured and needs help, mistress.'

Tom Skelton gasped behind him.

'Where is he? Can't he walk? All the rebels will be hunted down tomorrow. Some have been summarily hanged in the market-place. . .'

Adam winced inwardly at the thoughtless words which had further alarmed Isabel.

'He took an arrow between gorget and breastplate. I've knocked it through, but the pain is considerable. He lies in a copse near the gulley at East Stoke, but should be got clear tonight. Have you a cart, some means of conveyance?'

'Yes, a donkey cart I use sometimes for delivering larger objects, but where will you take him?'

Isabel said quickly, 'He should not come here. We may be searched.'

Adam nodded. 'I realise every house in the district is likely to be. He should be got home as soon as possible. If he could lie low for just another day, we must then leave for Leicestershire. You said it is believed he has come here to escort you home?'

'Aye, Sir Adam.' Someone else moved into the shadowed store-room and Adam recognised Wat Jessop. 'But if he must travel in a cart he's likely to be judged suspect should you be stopped on the way and questioned.'

Adam grimaced. 'If he could ride——'

Isabel cut in. 'Tonight he could stay hidden in my cousin's barn. It's not far from Fiskerton. They would help gladly.'

'Better still if they didn't know,' Adam said thoughtfully. 'That is, if the place is unbarred. Then, later, Wat here could join us with horses for the journey south.'

Tom nodded. 'It seems as fair a plan as any. I'll go and harness the cart.'

Isabel made towards the door. 'I'll fetch my herb chest from my room. He'll need tending.'

Adam said sternly, 'You cannot go with me.'

She faced him defiantly, her feet planted firmly astride like a boy's.

'It would take a stouter man than you are to prevent me, Adam Westlake.'

'Mistress, you cannot imagine what sights you will see out there in the gulley.'

'The dead, you mean? Can such sights be worse than nursing my own mother through the sweating sickness, seeing every moment of her suffering, watching her die, and knowing oneself to be helpless? You know well enough that my father's gravest peril now is infection in the wound.'

'That is true, but he does not bleed unduly——'

'Infection is far more serious. I need to dress the wound, and quickly.'

Adam drew a hard breath. 'Change into one of your maid's kirtles and bring a dark cloak or wrap, as old and ragged as possible.'

She didn't wait for further instructions, but gathered up her skirts and ran from the room.

Wat Jessop said gravely, 'How great is the mistress's peril?'

'Great enough if she's found with me and I am

recognised, but the men are busy about their own concerns for tonight. The biggest danger will be from those who plunder the dead.'

Cecily Skelton gave a horrified scream and Adam turned on her, smiling grimly. 'Yet those very devils may aid us. In the cart, dressed as we are, we may be taken for ghouls like themselves and pass freely through their ranks.'

Tom Skelton came back into the room and inclined his head. 'You are right, of course. This is Edwin's only hope. I know only too well you endanger yourself remaining with him. The cart is ready harnessed in the yard.'

'Once he is on the way to Swithland and clear of this district I can think of my own skin.' Adam turned to Wat Jessop. 'Do you know where this farm is, the one she speaks of?'

'Yes, Sir Adam; I'll join you there tomorrow with the horses, the moment I feel it's safe to risk leaving Newark.'

Isabel was back already, and clad, as Adam had ordered, in a dark kirtle and hooded cloak. Behind her, on the stair, Adam could hear Bess's hysterical complaints. Isabel ignored them.

'Come, Sir Adam, we waste time.' She went hurriedly to her aunt and was tearfully embraced.

'Dear Aunt Cecily, pray for us. I may not see you again for a while.' She bent and kissed the child's head tenderly, then, forcing her lips into a brave smile, she moved in front of Adam on their way to the back door.

CHAPTER SEVEN

ISABEL sat with her knees pressed very close together to prevent them trembling. The jolting of the cart thrust her shoulder to shoulder with Adam Westlake as he drove carefully through the archway leading from the goldsmith's yard into the street. He glanced sideways at her just once then gave his attention to the donkey.

'Keep your hood well up and, whatever is said to you, remain silent.'

She clasped her hands tightly on her lap. There had been no time to question Adam more closely about her father's condition and, despite her brave words to him, she was terrified at thought of what she would have to face on the battlefield.

Some distance from them men veered drunkenly across the street and whooped and shouted with amusement as Adam was forced to rein in or run them down. There were women with them, scantily clad, their hair streaming freely down their backs, singing as riotously as the men. Isabel wondered if they had accompanied the army with the baggage train as she knew whores did or whether they were local women who had been encouraged to join the company by the free-flowing ale and promise of costly trinkets looted from the fallen. She shuddered and averted her eyes.

A harsh voice challenged them to halt as they reached the last house in the town. Again Adam reined in and two men marched up to the cart. One, the elder of the two, appeared to be a sergeant, while the other, a brawny young archer, was clearly there to enforce his superior's orders.

Adam assumed the obsequious whine Isabel remembered from their first meeting.

'What is it, Captain? Be there orders to forbid our leaving town?'

The sergeant ignored the flattering greeting and ducked his head to peer into the cart's interior.

'Where are you bent?' The man's tone was uncompromising. His fierce eyes appraised Isabel where she sat huddled close to Adam, one hand holding her hood to hide her face.

'The wife and me are bound for Stoke.' Adam made no attempt to lie. He gave a grim laugh. 'We're bent on the same work as you've been, Captain, like as not. We've been told there's rare pickings to be had.'

The man's florid face, viewed in the flaring torch his subordinate held, flamed even more, as if he disliked the imputation.

'You're certainly up to no good. The devil take you,' he said contemptuously, 'for you're up to his work and no other. Get you gone; I've no orders to detain honest citizens about their business.' He emphasised the word 'honest' further to reveal his detestation of the purpose he judged they were about, out so late. Again his gaze dwelt broodingly on Isabel, then he gave a signal for the cart to proceed and stood back.

Isabel was shaking as the cart's iron wheels rattled from the cobbles of the town on to the harder ruts of the country road. The moon was up and she could view the coils of the river glimmering silver on her right. Now at last they were free of the town and unlikely to be challenged by men-at-arms. She moved a little nervously on the seat, further from Adam.

He gave a little harsh laugh. 'Don't be too venturesome, mistress; we could be challenged by far more dangerous folk than yon sergeant. Keep up the act of supporting your loving husband about his nefarious work.'

She said anxiously, 'Do — do many people go out to — to rob the dead?'

'Enough.'

'You say they are dangerous.'

'Aye, mistress, they are as likely to rob the living and, to make more certain of gain, render those as dead as their comrades.'

She did not utter the shrill little scream that her aunt had.

'Then my father is in peril from that quarter as well as from the effects of his wound.'

'I've hidden him as well as I could and my squire is with him, but you're right; we should not delay reaching him.'

'You are angry that I insisted on coming.' She read his feelings in the curtness of his phrasing. He did not answer and she said, 'Why, then, did you consent so readily to take me?'

He shrugged. 'You are not one to be turned, once your mind is made up, and I saw virtue in having you with me to tend your father. My rough and ready surgery was well enough for the moment, but I've seen more men die from infected wounds than did in battle and more horribly. I ask only one favour: you obey me absolutely. I promise to take your orders as to the manner of tending needed, but you take mine in the matter of decisions concerning our common safety.'

She considered. 'Even if they run contrary to mine as to the gravity of my father's condition and the dangers of moving him?'

'Certainly; there are worse deaths to be faced even than dying of wounds. Do I make myself clear?'

'As mountain-stream water,' she replied evenly.

He turned to shoot her an even more grim smile.

They reached East Stoke church without further incident and Adam turned the donkey in the direction of Fiskerton ford. Isabel leaned forward in horrified fascination as she saw lights bobbing about in the rocky gulley on their left. There were few sounds—rustling in the undergrowth, whispered orders, once a satisfied cackle. Isabel judged the lights were from horn lanterns carried by the despoilers. She turned a frightened white face to Adam as a scream of pain was hastily cut short. Her fingers pressing on Adam's arm bit into his flesh, but he gave no sign that he heeded her.

Now they were splashing through the ford and the lights and the ghastly sounds behind them. Isabel crossed herself and uttered a prayer to the Virgin for the souls so hastily dispatched and without the ministrations of a priest.

Adam was reining in their donkey and bent close to whisper in her ear. 'I've pulled as far off the road as I can. Now you must stay here and wait.'

She began to expostulate and he said with harsh deliberation, 'You promised you would obey and, in all events, it is necessary someone stays with the cart. Do you want it stolen? Of what use would that be to your father?'

'I'm sorry; of course I will do what you want.' She glanced about her uncertainly. 'How will you know your way in this darkness?'

'I marked the path. I'm used to hiding in copses. Woodland lore has had to become second nature to me.' He broke off abruptly and turned sharply towards the tree bole he had marked with his dagger to show him his way through the undergrowth back to his companions. There were marks of passage, a broken branch or two. Someone had gone this way, and very recently. He listened, and caught the sound of stealthy rustling, then, more ominously, panted breaths and a curse.

'Stay here,' he ordered, as Isabel half rose from her seat. 'Don't move. I'll have enough to cope with without troubling myself with your safety.'

He was off, bending his tall back beneath the low scrub, one hand pushing back the obstructing branches impatiently. Isabel's eyes peered anxiously into the gloom of the wood and her fingers tightened on the knotted leather reins. She swallowed and strained her ears for sound of him. Her heart jumped almost into her throat as she heard the noise she had feared most. Men scuffled some yards from her, and her father was in no state to defend himself from these human fiends who threatened his life. Regardless of Adam's orders, she scrambled down from the cart and secured the reins to a low-hanging branch. She could not wait helplessly while men fought so desperately.

It was soon clear to her that several men had passed

this way, for the ground was trampled and twigs and branches broken. She lifted her skirts and ran, faltering over the hummocks of grass hampered by creepers which tore at her unwary feet.

Once in the small clearing, she stopped dead, a hand to her mouth, as Adam fought doggedly with a shadowy figure whose rasping breath revealed he was certainly no youth. Another man's sprawled body lay only a couple of feet from her. His eyes gazed sightlessly up to the tree canopy, his horn lantern fallen from his nerveless fingers. Isabel's frightened eyes took in the rest of the scene. A man had been seated with his back to a tree bole. Another attacker lay slumped over his legs, and he was bending over the man to take possession of his weapon. Over the body of his assailant, Isabel's father looked wearily across to her, and she ran stumbling to his side. Crouching beside him, she turned towards the men locked in mortal combat on the far side of the clearing. The two were in a tight embrace like lovers until one gave a howl of pain and fell to his knees. Adam Westlake's hand did not falter as he bent over the pathetic, cringing figure of the vanquished thief, now sobbing and pleading huskily for mercy. Isabel hid her eyes against her father's padded gambeson as the *coup de grâce* was given and Adam stood up, kicking the flaccid body from him contemptuously.

'Where's the boy?' he demanded.

'I'm here, Sir Adam, sorr.' Sean stumbled into the clearing towards them, clutching at his forearm. Isabel saw how blood fell in great gouts from a wound, soaking into the grassy ground beneath. She rose immediately and went to the boy, stopping only to tear at her under-kirtle with hands and teeth.

'Stand quite still,' she commanded, as her fingers sought for a bleeding point above the wound to check the worst of the flow.

The boy stared at her blankly then stood docilely while she made a rough pad of the linen and bound it into place with a strip torn from his sleeve.

'It's a deep cut, but it will do well enough now until I

can cleanse it with salve when we have you all safe in hiding,' she said briskly.

Her shoulders were caught and she was swung unceremoniously round to face Adam Westlake's furiously scowling features.

'I ordered you to stay by the cart.'

She quailed under the intensity of his anger and tried to back away from him, but he held her fast.

'I heard — I heard you all scrambling and screams. I'm sorry, I was foolish, but I had to see if —'

'The harm's done now as like as not. Sean,' Adam ordered, 'go and see if the cart is safe. I left it at the entrance to the trail. What happened to your attacker, by the way?'

'I tried to tackle him. He was going to help the one who set on Sir Edwin, sorr. He struck me with his knife but I managed to hold on. Then he heard you coming through the trees, sorr, and took off like the devil hiself was at his heels. I couldn't catch him.'

'Just as well,' Adam said tiredly, releasing Isabel so that she was able to run back to her father. 'He might have done for you. Go, lad, find the cart.'

Isabel was sobbing wildly now that their immediate peril was over as quickly, it seemed to her, as it had begun. Edwin Hatfield gently stroked her hair where it straggled from her linen cap. Her hood had fallen back in her hasty scramble through the undergrowth. 'There, child, there's no danger now.' He looked up at his glowering companion. 'Don't be too hard on the lass, now, Adam. She was frightened and she didn't think.'

'That's just her problem; she doesn't think. Did that fellow wound you further, Edwin?'

'Oh, no,' Isabel breathed hastily, 'how bad is it?'

'No more than a scratch.' Sir Edwin chuckled. 'I tried the old game — played dead — and when the varlet came close enough I stabbed him to the heart. He'll not profit from any more battles, the devil take his black soul. What of you, Adam?'

'I'm well enough,' Westlake retorted quickly. 'We've

no time for more delays. We must get you to the cart. Can you stand, Edwin?'

'Aye, I think so, if you'll give me a hand up.'

Isabel scrambled to her feet, dabbing ineffectually at her tear-smirched cheeks, and stood back to allow Adam room to help her father.

Rustling in the bushes told them the boy, Sean, was returning. She prayed that no harm had come to the cart and donkey. It was needed to help her father to their cousin's barn and, also, she dreaded Adam Westlake's fury if, by her foolishness, they had lost their only means of conveyance, one for which he had risked his life in Newark.

'It's all right, sorr.' Sean sounded breathless but relieved. 'It looks like those men were the only ones to come near us, and the one who ran off must have run off the other way.'

'We can thank the Saints for that mercy,' Adam snapped, his fierce dark eyes flashing dangerously in Isabel's direction. 'Right, Edwin, if you can walk with Sean and me to support you, we can reach the road.'

'Now wait just one moment, Adam,' Edwin Hatfield said firmly. 'I'll not put Tom Skelton in any danger. You know what his fate would be if we were found in his house.'

'No, Father, we go to Ralf Blackburn's barn,' Isabel put in quickly. 'He would not be suspected and we can shelter there without them even knowing. That way, surely, they can come to no harm. Tomorrow, please God, we can be on our way again. Tonight your wound must be tended.'

He grunted agreement and winced as the first movements pained him, but, slowly, he allowed himself to be helped through the hampering undergrowth until the road was reached. Sean was sent to ascertain if there were any men watching and, on being informed that the way was deserted, Sir Edwin was helped up into the cart. Isabel watched anxiously for signs of internal bleeding. She was not sure yet just where the wound

was, but so far Sir Edwin appeared to be bearing up
well. Sir Adam ordered Sean into the cart.

The boy objected and insisted that Mistress Hatfield
take the seat, but Adam overrode him.

'Get up, I say. You look too obviously as if you've
been in the recent fray. That could betray us all.
Mistress Hatfield and I will pass as villagers returning
with our plundered loot.'

Isabel's hazel eyes looked straight into his to read if
he was punishing her for her recent disobedience, but
he showed no sign of malice and she realised that what
he had said was the simple truth. She was dressed for
the part and could walk by the donkey without coming
under suspicion from anyone who accosted them. Sir
Edwin and the boy drew back into the shadowy rear of
the cart and Sir Adam took the bridle and, under Isabel's
direction, they set out for the Blackburns' barn.

Fortunately they encountered no other looters or men-
at-arms on their short journey, for, short though it was,
Isabel soon began to feel the discomfort of the sharp
flints of the road on her tender feet. She had dressed
hurriedly in Bess's garments, but had not thought to
put on stout walking shoes, and hers of soft leather were
certainly unsuited for this purpose, but then she had
hardly thought she would be walking. Determinedly she
strode out, anxious that her limping gait would not
bring down upon her further disapproving glances from
Adam Westlake.

The barn proved deserted and no lock secured the
somewhat rotting door. Ralf Blackburn's animals were
out at grass, but there was some sweet-smelling hay and
straw, and Isabel watched as her father was helped down
and made comfortable on a heap of it. Adam moved off
to find some place to hide the cart. The donkey he
brought inside with them. A solitary animal grazing
near the barn might very well give them away or prove
too much of a temptation for passers-by in the morning
to steal.

Isabel unpacked her small box of medicaments and
insisted on her father removing his gambeson so that

she might examine the wound. She pursed her lips at sight of it. It was higher towards the shoulder than she had feared, and Adam must have been fortunate that he had not encountered the bone of the upper ribs when he had removed the shaft. The wound oozed sluggishly when she removed the pad, but the shaft's barb had left an ugly gash and she examined it carefully, feeling for any fragments of linen from his shirt which might have been driven inwards to cause further danger of infection. It seemed that Adam had taken care to avoid that pitfall, and she undid one of her pots of salve and smeared it on to fresh linen she'd brought with her.

'Is there much pain, Father?' she asked as he grunted at the gentle touch of her probing fingers. 'Can you breathe comfortably? There was no damage to the ribs, was there?'

'It's sore, my lass, and I feel weak as a mewling kitten. Why, God alone knows, since there doesn't appear to be much bleeding. I'll do well enough. See to the boy. The Saints know the knife used by yon thief was likely filthy enough to cause trouble.' He lay back tiredly against the hay. Adam had fashioned a cushion for him from his cloak, and his eyes closed contentedly.

Isabel insisted upon doctoring Sean's wound, though the boy stoutly averred it was naught but a scratch. The worst of the bleeding had stopped, but she smeared on a plentiful dressing of tansy salve then put her equipment back into the box, her eyes dilating in alarm at sound of approaching footsteps.

'It's Adam,' the newcomer announced, and he thrust back the rotting door and came in. 'How are they both?'

'I think they should do well now. I've cleaned and dressed both their wounds. Provided that arrow shaft touched no vital spot Father's wound should heal quickly.' She spoke very softly so that Sir Edwin could not hear. 'What about you, Sir Adam? I doubt that you escaped injury in the battle or in that tussle with the looter just now.'

He shrugged. 'Sundry cuts and bruises. Nothing

serious. I've taken worse on the Scottish border repelling marauding reivers.'

'Doubtless so,' Isabel retorted crisply, 'but then you could have the tending of your army surgeon and were not like to be taken for a traitor if your wounds later gave trouble. You've a long journey ahead of you. Take off that dirty houppeland and let me see what injuries you did suffer.'

To her surprise he complied without further argument, and she gave a little gasp at sight of the terrible bruising which disfigured his muscular chest. There were, as he had said, several cuts, which she deftly dressed, and then she applied comfrey salve and a compound of witch-hazel to ease the pain and discomfort given by the dark bruises.

He grimaced. 'The armour and under-tunic do their work of protection, but the blows do considerable damage to the tissue when the metal is dented. Thank you, Mistress Isabel. I shall be much more comfortable now and be able to move more quickly if that should prove necessary.'

'You found a safe place for the cart?' she questioned softly, for both her father and the boy seemed to be resting back against the hay and Isabel hoped that her father would sleep for the rest of the night undisturbed.

He nodded. 'I saw no one about. I'll see the donkey is watered. He can munch on some of that hay and we should be well hid now until morning. Wat assured me he knows where to come. If your father is able to ride we must be off as soon as we can right out of this district.'

Isabel glanced fearfully at her father and her brows drew together. 'You saw where the shaft was. Do you think it —— ?'

He gave the shrug she knew was characteristic of him. 'I pray not,' he replied curtly, and she forbore to press him further. Only time would tell if her father would take further harm from the journey, and it could not be delayed. Adam was taking the right precautions. She knew that and was content to trust to his guidance.

'You should try to sleep, Mistress Isabel, there, near
your father. I'll keep a close watch.'

'Surely you need rest more than I do,' she said gently.
'If you sleep for an hour or so, Sir Adam, I will call you
if anyone comes near. I have very sharp hearing, I assure
you.'

He blinked suddenly and, as before, she thought he
would protest, but he did not.

'That seems a sensible idea, mistress. Truth to tell, I
have had little sleep for some days and need to be fresh
in the morning to face what comes. Wake me just after
cock-crow and you must then sleep. If there is danger of
discovery, it will come then rather than now.'

Without further ado, he stretched himself out near
the barn door and appeared to fall instantly asleep.
Isabel seated herself, her back supported by the rough
wattle wall of the barn, near her father's side, her eyes
fixed upon the faint line of greyish light which came
between the ill-fitting, rough-hewn boards of the door.
It would be no hardship to stay wakeful. She felt no
inclination to sleep. Her eyes passed over her sleeping
companions and she reflected on the fact that they had
taught themselves to do so whenever opportunity arose,
whenever the circumstances allowed. A warrior, as
Adam had said, needed to be rested to face what came.
She shuddered at thoughts of the dangers to be encountered when the sun rose.

Would it really be safe for her father to return to
Swithland? She had told James Tarvin that his journey
north had been to escort her home, but would that tale
be believed? For the first time since she had been told
of the conclusion of the battle she thought of James.
Had he fought at East Stoke? Was he safe, or lying cold
and stark on that terrible field, his body plundered by
those fearful creatures she had glimpsed in her journey
out here? Tears rolled unheeded down her cheeks. Why,
oh, why, had men she admired and respected allowed
themselves to be used as pawns in this bickering for
power? James loyally served the King who had favoured
his family. Neither her father nor Adam could, surely,

fault him for that. Any other behaviour would have been
dishonourable. Yet she had constantly chided Adam
Westlake for those same allegiances to the cause he held
dear.

She watched his sleeping form thoughtfully. She felt
safe with him, and would have done so even if her father
had not been near. She trusted him, relied on him to
extricate her father from this deadly coil. How did she
regard him — as a brother? Even in the cool darkness of
the barn she felt her cheeks flush hotly. No, there was
nothing brotherly in her feelings towards him. She
allowed herself to consider how she would respond if he
made any amorous advances towards her. Would she
repel them angrily? She thought not. He had asked only
for one kiss of courtly parting to wish him well in the
coming encounter, and that she had readily granted.
Now her thoughts were less maidenly. Yet she thought
she loved James, had half promised him her hand, but
had not consented to plight her troth to him before
God's altar. What, then, had held her back? She had
told herself that there had been doubts in her mind,
memories of his uncouth behaviour to the pedlar, but
had that been all? Adam Westlake had come into her
life, and she was no longer sure of herself. She sighed.
She knew so little about the man, had never questioned
her father concerning him. She had been shy about that
and had never, until now, considered her own motives
for that reserve. She had not wanted to be told that
Adam was wed or that he loved some lady at Court.
Angrily Isabel shifted on the hay. She had never thought
herself wanton. No maid could love two men, or even
harbour such thoughts about them. Adam Westlake
would see them to safety and then make his own escape.
Likely she would never see him again. Certainly it
would not be safe for him to so much as set a foot in
England again. She must pray with all her heart that he
reach the Court of the Duchess Margaret and settle to a
new life with some stately dame of his choice. She sighed
softly. This conflict had done more than set the realm in

uproar; it had proved the cause of some soul-searching in her, as well.

Despite her promise to Adam, Isabel found herself constantly forced to take steps to remain wakeful. Her treacherous eyes tended to close and she deliberately strove to think of plans for their next journey and the problems that might well face them at the manor to keep sleep at bay. The hours seemed longer than she could have imagined and she strained her ears in the darkness for the raucous sound of the rising cockerel and the knowledge that her night vigil was ended. At length she rose and tiptoed to the barn door, thinking to open it and peer outside into the now greying light of the new day.

She almost screamed aloud as her shoulder was gripped from behind and Adam Westlake's voice warned, 'Gently, gently, now. There's nothing to fear.'

She turned instantly back to him. 'You frightened me. I——'

'Why did you go to the door? Did you hear something which frightened you?'

'No.' Her eyes roved to the outlines of the sleeping men. 'No, it was just that I had a job to stay awake. I got up to shift position, that is all. There hasn't been a sound, not even from the donkey.'

'Good.' He cautiously pushed wide the door and sniffed the cold morning air. 'The sun will be up soon. Now you get some rest.'

'That isn't necessary.'

'I say it is. You've just said yourself you've had your work cut out to stay awake.'

She smiled tremulously in the half-darkness. 'That was only because everything was so quiet and I was cramped.'

'Now get some sleep. You'll need to be fresh for the journey.'

'Are you going out?' She sounded alarmed.

'Only to see the cart is safe. I shall keep the barn within my sight.'

He pushed her gently but inexorably towards the

dents in the hay near her father. 'Settle yourself down. Are you cold?'

She shook her head. His very nearness, his touch, had inspired some bodily reaction, and she drew aside and reluctantly returned to her abandoned resting place. He waited until she lay down, wrapping her cloak tightly round her, then quietly left the barn.

Bright sunlight was bearing down on her lids when she woke and the boy, Sean, was already up and talking quietly to Adam near the door. Her father still slept on. She scrambled up and went to the two men.

'Is it late? Have I slept too long?'

Adam shook his head. 'No, it may be hours yet before Wat can join us. There have been villagers about but none have come close. Let your father sleep on for a while. He needs every bit of rest he can get. Sean has been to the river for water. I hope Wat thinks to bring food with him. We've all been on short commons since just after dawn yesterday and, to tell truth, few of us felt like eating then.'

It was the first intimation she had had from him that he had been concerned about the outcome of the battle. It somehow made him more human for her. She had always thought of him as a warrior of cold steel, without thought of danger both for himself and others he persuaded to join him in his cause.

'I thought of that last night,' she said hurriedly. 'Rushed as I was, I managed to get into the kitchen and put some broken meats and bread into a kerchief. I put it in the cart and must have forgotten it last night when — when the fight happened.'

Adam smiled. 'I'll go and look. Sean, step outside for a moment; you can see to the donkey, while Mistress Isabel makes a quick toilet.'

She was grateful for his consideration and shyly asked if she might go aside for a moment into the shelter of some low scrub which lay to the rear of the barn.

He nodded briefly. 'Go quickly, then; I'll stay on guard.'

By the time she had returned and washed with a small

amount of the water, her father was beginning to stir. He sat up and she hastily went to him.

'How is your wound? You seemed to sleep well.'

'Well enough, my lass.' He looked anxiously round the barn. 'Where are the others?'

'Sean has gone to water the donkey and Adam to search for some food I left in the cart.'

'Is there water? My mouth is foul as the bowels of hell,' he said feelingly.

She brought him the remains of the water the boy had managed to bring from the river in two abandoned steel salets. She looked at the empty helmets guiltily. Soon they would not be able to leave their hiding-place when villagers were up and about their business, and she had foolishly used up all their precious water. She rose and went to the door. Without waiting for her father to object, she murmured softly, 'I shall be back in just a few moments,' pushed open the door and slipped out.

The morning was fresh and full of the scents of grass and wild flowers. Isabel pulled up her skirts and ran along the road they had traversed the previous night. It was good to be out of the barn, which was becoming fetid with the closeness of bodies and would become more so as the temperature rose when the sun climbed to its zenith and they were cooped up with the donkey for company.

It seemed much further to the river than she had remembered and she was slightly out of breath by the time she came upon a spot where the access to the bank allowed her to bend down and fill her helmets. If only she had thought to bring a leather bottle with her in her hasty flight from the house. These helmets held little enough, but would have to suffice until they dared emerge from cover again. She had not realised how near she was to the ford until she heard the sound of cart wheels approaching her hiding-place by the bank and sank down as low as she could till she was partially hidden by the long grass and willows.

Some of her precious water splashed on to her skirt and she gave a little half-suppressed exclamation of annoyance. A burly young man was driving the cart drawn by a heavy plough horse, and he was exhorting it cheerfully through the shallow water. Isabel crouched even lower, but, perched as he was on the high driving seat, he saw her and called out a friendly greeting.

'Hello, there, mistress. It's a fine fresh morning after the troubles of yesterday. Can I carry you anywhere? I'm off to East Stoke village.' His rather protuberant eyes gazed at her curiously and at the water-filled helmets she had put down before her.

'I haven't seen you before. I be from Fiskerton.' He frowned. 'There's good spring water near the church in East Stoke, no need to carry it from here.' She knew he was appraising her, his gaze passing over her drab kirtle and torn bodice. She was conscious that there had been considerable damage to her apparel in her frantic rush through the undergrowth last night, and the young villager was making up his own mind about what had caused her dishevelled state.

She rose to her feet hesitantly. 'No—no, thank you. My man and I—we are camping back there.' She made a vague gesture behind her. 'I just came down here for the water.'

His large blue eyes narrowed. 'You be one of they camp followers, likely?'

'I. . .' Isabel groped for some explanation for her presence so near the battlefield. Already the young man was jumping down from the cart and approaching her. His broad grin had become a distinct leer and she understood he had made his own assessment of her presence here. She looked round for some way of escape, but knew if she ran he would, with the instinct of the hunter, immediately pursue. He was heavy-set but young and strong and used to hard work in the fields. The nearness of a young woman he undoubtedly thought to be a camp harlot seemed to him a gift from Dame Fortune. She could hardly complain to authority about his treatment of her, and he knew it. Who knew which army she had followed? She and her man were vulnerable to any accusation of treason. He came closer, undoubtedly beginning to enjoy his feeling of triumphant control over her.

Isabel looked about her huntedly. There was no one about to whom she could appeal for help. She backed, stumbled over her skirt, and half fell. Her intended ravisher stopped in his tracks, threw back his head, and gave a great bellow of laughter.

'Now, now, me beauty, ye're never going to play the modest maid.'

'Get away from me.' Isabel crouched, one hand behind her to balance herself on the uneven slope of the bank. 'If I scream my man will come.'

The youth came on, still grinning broadly. 'Aye, and what if he does? What'll he do? Is he bigger'n than me, eh?'

Isabel was still slithering her way sideways up the bank towards the track when he fell on her, catching at her ankle as she kicked out at him. She gave a startled cry of surprise and panic as she fell sprawling at his feet, totally at his mercy. Easily he was able to hold her frantically struggling body down on the grass with one hand, while he tugged at the lacing of his points. Not in the least concerned who heard him, he was whooping with laughter and clearly still thought her struggles were assumed to make the conquest sweeter. He was not brutal, not even rough, merely so sure of himself that he had no need to conceal his attack on her from anyone within earshot.

Isabel bit savagely at his restraining hand while her nails clawed at his cheeks. He gave a broad oath, aware now that his attentions were not welcome, grunted hard, but continued to hold tight to his prey. Isabel's teeth were clenched hard with effort and her breathing was becoming laboured. Horrified, she realised that she was powerless to prevent him from ravishing her now, at this moment, and she had no recourse even to justice afterwards. She made one last desperate effort to free herself, knowing it was but a forlorn hope. The youth was so much stronger than she was.

Suddenly, amazingly, the merciless hold which

pinned her to the ground slackened and her attacker fell heavily sideways across her body. Her eyes had been closed against the sickening realisation of her impending fate and she opened them at last and pushed ineffectually at his inert form. Someone kicked that slack body aside and leaned down an arm to help her up.

'In God's name,' stormed Adam Westlake, 'do you behave like this from deliberate waywardness or arrant stupidity?'

Isabel was trembling in every limb and could scarcely stand. She attempted to answer him, but words would not come and she burst into a storm of weeping.

Adam put a supporting arm round her shoulder. 'Isabel, let's not waste time by this foolish show of weakness. The fellow will come round soon enough, and we must be out of his sight. It may surprise you to know that I've no stomach for useless killing. I've done enough over these last days and I have to admit you asked for what you were about to get.'

The shock of his callous words brought her from her distraught state far more quickly than any show of sympathy would have done. She pushed herself free of his hold and moved from him, her fingers clutching at the torn edges of her bodice. He came close again and gave her shoulder an irritated shake.

'Did the fellow harm you?'

She shook her head, her eyes going worriedly to his sprawled form. She was still shaking, but she managed to find her voice at last.

'You say — you — you have not killed him?'

Adam gazed down at his fallen foe. 'I hit him with a boulder. He's likely got a hard head; I hope so, for his sake. He was so intent on struggling with you he didn't hear me approach. Granted I was keeping very quiet and hidden as much as I could be by the bushes on the far side of the path. Come, Isabel,' he said imperatively again.

She looked around her for the salets with their water.

'The water,' she impressed on him. 'We must have it.

I—I would not have risked myself if—if I hadn't thought it necessary.'

He followed her gaze, bent, and retrieved the helmets. One was empty and he moved back to the river and refilled it quickly, then, handing her the other, put a hand beneath her elbow and began to guide her back the way they'd come from the barn. It was later in the morning now and he impelled her into the shadow of the low trees which bordered the track, pointing the way ahead and then walking behind to guard the rear. Isabel found she needed every scrap of concentration to avoid falling on the tangle of roots and low brambles.

The struggle with her attacker had bruised her more than she had thought and one foot hurt each time she put weight on it. She must have wrenched it in the fall down the riverbank. Doggedly she pressed on, biting her lip against the pain. Adam Westlake must not be further hindered by her pathetic weakness.

She gave a sudden wince and he turned impatiently.

'What now?'

'I'm sorry, I——'

'You said you were not hurt.'

'It's nothing.'

'Then why did you wince?'

'I think I twisted my foot on—on a tree root.'

He muttered something unintelligible beneath his breath and came back to her.

'Sit down on this fallen tree trunk. Let me see.'

'It's nothing, really——'

'Obey me.'

She lowered herself cautiously as the bruises told their tale. His dark brows winged upwards sardonically.

'The fellow's love play was rough.'

Colour flooded her face and throat and she half rose. His arm held her down.

'Stay still, I say.'

His touch was firm but gentle on her ankle as he moved the injured foot experimentally.

'It is not broken; you've wrenched it and it will hurt

badly for a while. When you get back to the barn you
must strap it up.'

Her flesh tingled at his touch. She felt ashamed,
besmirched by the incident he'd witnessed, and tried to
pull her foot from his hold.

'I — I will manage.'

'You will not, without my help.'

'I'll manage.' She jerked away and rose, then agonising pain shot through her and she cried out.

'You see,' he snapped triumphantly, 'you can't, and
if we stay here arguing we'll be found by Royalist
soldiers.'

She turned her head away, afraid that she would
break into tears again.

'Stand still while I lift you on to my shoulder.'

'No,' she protested, 'I — '

He cut across her objections by lifting her unceremoniously so that her head and shoulders fell forward
over his left shoulder and his free arm hitched her
buttocks into position.

'Now, keep perfectly still while I stoop for the water.
We can't go back without that, can we?'

It was an uncomfortable journey and her body cringed
from the feel of his hard, soldier's muscles against her
yielding flesh. She clutched awkwardly at him for support, but he seemed to move effortlessly, showing no
danger of dropping her. She was furiously angry with
herself for the extra hazard she had brought on him. She
had been stupid and thoughtless when she had meant to
prove to him that she was capable of helping the menfolk
as well as looking after herself. She could feel his heart
beating steadily and knew he was in excellent condition,
despite the hardships he had faced over these last bitter
months. She gritted her teeth again to endure the jerky
discomfort of the ride and was greatly relieved when he
stopped at last and allowed her body to slide from him
to the ground.

'You should manage now.' His touch was cool on her
arm and he guided her on to smoother ground as the
barn came in sight.

Her legs almost gave way again when her father, waiting anxiously near the door, opened his arms to her with a low cry of gratitude for her safe return.

'Thank the Virgin, Adam, you found her in good time.'

Isabel's hazel eyes appealed to her rescuer to say no word of the attack, and his black eyes met hers unflinchingly, then he gave that little characteristic half-shrug and said curtly, 'I found her a little too near the ford for comfort. However, all is well now. Mistress Isabel must learn that, for all our safety, not least her own, she must continue to obey my instructions to the letter.'

Meekly Isabel handed the salet of water to Sean, who was listening open-mouthed to his master's explanation, and lowered her gaze from the furious stare Adam continued to keep on her.

She was still very trembly and sank down on the hay. Feeling her father's horrified gaze on her torn clothing, she opened her mouth to try and explain when Adam put in, 'I made her walk in the copse — there are more people about now. I'm afraid the branches and thorns have not improved her appearance.'

She was unfeignedly grateful for his explanation, but dared not meet his eyes just yet. Soon, she was sure, he would have more to say about the incident near the ford and a reckoning would be demanded of her. Now she was content to accept his domination and, if needful, his castigation of her conduct. Her father would have been so distressed to hear the truth that anything was better than Adam revealing it at this juncture.

Sean had found the food and busied himself in dividing it up between them. The manchet bread had become stale and, in any case, Isabel felt too shaky and sickened to eat, but with Adam's black gaze upon her she forced it down and swallowed a little of the water for which she had almost lost her virginity.

The morning hours seemed to stretch into infinity. The food finished, the four had nothing to do but wait. It was hot in the barn and as fetid as Isabel had feared it would be. Adam slipped out once to fetch more water for the donkey, but it appeared restless since Adam was reluctant to allow it out of the barn now to graze. Isabel busied herself after the food was gone in tending her patients' wounds again. Her father's looked somewhat red and sore round the area which the barb had penetrated, but he assured her the discomfort was not great. Then she sat by his side with the others, watching the closed barn door, listening intently for any sounds which would herald the arrival of mounted or foot soldiers searching the area. All they heard were the usual country sounds — cattle lowing somewhere close near the river, bird calls, once a man whistling as he passed near by on the track, but nothing to cause alarm. All the food was gone now and their water also. Adam waved aside Sean's offer to go out and try to forage from a nearby farm, for they still had some coin with them.

'No, boy, not today. We'll wait and suffer the hunger pangs until the hue and cry has died down or Master Jessop is able to keep his promise.'

'What if he doesn't come?' Isabel mouthed fearfully, stating their worst fears.

Adam shrugged. 'Then we must do our best without him and trust to the cart and my disguise, but we'd travel faster with good horses and your father's presence would be less suspicious if he rides as your escort.'

Moving closer to him near the door and noting that her father's eyes were half closed and he appeared to have fallen into a fitful doze, Isabel whispered, 'I'm afraid he may not be well enough to ride.'

Adam's gaze shifted to Sir Edwin. 'He must if at all possible,' he said curtly. 'To be noted carrying a sick man in the cart and so soon after a battle is bound to arouse suspicion.'

She swallowed but did not argue further. 'I — I am grateful that you did not tell him about —'

'No point in distressing him further. He has enough worries.'

'I am not usually so reckless,' she said stiffly. 'Always in the past I have had my father or Wat with me when I ventured abroad but — but it seemed that we must have water, and I had foolishly used it up for washing, and. . .' She was unaccountably anxious that he should not regard her as tardy about her own reputation. It seemed a trivial matter now, when their lives were at risk, but it seemed important to her that he should understand and not condemn her.

He gazed impassively back at her anxious, fearful little face. 'I was the best choice in this pedlar's garb of mine. Sean is likely to be recognised for what he is — a fugitive — but I realise none of us is thinking too clearly in moments of stress.' He looked down at her maid's kirtle. 'You must understand that, dressed as you are, without protector, you would be fair game for any man who comes upon you, especially in these dangerous days when a triumphant army is on the loose. Is your foot hurting as much now?'

'Thank you; it is better. I've managed to support it. A time of rest in the cart or on horseback and all will be well.'

She shifted uncomfortably on the straw. 'I swear to you I will wait for your instructions in the future.'

'Good.' He gave a little nod of satisfaction. 'Mistress Isabel, you must know that I am not entirely displeased with your behaviour over these last hours. Many women of your distinction would have given way to hysterics.'

'I think you judge women too harshly, Sir Adam,' she said smiling, but, none the less, she felt a warm glow of comfort for his avowed words of admiration for her competence.

It was late afternoon when the distinct sound of horses' hoofs were heard on the track outside. Adam was up on the instant and opened the barn door just a crack.

'There aren't too many of them,' he said crisply.

Sir Edwin had sat up abruptly and Isabel hurried to him and put a hand in his. Adam gestured to Sean to keep the donkey as quiet as possible. Cautiously he opened the door further and ventured out, one hand on the dagger he had withdrawn hurriedly from the hanging purse on his belt.

He made a muttered sound and stepped hastily back into the barn. 'Thank all the saints; it is your man, Jessop, with the horses.'

Sir Edwin echoed the prayer of gratitude and got painfully to his feet with Isabel's assistance.

Soon Wat was leading the horses inside the barn while Sean struggled with the refractory donkey, who took exception to their presence.

'Lead the beast outside for a while to graze. He should be safe enough for now,' Adam instructed.

Sir Edwin caught at the groom's hand and squeezed it hard.

'Wat, man, you have not endangered yourself or the Skeltons?' he questioned hoarsely.

'No, no, Sir Edwin, all is safe at the goldsmith's shop. Mistress Cecily and the child are well. The premises were subjected to a routine search, as were all houses and shops in the town, but, of course, nothing untoward was found. It was explained that Mistress Isabel had ridden out to her cousin's farm to bid them farewell before travelling home with her father.'

Sir Edwin gave a great sigh of relief. 'Then Tom has put it about that I arrived in Newark to escort Isabel home?'

'Aye, sir, it was said in passing, in case you should be stopped and questioned on the road.' He indicated saddle-bags tied securely behind the saddles and a small travelling chest. 'I have brought food and wine for the journey and Mistress Isabel's clothing. It would seem a good notion for Sir Adam to drive the cart with the goods inside. You might have need of it later.'

'But what of you, Wat?' Isabel queried. 'You have brought only two riding horses. Are you returning to Newark?'

'Later, Mistress Isabel. I've left Bess there. Mistress Skelton will see she is cared for and, indeed, Bess has become greatly attached to the child, as you know. In a few days I'll return and, if all is well, bring her home to Hatfield.'

Adam said gravely, 'I see you do not intend to ride

with Sir Edwin and Mistress Isabel. What is in your mind, Wat?'

The groom grinned. 'I have become friendly with the sergeant at the castle gatehouse. On several occasions I've been over to drink ale and dice with the men. This morning I went over and explained that I was detailed to ride south with my master and mistress but feared we might be molested on the way. My master would be safe enough, I said, but I was a comman man and might be thought to have taken part in the late disturbances. He understood my drift at once, went to his captain, and obtained for me a pass through the lines.' He held it out to Adam. 'I've brought some of my own clothing for you, sir. The jack should fit you well enough, though a trifle on the short side — we're much of a size, except for the height — but your own hose should suffice.'

'And you?'

'There is the question of your squire. I'll guide the lad north and put him on the road for the Dales. There he'll be safe enough hid by one of the late King's supporters till he can be got out of the country from some port in Lancashire or Cumbria.'

'While I take your place on the ride south,' Adam said thoughtfully. 'You take a grave risk, friend. If you should be thought to be implicated. . .'

'I think that most unlikely, sir. Who would question a groom travelling on his master's business and with one of the stable-hands? If the lad here keeps his mouth shut we should be safe enough. The difficult part will be getting clear of Newark, but I know my way hereabouts and can guide him easily.'

Sir Edwin leaned forward and again gripped his groom's arm. 'The Virgin will reward you, Wat,' he said quietly. 'You know as well as I that I have a fair chance riding with Isabel, but Sir Adam will be in grave danger once he leaves us, and while he is still in the area, even in that pedlar's guise. This way offers him a chance of safety.'

Impulsively Isabel hugged her groom and he grinned back at them, clearly embarrassed.

'It is nothing, sir, the best I could think of. You're sure you're fit enough to ride?'

'I'll do well enough,' Sir Edwin said stoutly. 'We'll leave immediately we've eaten.'

'We'll be on our way at once,' Adam demurred. 'To be riding late in the day could cause talk. We should be clear of Newark before nightfall, though Wat here and Sean would be better to stay in the barn until dark before setting out across country.'

He himself set out to retrieve the cart while Wat untied the bundles and chest from the horses. The men left the barn while Isabel changed her maid's dress for a gown and head-dress from the chest. She chose the simplest one available, since Bess was not here to assist with the back lacing. In the end her father completed that for her.

Adam was back now and Sean and Wat busied themselves harnessing the donkey. Adam went into the barn to put on the clothes Wat had brought. When he emerged he looked tolerably well in them, though, as Wat had said, the jacket was somewhat short. Not for the first time, Isabel marvelled at his height and lean, muscular figure. Would anyone really take him for a servant? His manner was so authoritative, yet she knew well enough that he could assume a subservient attitude when it was necessary.

As Adam lifted her into the saddle of her palfrey, she turned anxiously to look at her father, still concerned at how pale he appeared, but he mounted easily enough and gave her a reassuring smile as he took the reins from Wat.

The groom and young Irish boy stood near the barn door, their hands raised in farewell as Sir Edwin led the way towards Fiskerton ford. Isabel's eyes misted with tears. Would she ever see Sean again? He had been a faithful squire to Adam. She wished him well on his long, hazardous journey back to his own land. Wat, she knew, could take care of himself, but the task he had undertaken was undeniably dangerous. She murmured a prayer to the Virgin, then, catching Adam's sardonic gaze on her where he sat on the driving seat of the cart, she forced a smile and urged her mount forward to join her father.

CHAPTER EIGHT

THEY rode through the afternoon, Isabel's eyes constantly straying towards her father to assure herself that he was not too ill to sit his horse. He looked pale and a trifle strained, but his smile told her he was managing. They were forced to set a slow pace because of the cart, but, though she longed to eat up the miles quickly to get out of this district as swiftly as possible, Isabel knew her father was incapable of enduring a jolting fast gallop. They saw several armed bands, but were not stopped until they were approaching Bingham. Here there were signs of an army camp in the vicinity. Baggage wagons were in evidence, and the presence of men accompanied by the brassily haired women whose type Isabel had seen in Newark.

Within the village street a cart halted their progress and there were several brawny fellows attempting to replace a broken wheel. Isabel shivered nervously as a sergeant-at-arms came to their side as she drew rein. She did not recognise the device on his jack and thought he might well be one of the Welshmen in service to a Marcher lord who had supported King Henry at Redmoor. She deliberately avoided looking at her father or Adam, who drew up the cart close behind them.

Sir Edwin addressed the sergeant, and his voice showed no sign of alarm or weakness. 'You appear to be having some difficulty, man, but, by the look of things you should be soon on the road again.'

'Aye, sir, we've persuaded some of the village lads to help us.' The man's voice was accented, and he spoke with some trace of arrogance, as one who had fought on the triumphant side and was entitled to be proud of his achievements, at present recognising no man as his master. 'Where might you be going, sir, if you'll be so good as to inform me?' The last words were more conciliatory, yet still the authority in the man's tone could not be defied.

Sir Edwin regarded him mildly. 'I am Sir Edwin Hatfield, since you ask.' There was steel beneath the silky note, and the fellow had the grace to blush. 'I am escorting my daughter back from Newark to our home in Leicestershire.' He eyed the man determinedly. 'I consider it unwise to remain in the area of the battlefield. Newark has become distinctly unpleasant for the susceptibilities of gentlewomen.'

'Aye, it would be.' The fellow quickly recovered his cockiness. 'Folk who are loyal to His Grace'll understand why.'

'That may be so,' Sir Edwin acknowledged, 'but the behaviour of some of the men-at-arms may be termed excessive and doubtless will be curbed soon when the King is able to give his attention to such matters. For the present it seems sensible to get my daughter clear of the district.'

The man's gaze passed over Isabel curiously and went to Adam on the driving seat of the cart. 'And who might this fellow be?'

'My groom. We should not be here now had not one of our horses gone lame—a sturdy beast we employ to carry our baggage—which delayed us considerably. My kinsman, Master Skelton, a noted goldsmith in Newark, has kindly lent us the cart to get our goods home.'

The man nodded slowly. 'He looks a well set-up fellow, this groom of yours, one as could have been fighting for his King.' His meaning was clear enough, the implication that Sir Edwin would have been better so employed also.

Sir Edwin rejoined frostily, 'My man knows where his duty lay. He was sworn to keep safe my daughter, who was in Newark to care for her sick aunt. Knowing we might have this problem, we took the precaution of obtaining a safe conduct for Wat from the captain of Newark Castle. Show this fellow your pass, Wat, and let us get on.' There was a peremptory note in his voice now which the sergeant reluctantly acknowledged.

Adam produced the pass Wat had given him and the man gave it only a cursory glance. More than likely he couldn't read, but he recognised the seal of the castle seneschal and nodded.

Adam said in the subservient manner Isabel knew well, 'My master was injured at Redmoor. He is no longer fit to support the King in battle, but his loyalty has never been challenged.'

'That will do.' Sir Edwin's voice was decidedly angry now. 'My affairs are none of this fellow's business. Stand aside, man, and let us by. Can you not see my daughter is wearied and anxious to reach our designated inn for the night?'

The man stepped back sulkily. He bawled to his inferiors to clear the way. The cart was edged to one side and the two riders and donkey cart were able to pass at last. Isabel was shaking violently at the encounter. She forced herself not to look back until they were well out of sight of the armed men.

'It seems Wat was right to take precautions,' her father said evenly. Isabel looked at him sharply. For one moment it looked as if he was about to fall in the saddle. He waved away her concerned questions, and urged them all forward.

She tried not to turn to look at him too closely, but she was now thoroughly alarmed. They managed about another mile before he made some inarticulate sound and, riding up close, for she had spurred slightly ahead, she saw he was swaying and his hands were slack on the reins. Isabel gave a frightened shout to Adam in the rear and jumped clear of her saddle. Her father's hack was sidling nervously and it was all she could do to hold him upright until she was joined by Adam, who took charge instantly.

'Lead the cart up; we must get him into it at once now.'

He took the reins of both horses and she ran to do his bidding. The little donkey was docile and Isabel thanked the Saints that they were on a clear stretch of road with, apparently, no one in sight. Between them they managed

to lift Sir Edwin down from his horse and into the cart.
His eyes were closed and he had lost consciousness.
Isabel noted that his breathing was bad.

'I was afraid of this,' she said frantically. 'We must
get to the inn at Normanton. The landlord knows us
and——'

'No inns,' Adam said firmly. 'We must get off the
road and into the shelter of some small copse.'

'He must be got to bed,' Isabel snapped furiously.
'We are well clear of the battle area now. He must have
tending. Can't you see how ill he is? He's kept up till
now despite all——'

'Listen to me.' He took her firmly by the shoulders
and shook her hard. 'Take a hold on yourself and listen.
He is injured. We cannot trust to some landlord to know
such a thing. Injuries are suspect at these times. The
man himself could be charged with treason for sheltering
your father if he does not inform against him. Do you
understand?'

Eyes wide with terror, she bit down savagely upon
her bottom lip and, at length, nodded.

'Come, now, I need you to handle your father's horse
as well as your own, for I must drive the cart.'

She gave one despairing glance at the cart's darkened
interior, and went to mount her palfrey. Adam moved
to her side and put his hand to lift her up.

About three miles further on Adam discovered the
small copse he declared suitable for their needs. He
drew up the cart and instructed Isabel to lead the horses
down a scarcely used track. It was not easy for the cart,
and his patient was sadly jolted on the rough ground,
but he drove skilfully into the middle of the copse,
where he was sure they could not be overlooked from
the road, before he ordered Isabel to make fast their
mounts' reins to an overhanging branch and, at last,
allowed her to give her attention to her father.

His breathing was certainly not improved by the
rough ride, but his eyelids fluttered open and he reached
out desperately for her hand.

'Isabel, my lass, what happened?'

'Lie quiet, Father. You almost fell from your horse. We managed to get you into the cart without anyone seeing us. Hush, now, let me see the wound.'

'Adam?'

'Edwin?' Adam came instantly to the side of the cart. 'Do what Isabel bids you. Rest quiet. We're well hid, safe enough for the night. In the morning we'll get you home.'

'I must ride again.'

'More than likely you'll be well enough to do that. We'll cross country. Isabel knows the way well enough to guide us. Best if we avoid inns and villages if possible.'

'Aye.' Sir Edwin's face contorted as Isabel opened his shirt and laid bare the wound. She grimaced at sight of it. There was an area of discolouration surrounding it, and some yellowish pus.

'Dare we light a fire?' she asked Adam.

'I see no reason why not. If the smoke's seen from a distance it will likely be thought to be some woodcutter cooking supper or disposing of rubbish.'

'I need to make a heated poultice.'

He nodded and went off at once to find brushwood. Soon he had a fire going and was able to boil water in a small pot provided by Wat, who appeared to have thought of every contingency.

Isabel busied herself with the herbs in her chest, determined not to give herself time to think. She made the poultice and applied it to the wound, binding it into place with strips torn from her shift. Adam had disappeared for a while and later returned with a rabbit for the pot. Isabel made stew with the meat and wild herbs and garlic he'd found and was gratified to see her father take some nourishment. He declared he was no longer in pain, but she did not believe him. There were beads of sweat on his forehead, but, as yet, his skin did not exude that hot, dry touch which preceded the dreaded fever she most feared. At length Sir Edwin fell into an exhausted doze covered by Adam's cloak.

Isabel came to the fire and forced herself to eat some

of the stew. Her hands were shaking and some of the hot liquid fell on her forearm. Gently Adam took the wooden dish from her and laid it down by the fire.

'Here, steady, now; you'll need some of your healing herbs for this scald.'

'It's nothing.' Fiercely she scrubbed at her eyelids, for she was determined not to weep. Her father needed her. She must not give way to despair. Uneasily she looked into Adam's unfathomable dark eyes, lit curiously in the light of the camp fire.

'He will not die. I'll not allow it.'

He inclined his head. 'He has a good nurse and a brave one. I'm sorry, Isabel, that I snapped at you back there on the road, but you have to realise his peril.'

She gave a great shuddering breath. 'Even if we get him home safely, how can we conceal his injuries?'

'Do you not trust your servants?'

'Yes, yes, I think so; they all love my father, but you explained how dangerous it could be for them. . .'

'And for you,' he agreed gravely. 'Isabel, once home, he has every chance. You must give it out that he is sick of a tertian fever. You alone will enter the sick-room except for a trusted servant to bring up the food. I should not send for a physician.'

'Even if—'

'Even if you fear for his life. Best, if die he must, he does it in his own bed, not on the scaffold at Tyburn.'

She gave a terrible cry, hastily caught back, and he drew her gently close to him.

Wat's borrowed clothes, though well worn, smelt only of grass and horses and leather. She hid her face against his shoulder and cried weakly, giving way at last after holding in her terror for so long. He held her silently, then gently he put her from him and rose to his feet.

'I must see the horses are safe. Get into the cart beside your father, Isabel. It's chilly tonight; the closeness of your body will warm him.'

She stared at his back as he strode away. She had needed his comfort so much, yet he had so quickly withdrawn from her. She wiped away the foolish tears and moved to the cart, knowing he would keep watch throughout the night.

She woke in the chilly dawn, sat up in the cart, and looked anxiously towards the camp fire for Adam. There was no sign of him and the fire was almost burnt out. Her father stirred stiffly and uneasily at her side.

'Isabel?'

'It's all right, Father. The sun will soon be up. I was looking for Adam.'

'Don't fret, lass; he'll not abandon us.'

'I know that. I'm frightened that some harm might have come to him.'

Her father gave a weak, hoarse little chuckle. 'I doubt that either. That man has more lives than a cat.'

Isabel scrambled awkwardly down from the cart. There was still a little water in the leathern water bottle they'd brought from Newark, and she carried a cup to her father, who drank thirstily. She regarded him anxiously. He was more flushed this morning. She had no wish to alarm him by feeling his brow, and he was determined to be cheerful, chiding her for her concern.

'I'm in less pain today, lass, very stiff after being cramped in the night. I'll soon be up and ready to ride again.'

Isabel strove to put to rights her dishevelled appearance and was thankful to see Adam at length come striding into the little clearing.

'I was worried about you,' she said reproachfully. 'Why didn't you tell me when you were going?'

He smiled down at her. 'I've been foraging; it's second nature to a soldier.' He handed her an old canvas bag. 'You'll find bread — coarse rye bread, I'm afraid — and cheese, but it will suffice. There's a little stream over there. I'll fetch some water to wash it all down. How's your father?'

She had moved nearer to the horses and lowered her voice doubtfully. 'He insists he is better, but I fear the fever is rising. I doubt he should ride.'

Adam frowned. 'Well, we can proceed in the cart, at

least until we are somewhat nearer the manor. Then we must see.'

They made a hasty meal. Sir Edwin ate very little and Isabel was further alarmed by the amount of water he craved. Adam stamped out the remains of the fire and began to harness up the donkey.

'I've already watered the horses, taken them all down to the stream.' He smiled at her confidently as he put a hand to lift her into the saddle. 'Take courage, Isabel. A few more miles now and you will be safe home.'

She leaned down to take the reins of her father's horse from him.

'What — what will you do then? Will you come to the manor with us?'

He considered. 'How long should it take us now?'

'Perhaps four or five hours. We dare not travel too fast.' Her hazel eyes were clouded. Soon now he would leave her, and she could not bear the thought. She would be totally bereft, yet, for his own safety, he must soon head for the East Coast and a port from which he could sail to Burgundy. Panic struck her as she realised for the first time that she might never see him again.

He looked back towards the cart where her father had been persuaded to remain resting, grumble though he might.

'We must see how he is. You may need my help to get him into the manor house.'

He squeezed her hand briefly and moved back to climb up on to the cart's driving seat.

She gave a little thankful sigh. She was reprieved. For a while she could continue to rely on his strength and resourcefulness.

Isabel now took the lead, knowing the country more intimately than Adam. They bypassed Radcliffe-on-Trent, where King Henry's army had camped on the way to East Stoke to engage the enemy, then moved steadily south through gentle wold country, passing near to but avoiding the villages of Normanton and Clipston, where her father was known and had previously stayed. At Wymeswold Adam managed to obtain more food and ale for them and then they pushed on to Barrow-on-the-Soar. Isabel was determined her father should not spend another night in the open. Here she was able to move into Charnwood Forest, well away from the road. So close to home ground now, she led them unerringly down hidden tracks just wide enough to allow the cart passage. Within a stone's throw of the manor, she drew rein in a clearing, lifting her hand as a signal for Adam to rein in the donkey.

He hurried to her side and lifted her down from her mount.

'We are very close now. How is my father?'

'He seems better, has managed to rest. He should be well enough to ride the rest of the way. I'll help him from the cart.'

Sir Edwin was clearly cramped by his stay in one position and stamped about for a while then nodded, smiling, as Isabel led up his favourite hack.

'Now, Adam, you will come to the manor, at least for tonight. God knows you need to sleep in a clean bed for once.'

Adam's eyes were narrowed as he surveyed the clearing.

'This is the place you instructed me to meet with Wat when I brought Lord Lovell to Hatfield?'

'Yes, it is.' Sir Edwin's eyes clouded at mention of the man who had been friend to both of them and who now must be believed dead.

'I'll change into my pedlar's clothing and reconnoitre.' He turned to Isabel. 'I insist that you both stay here until I've made sure it is safe to approach the manor.'

Isabel's eyes widened in shock. 'You think it is possible that the King's men — ?'

'Anything is possible, Mistress Isabel. Your father has been away from his own manor and during a period of time when rebels have challenged the King's rule. We must be sure.'

She leaned wearily against the bole of a gigantic oak. It was already growing dusk. These last hours she had set a hard pace, longing to have her father in his own home again.

'You are right to take precuations. We shall obey you.'

Adam had moved to the cart, where he was pulling the shapeless houppeland over his jack and hose. He jumped down and came very close to Isabel, peering deep into her eyes.

'I can really trust you to keep your word this time, whatever happens?'

She coloured, recalling the incident near the ford at Fiskerton.

'I swear it, Adam.'

'If I'm delayed or fail to return to you at all. . .'

Again her eyes widened in horror.

He continued grimly. 'If that should happen, on no account approach the manor. Get your father to some secluded place, preferably on the way to the East Coast, before you attempt to go home.'

'But what about you?'

'If I don't come back, you must assume I am taken and look to yourselves.' He bent and took her hand. Sir Edwin was some feet from them, adjusting the harness on his horse. 'Isabel, never trust to Henry Tudor's word. Accept no offer of pardon for avowed rebels. Get your father to sanctuary or abroad. Remember what happened to the Staffords.'

She was pale now and trembling. He felt her fear in the quivering of her fingers, but she controlled her agitation and jutted her chin determinedly.

'We shall do as you advise.'

He grinned almost boyishly and bent to kiss her gently on the cheek. 'A brotherly kiss only, nothing James Tarvin might disapprove.'

He moved off quickly after grasping her father's hand and was soon a shadowy figure, lost to sight within moments. Sir Edwin sighed gustily as he looked after him.

'There goes a true knight, whom King Richard would have honoured, had he lived.'

Isabel hesitated then she said softly, 'Father, is—is Sir Adam married?'

He stared back at her, astounded. 'Wed? Adam? Bless you, no, lass. Whatever made you think it?'

'He is past the age for wedlock.' She faltered. 'It seemed—most likely. He has never spoken of a wife, but I know men at Court often leave their dependants on their manors and——'

'Nay, Adam never got round to wooing a maid. Doubtless he was too busy with Richard on the border, then, when His Grace was crowned, God knows he needed his loyal men close to him in London.' He scratched his head thoughtfully. 'I imagine, had things gone well at Redmoor and the realm settled in peace, he would have made a good marriage for Adam. Come to think of it, there was once some talk of a maid, but nothing came of it.' He grinned. 'Likely they did not take to each other.'

Isabel turned away so that her father would not see the hot blood crimson her cheeks. Who was this maid he spoke of? Surely she must have found Adam Westlake comely enough. Perhaps the girl herself was found wanting in his eyes. It was certainly unlikely now that, masterless and landless, he would find a suitable wife.

Uncertainly she looked down at her own dust-stained gown. Had Adam Westlake once seen her to advantage? Even on her own manor she had either been in mourning or her old, shabby gown. She remembered, with a little blush, how they had sat together companionably in the straw of the stable, tending Cass. He had kissed her hand gently, like a brother. He must have thought her a country bumpkin indeed compared with the noble-born maid he had thought to wed. When he returned to Burgundy there would be courtly dames in plenty to listen to his tales of daring, both on the battlefield and during the flight following. Would he speak of her, Isabel Hatfield?

She sighed beneath her breath. She would never

forget him, but she could talk about him to no one, save her father, not even to her Aunt Cecily.

Her thoughts flew, perversely, to James. How could she face him, lie to him? Would he still wish to court her? She could no longer hope for marriage with him. There was too much between them — and, always, there would be memories of Adam Westlake and the way he had saved her from her bucolic attacker, his fury at her folly, and the way her heart had beat in tune with his as he carried her through the wood. Her foot had healed now; she could walk without pain — another reminder that their short time together was coming to an end.

Isabel was caught completely off guard when the sound of a horse's hoofs trampling down the bracken told her someone was approaching the clearing. She straightened hastily and turned towards her father. He, too, was listening intently and thoroughly alarmed. Soon the rider emerged from a side-track, one arm slightly raised, revealing his reason for being abroad. His falcon fluttered its wings impatiently while her owner soothed her with calming words.

'There, there, my beauty, be patient awhile; you will have your chance soon enough.'

Sir Edwin's hand was on his horse's bridle and Isabel was about to move to her own mount when she recognised the falconer. Sir Gilbert Tarvin was accompanied only by a groom whose horse followed delicately along the track behind him. Sir Gilbert's eyes slewed from his bird to his neighbour and he gave a start of surprise, then his free hand moved towards his dagger sheath. The action, slight as it was, stirred Sir Edwin into action. He stood clear of his horse and deliberately drew his own blade.

'Isabel,' he snapped, 'stand well behind me.'

Sir Gilbert sat arrogantly, staring down at his erstwhile neighbour. The falcon rustled its feathers again, indignant at being ignored.

Sir Gilbert spoke in that accented tone, softly and yet with menace.

'I see you have deigned to return home, Sir Edwin.

We have been waiting for you. The King's men are anxious to question you concerning the reasons for your absence.'

'My absence from my own home is no concern of yours, sir.'

'I fear it is, since the King has appointed me to act in his stead in this district to root out all traitors.' The silky note had vanished now and Sir Gilbert showed his hand clearly enough.

Isabel was about to put in, but her father gestured imperatively with raised hand for her to remain silent.

'I think you trespass on my land, Sir Gilbert,' he said stiffly.

'If the King's suspicions are correct, Hatfield may not remain your land for much longer. I must ask you to accompany me to your manor hall, where you can satisfy our curiosity as to your recent destination, if you will, Sir Edwin.'

'And if I will not?'

'Then my duty is plain. I must declare you my prisoner.'

Sir Edwin snorted his contempt. 'First you must take me, Gilbert Tarvin.'

Without warning Sir Edwin launched himself at the other man and pulled him clear of the saddle. The falcon's frantic flutterings and raucous cry of rage filled the quiet clearing and, as if in answer, all other birds in the vicinity took flight. Isabel stood petrified as the two men struggled together. The groom, no trained fighting man, and as surprised by the encounter as she was, sat still in the saddle, watching the combatants with huge, startled eyes. The falcon abruptly, with a supreme effort of will, tore herself free from her jess and launched into flight. Sir Gilbert was a big man and the fall from the saddle had jarred him sorely. It took some moments for him to hold his own with the furious man who was attacking him. He gave a bellow of rage, his dagger hand stabbing furiously, quite blindly. Isabel warily watched the groom, who remained where he was, like a rabbit caught in the basilisk stare of the stoat. She looked

huntedly around for some weapon with which she could
aid her father. For the present it seemed the two men
were well matched, but Isabel knew her father to be too
gravely injured to hold his own for long. If Tarvin's
words were true, then Adam must have fallen into a trap
and could give no help. The sounds of struggle eventually must bring men to the spot, and she had no idea
how many were in the hawking party. Could Sir Gilbert
have come from his manor alone? She prayed that were
so, but her father must have help, and soon. Sir Gilbert
must be laid low and she and her father got well away
from this place as Adam had warned her.

She flew straight at Sir Gilbert's back, where he
panted and grunted in the remorseless battle for mastery
with his adversary. He was taken by surprise by her
futile, clawing fingers, but easily flung her off. The
groom dismounted and stood stupidly, mouth agape at
the sight of a well born lady indulging in a useless brawl
with his master. He was one of the Heywards' servants
and could not imagine himself dealing harshly with
Mistress Isabel Hatfield. He waited, swallowing
uncomfortably, for the outcome.

Isabel's body hit the ground with a spine-jarring jolt
and it was seconds before she could pull herself again to
her feet. Her father was tiring; she could see that, and
hear the uneven, laboured breaths as he moved in that
clumsy, horrifying dance of death with his opponent.

Now Tarvin had him down and his arm was upraised
to strike. Isabel uttered a shrill scream and flew at him
again, her fingers striving frantically to stay that hand.
He muttered a round soldier's oath and grappled with
her. She rolled over and over with the knight's heavy
body pinning her down, spitting and clawing like a wild
cat, further and further from the prone figure of her
father, her fingers ever straining for that weapon glinting
and winking in the sunlight which pierced through the
interleaving branches of the trees. Gilbert Tarvin had
no wish to harm the girl, simply to free himself from
her hold. This put him at a disadvantage and he yelled
at her hoarsely to, 'Let be, let be.' Isabel had no

intention of allowing him leeway to strike again at her father. She held on to his arm relentlessly. How long they struggled she would never know; it seemed like an eternity. She had no thought for her own safety, nor the foolhardiness of her conduct in believing she could best a trained warrior like Gilbert Tarvin. The dagger weaved uncertainly from side to side above her. She was intent on nothing else but that menacing blade. As from a distance she heard another hoarse shout and judged the groom would, at last, try to intervene, and weakly redoubled her efforts to deflect that dagger from her own body and, at the same time, keep Tarvin pinned down so he would be unable to turn his attention once more to her father.

They both pushed and strained for control, then, suddenly, Sir Gilbert rolled free. Her arm was still desperately thrusting downwards. She gave a muffled cry of terror as the blade tore down her forearm. If she continued to hold on she knew it would plunge itself into her breast, yet still she would not relinquish it. She flung herself once more down on to the knight's body, then felt herself seized from behind. She gave a yell of fury and turned on her attacker, her fingers slackening on the weapon. How dared this man stop her now — now, while she had momentary mastery?

'Gently, gently, Isabel, my love,' a voice urged, and she collapsed sobbing into Adam Westlake's arms.

He lifted her to her feet and stared soberly down at the fallen Sir Gilbert. That last lunging thrust of Isabel's had taken the man full in the breast. He had half struggled upwards and their two hands had forced the dagger blade up to the very hilt into his heart. He lay unmoving, a trickle of blood issuing from his half-opened lips.

Isabel stared down at him wildly. 'Stop him,' she exhorted Adam. 'He will kill my father or take him prisoner. . .'

Gently he tried to guide her away from the scene of carnage. As yet she had no knowledge of what she had done.

She tried to thrust aside his constraining arm and knelt down over Tarvin's body, hunting for the dagger. 'I have to find it. . . I have to. . . He will. . .' Her words trailed off uncertainly as she stared down at her fallen opponent. 'Is he. . .is he unconscious?' Kneeling, she looked anxiously at Adam's frowning countenance. 'Shouldn't we pinion him? Where is the groom? He may warn the others. . .'

'He's safe enough; for the second time in two days I've had to deal with your attackers. I caught him with a heavy branch. He'll lie quiet for a while.'

Isabel was staring with growing horror at her reddened hands. 'Sir Gilbert. . .he's not moving. . . He cannot be. . .dead?' The final word rose to a shriek. 'Dear God, Adam I didn't kill him. . . I didn't. . .'

Firmly he lifted her to her feet, turning her face to his shoulder. 'He fell on his weapon. You were struggling. I saw what happened when I came into the clearing. Isabel. . .' He shook her roughly as her mouth opened to give a scream of hysteria. 'Isabel, don't give way now. We need you, your father and I, as much as when you ran at Sir Gilbert. Come, now; we must get away from here.'

She was shuddering violently, her hazel eyes wide with shock and torment, and she made no resistance as he guided her towards the cart.

He was talking steadily, quietly, as much to keep her mind from dwelling on the horror she had just realised as for any real purpose. Obediently she allowed him to half lift her into the cart and sat passively, staring down at her bloodstained hands, when he moved back to her father.

Heaving Sir Edwin to his shoulder, Adam carried him to the cart and called to Isabel to help lift him up into the back.

'You must help me, Isabel. I can't manage him alone.'

She obeyed him at last and, between them, they pulled the unconscious man down on to the floor of the vehicle. Isabel cradled his head in her arms. Adam rushed back to the horses. He smote them all on their

withers and saw them take off into the undergrowth. It
was likely, since all were from the adjoining manors,
that they would find their way home, which would not
allow him much time to get clear. He muttered an oath
between his teeth, raced back to the cart, and sprang to
the driving seat.

He cast one glance behind him at Isabel, but she was
staring down at her father, and he turned the cart
awkwardly in the confined space and made for the way
they had come. Isabel was in no condition to guide him
and he was thankful that recent experience had made
him a good woodsman and he was able to follow the trail
they had made. He pulled up near a second small stream
which bubbled over boulders between the peaty soil and
bracken, and turned back to Isabel. Reaching into the
cart for the bundle of clothing she had discarded earlier
near East Stoke, he thrust it into her arms.

'Go down to the stream, Isabel; do it now. Wash off
the blood and put on Bess's clothes again. We must hide
your own.'

He climbed down and reached up to help her out. She
avoided his grasp, as if unwilling for her stained hands
to come into contact with his, and climbed down
unsteadily, then she nodded and moved to the stream to
do as he ordered.

He gave a passing glance at Sir Edwin. There were
fresh bloodstains on the man's doublet. He was breathing unevenly and still deeply unconscious. Again Adam
cursed beneath his breath. The struggle with his enemy
had undoubtedly weakened him further, possibly torn a
vital organ already damaged at East Stoke. They would
be fortunate to take him living to safety. For the moment
his thoughts must be for Isabel.

She turned, recoiling nervously as he joined her at the
stream. She had stripped off her gown and half
crouched, washing her hands and arms in the chill
water. Her shift clung wetly to her body and she was
shivering violently.

'Come here,' he commanded.

She stared at him wildly.

'Come here; I must see if he injured you.'

She shook her head mutely, but came meekly to his side.

Gently he took her by one shoulder and examined her minutely. There was an ugly gash along her right wrist, and he stooped and tore off a portion of the damp shift to staunch the blood.

'It's not deep. We can dress it with salve later. You are sure there are no other wounds?'

Again she shook her head dumbly.

With patient fingers he helped her to dress in Bess's sober kirtle and bodice.

'Now you must be the pedlar's wife again, sit beside me on the seat. You understand?'

Her teeth were chattering from the water's cleansing coldness, but she nodded and forced a smile.

'Don't be alarmed, Adam. I will be sensible.'

He ran a gentle finger down the contours of her face. One solitary tear ran down and he checked it smilingly. 'Remember, tell yourself always you did no wrong. You thought only to save your father. You must continue to be brave. We have a long way to go and there must be bands of armed men in the area.'

She swallowed the bile which rose in her throat, her gaze going back to the cart.

'Is he. . .is he. . .?'

'He has been hurt again. I do not know, Isabel, if he will survive, but we, and we alone, can save him if God wills it so.'

'Sir Gilbert. . .lying alone there in the forest. . .'

'Men will come soon and find him. The groom will come to his senses and summon help; that is why we have no time to waste. We must make for Melton now and get him clear across the fens to Bishops Lynn.'

'The horses?'

'I scattered them. We cannot ride now; our only hope lies in being taken for poor travelling folk.'

She gave him a tremulous smile and walked before him back to the cart.

RELUCTANT REBEL 155

He bundled up her bloodstained clothing and sought for some boulder under which he thrust it. He gritted his teeth in a mirthless grin as he thought she was now entirely lost to James Tarvin.

CHAPTER NINE

ONCE near to the main highway from Leicester to Loughborough Adam knew his bearings and crossed it, moving steadily east. Isabel had scrambled into the back of the cart and sat huddled against the supports which held the canvas cover in place, her father's head on her lap. Adam asked only once how he was and received a husky answer that he was dozing. He did not press her to talk.

He was intent now on leaving the area as quickly as possible. Sir Gilbert's body would be found before nightfall, more quickly than that if the groom came to himself sooner than Adam hoped and managed to reach the manor to tell his tale. The man probably knew Isabel, so it would not be believed that Sir Gilbert had been set upon by footpads. He himself had seen the company of men-at-arms surrounding Hatfield and surmised they were waiting to snare Edwin; therefore men would be sent out to comb the area for the fugitives. Likely it would be supposed that, once warned, Edwin Hatfield would attempt to make for the coast. Every highroad would be alerted, for Adam knew, to his cost, that King's spies were everywhere. Henry trusted no one. Adam smiled grimly. How could a man who had usurped a throne and killed its rightful king afford to rely on his nobles? As he had seized the opportunity to encourage insurrection, so others would do also, so he must always be on his guard.

Yet he dared not drive too far. Edwin Hatfield needed further attention and the Saints knew Isabel was in no state for the rigours of the road just yet. Fortunately the groom had not really seen him closely, if at all. All the man's attention had been on the fight, so Tarvin's men would not be on the look-out for a pedlar. He ground his teeth in helpless fury as he wondered if James Tarvin had yet arrived home and was informed of his father's death. The groom had not witnessed the end of the fight. He could not know that it was Isabel who was instrumental in causing his master's death.

Her voice came to him now, hoarse, as if she was holding back rivers of unshed tears.

'Adam, the jolting cannot be good for my father. Dare we stop?'

'Soon now,' he promised. In an hour or so it would be full dark and they would not be able to proceed further. Already their sturdy little donkey was tiring. He must be watered and fed.

They crossed the Wreake river by a ford and Adam drew up on the further bank not far from the village of Frisby. Here was common pasture land where the donkey could graze and they were near to water.

He jumped down and surveyed the terrain. It was too late now to try to obtain fresh food from a nearby farm, but there was still bread and cheese and salt bacon in the cart, and he would be able to build a camp fire. He could see that Isabel was still shivering violently — from shock, he thought, rather than cold, for the summer night was mild enough.

She lifted her arms submissively to be helped down. Her eyes were huge in the dim light, for the moon had not yet fully risen.

'Is it safe to stay here?'

'I see no reason why not. In my guise as pedlar I can show my wares in the village tomorrow and buy fresh supplies.'

'Can you light the lantern so that I can tend Father?'

He nodded, placing the kindled ox horn lantern with its stub of candle down on the floor of the cart. He watched her take out her herb chest and moved off to find dry kindling after first unharnessing the donkey and hobbling it so it might graze freely in the vicinity. It was best for Isabel if she occupied herself with her father for a while.

Soon he had a fire going and rigged up branches as a support for the hanging cooking pot in which he was able to boil the last of the bacon Wat Jessop had provided.

He turned as the rustle of her skirts across the grass told him she was near, and he indicated a place by the fire.

'Is he asleep again?'

'Yes, I do not think we should disturb him to eat or even drink anything yet.' Her voice faltered. 'He seems so very weak. I cannot find any serious fresh wound, just scratches and gashes on the sword arm where they struggled with the blade——' she broke off and swallowed awkwardly '—as I did with. . . His breathing is still poor. I think he tore open the earlier injury.' Her eyes appealed to him to contradict her, but he could not and he looked away.

'Come and sit down and eat.'

He put out a hand to draw her down and she recoiled, then recollected herself and seated herself by him. 'I'm sorry; I feel that I do not want anyone to touch me. I am soiled by what—what happened back there.'

'Because you were instrumental in killing a man? Note I did not say "killed", for he brought it upon himself. Who can say whose hand was the stronger and jerked the dagger into his breast? Isabel, would you recoil from your father's touch because he came to you fresh from the battle, having killed and wounded men?'

She blinked back tears. 'That—that is different.'

'How different?'

'He and you are soldiers. . .'

'And you were a warrior back there, fighting to preserve your father's life.'

'I have committed a mortal sin.'

'It is no mortal sin to kill in self-defence. When I can, I will find you a priest who will absolve you, I swear it.'

He put a hunk of bread and bacon into her hand and though she shook her head he pressed her hand towards her mouth.

'Eat. You can do no good by starving yourself, rather harm. I cannot have you show weakness now.'

'What do you intend to do?' Her eyes filled with tears

again. 'You should not be burdened by us. The fault is mine. . .'

'Don't start that again,' he retorted grimly. 'What's done is done and cannot be helped. There was no other course. I must try to get you both to Burgundy.'

'But the ports will be alerted?'

'Aye.' His fierce black eyes were on her again and she obeyed him and began to eat, though reluctantly.

'You said you saw soldiers at the manor. How could they know? No one knew he was injured.'

Adam sighed. 'He was absent—suspicious enough, in the circumstances. It's likely Sir Gilbert was aware he had been in the vicinity of Newark. It left him open to questioning.'

'But no one knew where he had been. . .' Her voice trailed off. 'You think it was James Tarvin, don't you? He must have sent a messenger that night he spoke to me in Newark.'

'It's probable,' he said guardedly. 'Didn't you tell him your father was possibly visiting your kinfolk near Fiskerton?'

She nodded and looked away from him over the darkening meadow. 'How could he have done it?' she said at last, brokenly. 'Even if he really *did* suspect. He said he loved me.'

Adam was silent and she turned back to him suddenly. 'Why?'

Adam shrugged. 'He thought it his duty?'

'Would you have betrayed a friend to your King?'

His dark eyes held hers. 'That would depend.'

'On what?'

'On whether I thought my King's life threatened.'

She munched silently for moments on the hard bread. She had believed herself not hungry, but found now that she was. She shivered again. 'I think—I think my father might die.'

He drew in his breath. 'You must be very brave, Isabel, whatever happens. I know you can be; I've had evidence of it.'

He felt her whole body tremble beside him and she said piteously, 'I'm so afraid.'

He put an arm round her and drew her close and, this time, she did not resist. She said haltingly, 'Talk to me, Adam. Keep me from thinking what—what might be. . . Tell me about yourself and—and how you came to enter King Richard's service.'

He moved slightly, so that she was sitting comfortably supported by his shoulder.

'It's an unusual tale; at least, few men have had the fortune to enter a noble household so. My father was killed at Empingham; ironically the place is not so far from here.'

She nodded. 'He was fighting for King Edward?'

'Yes. Until then he had not involved himself with either faction, but my mother believed he could better himself by supporting his sovereign, though how she thought he would ever have come to the King's attention I cannot think. He had a small holding in Lincolnshire near Grantham and the land barely kept us all alive in times of bad harvest.' He hesitated. 'I truly believed she loved my father—at all events made him a good wife—but—but she married very soon after, one Walter Pilton, a younger son of a Northamptonshire gentleman. He had no prospects, had become acquainted with my father during the short campaign, and came to us with the news of his death bearing messages, so he said.'

'You had no liking for the man?'

'I detested him. He was handsome enough—far more so than my father, I suppose—though, as a grieving son of just thirteen, I was hardly likely to welcome him to my mother's bed.'

His tone was bitter, but Isabel did not interrupt at what was obviously an important point in his story.

'I made it very plain. That was obvious. He disliked me as much and very soon managed to make life hell for me. My mother, God bless her soul, loved me well enough, but she was besotted with the fellow—then, at least. I shall never know how it was with her later. We struggled along together for some time—about two years, it must have been. I was putting on a man's shape by then and did not take his strictures or physical abuse without complaint. Mother began to fear for me. One night he beat me so badly, after some minor misdemeanour, that I could scarcely stand. She decided that I must leave our home. She was carrying his child by then.'

'Did he treat her well?'

'At first. He liked her well enough and she was comely. She had black hair, like me, and big, dark eyes, but she was not strong. Even then, when I left her, I could have circled her body easily with my two hands, and she with child, she was so small of stature.' He fell quiet for a moment and Isabel thought he was recalling his mother's loved features. Hadn't he seen her again?

Adam found her grave hazel eyes on him searchingly and continued.

'Her father—my grandfather—had once served Lord Scrope of Bolton and done him some great service. I was never told the details. He had died, of course, by then, but my mother furnished me with a letter to the present lord requesting that he take me into his service. As I said, I was thirteen—young, but old enough to be trained as a man-at-arms. She thought it was the best possible hope for me. It was winter and clearly not the best time to travel. I had to make for Bolton in the Yorkshire Dales, but my stepfather was temporarily from home and we both thought it wiser for me to be gone before he returned. I had my own horse——' Adam smiled grimly '—though I doubt Walt Pilton would consider him to be rightfully mine, so I set out.'

'That was a long journey at that time of year and you so young. Had you money for accommodation at inns?'

'Some. My mother had little to spare and that only what she hoped Pilton would not notice had gone. At first things did not go too badly. I was borne up by hopes of a brave future as a man-at-arms. I would make my fortune later as a mercenary and return to rescue my mother from Pilton's hands.' He smiled a trifle bitterly again and Isabel waited, silently, for the rest of the tale.

'I lost my way, then my purse was stolen while I slept

in the common room of an inn near Doncaster. After
that I was forced to sleep under hedges or in ditches.'

'And your food had run out?'

He nodded ruefully.

'The weather worsened suddenly after I left the Great
North Road and was travelling in the Dales. My poor
beast was making slow going, but I was determined to
reach Bolton instead of spending another night in freez-
ing misery so I pushed the brute far more than I should
have done. I could have begged for shelter at the Abbey
of Jervaulx, but I was too proud to do so — rank
foolishness, as it fell out. I was riding out of Masham
when I met a lone rider muffled hard against the
weather. He hailed me pleasantly enough and rode with
me part of the way when I requested direction. I
remember him looking up at the sky when I spoke of
Bolton and he said, "Take my word for it, we shall have
blizzard conditions before morning. You shouldn't try
to reach Bolton tonight. Turn back to Jervaulx or make
for Middleham and take the road north when the
weather eases." I could not confess I had no money for
food or accommodation, so I thanked him kindly, and
we parted company and I struck out northwards. He
was right. By late afternoon the sky darkened and snow
fell so heavily I couldn't see a hand's breadth before my
face. My mount was foundering in deep drifts and I
knew we should be benighted, so, in desperation, I was
forced to turn back.'

'To Middleham?'

'Aye, to Middleham. How we made it I shall never
know. Once my horse fell and wouldn't get up again. I
remember belabouring him and cursing and, to please
me, he struggled up again and then I had to dismount
and lead him. I knew I was likely killing him, but, by
that time, I had no other course. I knew if we didn't
reach Middleham we should both perish in the drifts.
My fervent prayers were answered and at last I saw the
castle gatehouse looming up before me out of the snow
and pulled my suffering beast in against the partial
shelter the wall offered against the biting wind. I had

little hope I would be admitted and dared not ask for shelter at one of the houses clustering near for lack of coin for payment. So we stayed there. The drawbridge was raised; it was night,' he laughed, 'and the Duke not expecting callers, but my luck was in, or the Saints intervened for me. A small party of men-at-arms arrived and demanded admittance. The sergeant saw me, dismounted, and came up close, demanding to know who in God's name I was and what I was doing out so late.'

'During the civil wars, I imagine lone visitors were not made welcome. You could have been a spy, even one so young. It was not unknown.'

'Indeed. Before I could utter a word I was hustled into the gatehouse guard-room and ordered to explain my business. Things might have gone hard with me had not my companion of the morning not entered the guard-room suddenly and he, thank the Virgin, recognised me instantly.'

Adam's lips were smiling now and Isabel's eyes widened as she began to understand. 'It was King Richard? He was Duke of Gloucester then and lived much of his life at Middleham and you had not known him?'

'Yes, it was Richard. He greeted me kindly, reminding me that I had been foolish to ignore his warnings. I told him why I was bound for Bolton and offered him proof — my mother's letter to Lord Scrope. I didn't know who he was then, of course, only later, though I should have realised by the deference he was accorded by the guards.'

'You were granted shelter then?'

'Aye, I was given a bed in the pages' dormitory. As it happened, one of the squires and two of the pages had been granted leave to visit their homes for Christmas, and the worsening weather had delayed their return. I was able to make myself useful to Her Grace the Duchess. She was big with child then and found it hard to climb the stairs too often.'

His voice had softened and Isabel guessed he was remembering the Duchess and her untimely death

before Bosworth. She said diffidently, 'There were
rumours that he — Richard — wanted to be rid of her in
the end, that he —— '

'They lied through their teeth.' His voice was hoarse
with suppressed fury so that she quailed before him,
and he put a hand on her shoulder to reassure her. 'I am
sorry, Isabel, if I snapped at you, but, you see, I loved
them both, and I had years to see how dearly they loved
each other.'

She nodded, her head bowed, ashamed of her own
foolishness in suggesting that the man he admired so
greatly would have stooped to such dishonour.

'So you stayed in service at Middleham?'

'Aye, I learned that Scrope was away from Yorkshire
and, when he returned, Richard requested that I be
allowed to remain in his service, which boon my lord
gladly granted.'

'Did he know — how it had been with you at home,
about your unhappiness?'

'Aye. I told him everything.' Adam's lips curved
again in wry humour. 'I do not think his own family life
had been easy. He understood my need. I served first as
page then was trained to arms. I fought by his side on
the border against the Scots and there he knighted me.
When Edward died and he came south, I was in his
train.'

He shifted and put more kindling on the dwindling
fire. Isabel was tempted to ask him about the fate of the
princes whom Gloucester had sworn to serve as loyal
subject and then usurped the throne of, but Adam's
expression was remote and she dared not. She felt a
great rush of tenderness for the boy who had fled his
stepfather's ill treatment and found happiness and security in Richard of Gloucester's service. For the first time
she fully understood how it had been for him. He had
been received with kindness and she surmised that the
Duchess had shown the lonely boy some measure of
affection. No wonder Adam's allegiance to the man who
had given him shelter and later advanced him in service
had never wavered. It never would. Adam would never

cease to join any cause which would bring a Yorkist King once more to the throne of England, the only service he could now render his dead friend and liege-lord.

She said quietly, 'That is a fascinating tale, Adam. What of your mother? Is she still living?'

He shook his head, the dark eyes becoming opaque once more. 'No, she died in childbirth, some months after I left. Pilton stayed on in the manor house, though by rights it was mine. He was killed about a year later in some drunken brawl in a Grantham tavern—a dis-agreement over dice, it was said. The Duke arranged for a steward to care for the estate. I have returned to it only briefly and——' he shrugged again, regretfully '—it is lost to me now.'

He stood up as if, suddenly, he was aware that he had revealed more of his feelings to her than he would have wished. 'We should look to your father.'

She rose hastily and, scarlet-faced, went from him to the cart.

Sir Edwin appeared to be breathing more easily now, though Isabel was still alarmed by his pallor, and his lips were blue-tinged. Adam leaned down to look and his eyes met hers.

He sighed heavily. 'It is good that he sleeps. We can do no more for him now. You should try to rest also.'

Isabel swallowed hard. 'Yes, I must, but. . .' Her voice trailed off, but she knew he understood. Visions of the afternoon's tragedy would continually intrude, as well as the nagging uncertainty about her father's con-dition, making it almost impossible for her to sleep.

Her father was lying full across the width of the cart and she had no wish to disturb him so she stretched out, wrapped in her cloak, some little distance from Adam on the far side of the fire. As she had dreaded, her mind was full of doubts and forebodings, and she shifted fretfully and often in an effort to get comfortable. He lay with his back to her, a short cloak of Wat's thrown over his legs. He was still and she judged that, with the practice of long campaigns, he slept more easily than she did.

She forced her mind from her worries back to the story he had told. How unfortunate that a youth who had come to some prominence in the late King's household, from comparatively humble beginnings, should now find himself back where he started, and have the need to carve out a new niche for himself. Her father, should he live, was in little better state. He, too, would be forced to live in exile and she with him. There was some little money — Sir Edwin had naturally carried sufficient for his needs on his person when he had ridden out to war — and there were her few jewels which Wat had brought to the barn with her other possessions, but Hatfield would be forfeit, and she without dowry. Her face flamed as she thought of James. Had she really loved him? There had been times when she had believed it possible that she could spend her life contentedly with him. Now she could only remember his betrayal, for that could only have come from James. Regretfully, she realised that Adam had feared this all along. That night at Hatfield when he had accosted her going to tend Cass, he had feared she would meet James and that he would learn of Lord Lovell's presence in the house. She must put all thoughts of James aside and settle to her new life in exile, tending her father, who might be able to attach himself to the Duchess of Burgundy's household at Malines.

For the first time the full horror of her situation struck her. If her father should die. . . She could not continually rely on the good offices of Adam Westlake to protect her. Possibly he had other responsibilities at Margaret's court. A man so personable and gallant would not need to beg for women's favours and, if he was wise, he would look to bettering his fortune by an advantageous marriage. The thought of that was horrifying to her. Had she come to love Adam Westlake? If so, she must not let herself hope that her feelings would be reciprocated. She must not allow him to guess that he had come to mean any more to her than a good and trusted friend. Once safely abroad, she and her father must go their own way, and, if necessary, she must face the future alone. She had some skills. Her needlework was passable and she was knowledgeable with herbs and salves. Some noble or merchant family might agree to take her in. She would manage. She must. Swallowing back hot tears of panic, she turned away from the sight of Adam lying so still and sturdy only feet away from her.

The next morning her father seemed a little improved. His breathing was still hard, but he expressed himself hungry, and Isabel was glad when Adam returned from the village with food for them, the simple fare she had come to expect — rye bread, cheese and a leathern bottle of ale.

They left after Adam had helped to tend her father's needs and assist him once more into the cart. He managed to lash a framework of heavy fallen boughs to the side-support of the cart to allow Sir Edwin a more comfortable, half sitting posture, which eased his breathing and made tolerable the jolting of the diabolically uncomfortable vehicle. Isabel, seated by Adam's side on the driving seat, found herself clinging on for dear life. The June heat worsened their discomfort and she did not enjoy the quiet scenes of the countryside as much as she would have done in different circumstances.

They passed through the village of Gaddesby where men could be seen busy in the fields already reaping early bean crops, then on to the market town of Oakham where Adam peddled his wares before the market cross and did well enough to allow him to spend money on more tasty fare of venison pasties and a bottle of wine. Sir Edwin was still clearly in pain, but he made light of his suffering and enjoyed the meal.

Adam had also managed to obtain news which filled them all with despair. The death of the Earl of Lincoln had been confirmed.

Adam said grimly, 'Rumour has it that Henry left him there, buried on the field with a stake of willow

through his heart. I doubt the truth of that last part—
foolish peasant superstition.'

Sir Edwin crossed himself. 'Did you hear anything
more about Frank Lovell and the boy?' Isabel noted
that he did not term the lad 'King' any more.

'No news of Lovell. There is a hue and cry for him
throughout the realm, but it seems he must have
drowned in the Trent as we first thought. As for the
boy, that is the strangest story of all. I was told by a
travelling friar, fresh from Nottinghamshire, that the
King has shown the lad uncommon mercy, had him
conveyed south to London in his train. Henry gave it
out that, since the boy was clearly of servant stock, he
would find him work in the palace kitchens. That, too,
is probably scurrilous gossip which we shall find later to
be totally false.'

'It would be like Henry to so completely humiliate his
captive, in some way a more unendurable punishment
than death on the block,' Sir Edwin said thoughtfully.
'How much pleasure it will give him to think of the boy
scouring pots, especially if he believes, in his heart, that
the boy he calls so jeeringly Lambert Simnel *is* George
of Clarence's son, the true Earl of Warwick.'

Isabel frowned as she considered, not for the first
time, the Queen's feelings in this matter. Lincoln was
her cousin, so dishonourably buried, and the boy might
well be her nephew. She had borne the King an heir and
had the fortunes of her child to think of, but there must
be times when she considered the fates of her Yorkist
kin with some disquiet.

She was surprised when Adam drove straight through
the busy market town of Stamford. Since it lay on the
Great North Road and might be watched for all those
suspected of treason, she had thought he would try to
avoid it, but he merely observed that in such a motley
crowd which thronged the town they would be hardly
noticed, and so it proved.

He made camp once more just outside the village of
West Deeping, and with more of the supplies he'd
bought in Oakham they made a good supper. Sir Edwin

settled in the cart and Isabel wandered back to Adam
where he sat near the camp fire.

'You look very abstracted. Are you getting alarmed
about our journey?'

He gave a faint smile of welcome as she seated herself
beside him. 'Not really, though the closer we get to the
ports the more care we must take. King's men are
always on the look-out for emigrants to Burgundy, and
spies bound for the French Court. No, I was thinking
about our friends who seem lost to us.'

'You really think there is no hope for Lord Lovell?'
She had a mental picture of the man who had so charmed
her and made light of the discomforts of his dangerous
journeying.

'We should have heard if he had been taken.'

'But he has friends. Could he not have gone to ground
with one of them, as he did before?'

'Yes, that's possible, but Frank would know, only too
well, how dangerous his arrival there would be to any
one of them. Now there can be no doubt of his treason.
He could have made for home — Minster Lovell in
Oxfordshire — but I think that doubtful, for the same
reason.'

Isabel could only share his pessimism. Experience had
shown her that there was no shelter in their own homes
for rebels. 'How dreadful for that young man in the
King's kitchens. He will have to endure constant bait-
ing. Adam, when you were in King Richard's household, did you ever see the Duke of Clarence's son?'

He shot her a piercing glance as if he read the doubt
in her mind concerning the boy's identity and, in it, the
madness of fighting for so doubtful a cause which had
brought them all to disaster.

'Just once. He had been under the control of the
Marquis of Dorset, the Queen's son by her marriage to
Lord Grey. He seemed——' he hesitated '—somewhat
backward for his age and very nervous. Richard was
concerned about him, and removed him from London
to Sheriff Hutton, where he could be tutored with other
members of the royal household.'

'And——' Isabel bit her lip '—when you saw this Simnel boy, did he resemble the young Earl?'

'He was certainly Neville-fair and personable like the two sons of King Edward.' He looked thoughtfully into the fire. 'The fact is, both your father and I were never sure if the boy—the one who was always in Henry's hands—*was* the true son of Clarence. Truth to tell, he never bothered himself too much about the lad. As you know his own death was brought about by an altercation with Edward concerning the inheritance.'

'Then you, too, thought the tale of his baby son's being conveyed abroad was possibly true.'

'Yes.'

Isabel hesitated. It seemed a good time to broach the fate of the two lost princes, since Adam had himself mentioned them.

'And the sons of King Edward, the royal bastards. You believe them to be dead?'

His head shot round and she felt that fierce gaze on her again. Any hint that she believed Richard to have been a murderer of helpless children would bring down on her his full fury, and she dreaded that. She was trembling as she waited for his answer, yet that very answer meant much to her.

'The boys were taken north, as young Warwick was. After that I do not know what happened to one of them. The other, please God, still lives. If the elder boy fell into Henry's hands, as it seems likely, then all hope must be lost.'

'You say you know for certain that one boy still lives?' Isabel was astounded. 'Then why did you not support him instead of this lad who might have been an impostor?'

'The younger boy, Richard of York, was taken from the realm soon after Richard's coronation by one of Richard's most trusted knights. I know that to be fact. It was thought advisable to separate the boys, both for their own safety and for Richard's security. It is best if you do not know where. I am not sure exactly, at least at this time. The children of Edward and Elizabeth were

declared bastards. I believe that also to be fact and
Bishop Stillington's assertion that their parents' marriage was unlawful perfectly true. While a legitimate
heir existed, my duty was to support him. Two did—
Lincoln and the boy we thought was Warwick. Now
both are lost to us and we must consider where our
allegiance lies.'

Isabel regarded him open-mouthed and his lips
twitched in a little grim smile. 'You did not think I
would continue to loyally support a man who could
murder his brother's children, did you? Richard half
worshipped Edward. Some of us thought his devotion
too great at times. Edward could be ruthless and cruel.
Richard would never harm the children. Warwick was a
much greater threat to his claim, being legitimate, yet
the boy remained unharmed throughout his reign; no
one doubts that. Why should he harm his cause—a
cause which Parliament sanctioned—by the pointless
murder of two innocents?'

'Yet there were rumours. . .'

'Foul calumnies, spread by his enemies, which
Richard would not stoop to deny. Surely you must see
that the princes, should they live, prove a far more
serious threat to Henry. He insisted on their sister being
declared legitimate before he wed her.'

Isabel's thoughts were racing. Then, if what Adam
said was true, there was another Plantagenet prince
living, one whom Adam would wish to support. Her
father, too. Was this uncertainty never to end for her?
Was she to continue, all her life, to live in fear that those
she loved would again deliberately place themselves in
danger?

A cool light breeze had sprung up and, after the heat
and humidity of the day, Isabel found it easier to sleep
than she had on other days on the journey. She was
wakened abruptly, just before dawn, by a terrible choking sound which brought her instantly to her feet. Adam
was already up and bending over the cart. Isabel raced
to his side, an icy dread seizing her vitals.

Sir Edwin was finding it almost impossible to get his

breath. He had haemorrhaged. There was blood staining
his doublet and trickling from the side of his mouth.
Isabel stifled a cry of panic and took one slack hand in
her own.

'Father, it's Isabel. I'm here, beside you. Can you
hear me?'

He nodded, trying to force a ghastly smile. His clasp
on her hand tightened. Adam was supporting his head
and, at last, he managed to croak, 'Get me — out of this
damned cart, lad. . . Can't breathe. . .'

Adam gestured to Isabel to release her father's hand
and move back. It was an awkward business, but, with
Isabel waiting beside him to support her father's body,
he managed to lift him down on to the grass.

'Get my cloak for his head.'

She hastened back to the fire then returned to the cart
for her herb chest. She had little hope that there was
anything she could do for him. It was as she had feared
from the beginning. The lung was pierced by the arrow
and the wound had worsened in his struggle with Gilbert
Tarvin. Her whole body was trembling, but she took
hard breaths, forcing her limbs to move back steadily
and surely to where Adam sat cradling her father's head
and shoulders against his breast. She could not quite
catch what was said, for Adam's head was bent low to
hear the dying man's words.

'Adam, remember what. . .what you promised. . .
after Stoke. Isabel. . .she's in more need of you now. . .
than ever. . . You'll. . .see her safe. . .'

The eyes were imploring and Adam said quietly,
'Give your heart peace, Edwin. Isabel means more to
me than even the cause.'

Sir Edwin's lips contorted again into that travesty of a
smile. 'You will wed my lass, Adam?'

'If she is willing, but her heart may still be held by
young Tarvin.'

'No, Adam, lad. . . I have watched her. . . She. . .'
He broke off into a bout of horrifying coughing which
brought with it a fresh flow of blood.

Isabel was by his side again now and he clawed for
her hand.

'Nay, lass, don't fuss with your potions. . . Won't. . .
do. . .a mite of. . .good. Bend very. . .close.'

She sank to her knees on the grass and bent to catch
the sound of the weakened voice.

'Don't try to talk. Rest, Father, you must!' Her own
voice broke in a half-sob.

'For what. . .daughter? To save. . .a few moments?'

She swallowed back her tears.

'Obey Adam. He will get. . .you to safety. . . Trust
yourself to him. Swear to me. . .you will do that.'

'I will, Father.' Despite her intentions to remain calm,
the tears were raining down her cheeks now as she bent
to kiss his loved face.

'Isabel?' He tried desperately to rouse himself into a
sitting position, and Adam moved to help him.

'Adam. . . Adam. . .'

What he needed to say most had been left too late.
She could not get those last words which meant so much
to him. He gave a final spasmodic cough and there was
a further rush of blood. Mercifully the agonising choking had eased. There was a last rattle of breath and his
hand slackened in hers.

'Father? Father?' Her voice rose to a little shriek as
she tried to rouse him to finish the sentence, though, in
her heart, she knew he had already gone from her.

Adam laid down his burden and scrambled awkwardly
to his feet. He walked back to the fire, leaving father
and daughter together.

She lifted his head on to her lap and sat there, how
long she would never know, while she crooned to him
and cried softly at the same time. She had prepared
herself for this from the moment she had known about
the position of the arrow. Only last night she had
rationally considered her situation, should her father
die, yet now, in the final moment, it still seemed unreal
to her. She could not bring herself to accept that they
had lost the fight. Since Redmoor she had feared he
would take arms again. She had blamed Adam, though

she knew he was not responsible. After Stoke he had
done everything to try to save her father, putting himself
in considerable jeopardy. It had all been in vain. She
had killed Gilbert Tarvin for nothing. Her father was
dead and, despite her brave determination last night,
she felt utterly bereft.

At last Adam came back to her side and reached down
his hand.

'Let me lift him back into the cart, Isabel, and. . .and
do what I can to arrange his body reverently.'

She shook her head fiercely, unwilling to relinquish
the loved form even to Adam. His hand pressed gently
but inexorably upon her shoulder-blade.

'You know it must be done before. . .before he
stiffens.'

'I. . .must wash him. Is there. . .is there enough
water?'

'I'll see to it.'

He worked at her side silently and efficiently. She
stripped Sir Edwin and washed him for his winding
sheet. There was nothing suitable but Wat had furnished
a clean shirt for Adam and they dressed him in that.
Adam lifted him into the cart for the final journey and
arranged his limbs decently, then covered him with his
own cloak.

Now it was done Isabel stood a little apart, her arms
slack by her sides, the tears drying now into runnels
down her cheeks, but she was mercifully calm.

'What. . .what can we do with him?' she questioned
piteously. 'We cannot. . .cannot leave him here. . .'

'I swear to you he shall lie in sanctified ground,' Adam
said quietly.

'But where? We are fugitives and——'

'Leave that to me. Do what he asked. Trust me,
Isabel.'

He came very close and took her by the shoulders and
into his arms. She did not resist. His hand rumpled her
tangled red-gold hair, for she had flung aside her hood.
She laid her heated face against the roughness of his
pedlar's frieze houppeland. His heart beat true and

steady near her own and she felt one hand move comfortingly against the small of her back. It was good to be here, and she caught back a sob of despair.

She had promised her father she would obey Adam and trust him. She longed with all her heart to belong to him completely, never to leave his side, yet she must face facts. He had equally sworn to her father he would protect her. To keep that vow he would even offer her his hand. She must not take advantage of that. She would accept his protection, no more. She would never tell him she loved him. She would go with him to safety, then she must leave him to find his own happiness. Already he had done so much for her that he must not sacrifice himself further. She was a dear companion, the daughter of his true friend, no more.

She withdrew herself from his embrace, lifting her face to his courageously.

'Thank you, Adam. It was good to have you by me . . .at. . .at this time. I will sit by the fire alone for a while. It will soon be full dawn. Can you not sleep for an hour at least? I know. . .there will be much to do in the morning.'

He stooped to kiss her gently upon the forehead.

'Aye, lass, you go over there and sit for a while. I'll watch by Edwin.'

Her lips trembled piteously once more and she turned her head away, then steadily she moved away from him.

CHAPTER TEN

ADAM came to Isabel the moment there was enough light to travel. She understood the need. If the coming day's weather should be anything like the stifling heat of yesterday it was imperative that her father's body be conveyed swiftly to its final destination. She bent over the cart, lifted the cloak which covered him, and kissed the still face. He looked peaceful, almost happy. She crossed herself, praying to the Virgin that, despite the fact that he had no time to confess himself or even to utter an act of contrition, he would be, even now, with her mother in Heaven.

As she took her seat by Adam he smiled encouragingly and squeezed her hand. 'Don't fear for him. He committed no sins since he was last confessed before Stoke battle.'

She did not remind him that there was the death of a man to be accounted for, the one he had slain in their hiding-place near Fiskerton, besides those he had slain in the course of the battle. Surely the Virgin would hear her prayer and intercede for him? All his sins had been committed without malice.

'When it is safe I must have a mass said for his soul,' she said softly. 'I still have sufficient gold.'

He nodded and whipped up the patient donkey.

She did not even question him as to their destination. She trusted in him implicitly.

The countryside had radically changed now. On previous days they had journeyed through acres of rich farm land and pasturage; now they were in the flat, featureless fen lands. Some dikes had been constructed to draw off the brackish water from the low-lying swampy ground, but travel was slow, since it was necessary to wind their way around them, sometimes crossing roughly constructed board bridges to which the

176

donkey objected strongly and Adam needed to jump down and lead the animal across, and in other places splashing through the marshy ground. As the sun rose the heat increased and Isabel wrinkled her nose against the peaty, strong scent of the waters.

Through the busy little town of Market Deeping and on through smaller villages, then more flat ground, but here the abbey monks at Croyland had drained the land more efficiently and the dikes were regular and well maintained. Isabel marvelled as she realised that Adam was aiming for the wealthy abbey itself.

They had journeyed some miles by the banks of the River Welland and entered the little town which had grown up by the abbey gates across the strange triangular bridge where the two arches spanned the two streams of the river which had divided here. It was past midday now and a small crowd had gathered in the market-place by the bridge. Adam clicked his teeth to encourage their donkey and made for the abbey gatehouse.

He conducted her to the guest-house and hurried into the abbey itself. She, of course, could not progress further into the enclave. A young monk had taken charge of the cart with its silent passenger. Another young monk showed Isabel into a small cell-like room where she was provided with water and towels for washing. She made a hasty toilet and waited impatiently for Adam to return. When he did so, he was accompanied by a grave-featured monk who must have been roughly the same age as Adam.

The man greeted her warmly. He was a big man, whose cleanly cut features and aristocratic nose spoke of noble blood.

'Brother Eustace is ordained. He will hear your confession, Isabel. Don't be afraid. He is acquainted with the difficulties of our circumstances and is already making arrangements for your father's burial,' Adam said gravely.

A glance was exchanged between the two men and Isabel wondered if this solemn-faced monk had once been a companion-at-arms. Despite his quiet demeanour

there was something about the man which suggested he
understood the ways of the world far away from this
abbey only too well.

He reverently kissed and donned his scapular and,
after Adam left them together, seated himself and
gestured for Isabel to kneel at his feet.

'And now, my daughter, I understand you have great
need to unburden yourself.' His voice was mellifluous
and Isabel instinctively felt that she could trust him and
that he would understand her agony of mind.

Haltingly she told her tale, not sparing herself anything. He listened in grave silence, then placed one hand
on her bent head. Her voice had broken with emotion
and she was weeping now.

'My child, I will absolve you now. It is clear to me, as
it will be to Almighty God, that there was no hatred in
your heart for the man who was killed by your action.
You wanted only to save your father and you must not
believe now that Sir Edwin's death in any way makes
your behaviour any more reprehensible. First, are there
any more sins you would reveal to me?'

She lifted her head to stare into his cool grey eyes and
then hot blood raced from her face to her throat.

'I have committed no carnal sin, Father,' she said
softly. 'Sir Adam Westlake has behaved towards me
with the utmost propriety throughout our journey.'

He nodded and gravely pronounced the words of
absolution, exhorting her to pray within the abbey
church and, when she had opportunity, to offer masses
for the good of her own soul and the welfare of her
father's.

She rose to her feet, greatly comforted, and thanked
him softly.

He said smilingly, 'Sir Adam has requested that I
witness the plighting of troth between you, before the
continuation of your journey into exile. Is this your true
wish, my daughter?'

Isabel gave a great gasp of astonishment.

'I. . . I do not know if. . .he asked you just now. . .'

Brother Eustace inclined his head. 'There have been

no words of love between you? I understood your father approved the match.'

Her lips parted slightly and she turned away from him to look from the glassed window across the busy abbey courtyard.

'I think such a match would have pleased my father, who had great affection for Sir Adam, but. . .'

'Yes, my daughter?'

'I am not sure I should agree.'

'You do not love him?'

She swung round, startled by the frankness of the question, and his grey eyes twinkled at her. 'Forgive me, child, but I read another message in your eyes when we entered.'

Again her face flamed. 'I. . . I *do* have strong feelings for Sir Adam. He has rendered me a great service which I can never repay. I shall always hold him in my heart with sincere affection, but. . .'

He waited silently and she plunged on urgently. 'I have nothing to offer him.'

'But your love, and you *do* love him, don't you?'

'Yes.' The single word was whispered.

'And you *do* wish for the marriage. My daughter, you must see that to arrive in Burgundy at the Duchess Margaret's court escorted by an unmarried knight, and unchaperoned, could prove embarrassing for you both.'

Again Isabel drew a hard breath. 'But, Father, it is just this aspect of the betrothal which disturbs me. Sir Adam has never said he loves me. He offers me his hand to protect me. I have no land, no dowry, barely the means to keep myself in tolerable comfort for a few months. He deserves better.'

'He has spoken to me of another man. Did you pledge yourself to him, my daughter?'

'No, Father, his own father disapproved of our association and, though there were words of love between us, there was no real promise made, nor any conduct which would displease God or man. Now ——' she broke off on a hard sob, '—I have been responsible, however unintentionally, for the death of his sire. There could be no match between us, even should I still want it. . .'

'And you do not?'

She hesitated. 'No,' she said evenly at last, 'I do not love James Tarvin. I don't think I ever did. He flattered me and, childlike, I revelled in that. At that time in my life I had experienced much unhappiness and my heart responded like a flower to the warmth of his kindly words. And he was—personable.'

'And you have now found him unworthy?'

Again she hesitated. 'For days now I have been in Adam Westlake's company and witnessed his courage and constancy towards those who rely on him. I could not fail to be moved by that. Then—then I realised something which—which altered my attitude towards the—other man.'

He nodded, satisfied. 'Then, in your heart, you would be perfectly willing to pledge yourself to Adam?'

'If I believed he truly wanted me.' Her words were very low.

He rubbed his chin reflectively. 'A solemn betrothal is naturally a binding undertaking, but it could be broken by appealing for a dispensation, should the circumstances warrant a change of mind, which might be allowed in this case.'

Her eyes were troubled as she regarded him. 'I would not wish to enter a betrothal with such a proviso in mind, Father. It would not be proper.'

'No,' he agreed, his grey eyes twinkling again, 'but it would allow Adam freedom if, as you fear, he would regret the match once back in Burgundy, but, at the same time, it would protect your honour, which is important to him.'

Isabel bit her nether lip. 'You are counselling me to accept him, Father?'

'From what Adam has said to me I see no obstacle to this betrothal. He wishes it, and I know him to be a deeply honourable man. Naturally my thoughts are for you, my daughter, left unprotected in a dangerous situation. If the worst occurs and you should be taken by King's men, your position would certainly be worsened by slurs concerning your journeying with this man. Until now your father has chaperoned you; now matters are changed considerably.' His beautiful voice was very gentle as he saw her eyes fill with tears again.

Bleakly she reviewed the picture his words conjured up. Should she be taken and charged with treason, as well she might be, since she had helped a known rebel, even if the worst was not known — that she had killed a King's officer — she would be publicly arraigned as a whore. The thought of that was unbearable. Also she had no knowledge of courts. Her upbringing had been unworldly in the quiet Leicestershire manor. By a refusal to carry out Adam's wishes, which had also been her father's, she might well bring opprobrium on his name also. She swallowed uncertainly.

'I will speak with him about this, Father, and if it is truly his wish I will obey him.'

Brother Eustace rose to his feet, clearly well satisfied.

'I will send him to you and, in the meantime, I will complete the arrangements for your father's burial in our lay cemetery.'

She waited nervously until Adam came. His expression was grave but encouraging.

'Brother Eustace has spoken to you of my intentions?'

She nodded.

'And? It was your father's dying wish, Isabel.'

'But is it truly yours?'

His brows drew together slightly as he regarded her thoughtfully, then he said, 'Yes, it is mine.'

She drew a hard breath and offered him her hand. 'As Brother Eustace thinks it is the wisest course, I will agree, only on the understanding that, if you should have a change of heart later, you will feel free to ask for a dispensation to annul the contract.'

He opened his lips as if to gainsay her, then, eyes narrowed, nodded his acceptance of her condition.

A young novice came to tell her it would soon be time for the burial, if she would care to spend some time with her father in the chapel. She hastened out to follow him.

Kneeling alone in the silent chapel, she gazed down at her father's serene face.

'Oh, Father, I tried so hard to keep you with me.' Her voice broke in a sob. 'Yet I know it was your heartfelt wish to follow your allegiance. I pray you may now be with Mother — and your fallen companions in the field. I have fulfilled your wish in allowing Adam to make what he thinks the proper arrangements for my future, only, Father, I do so love him now that I cannot go through with the wedding if I believe he does not truly want me. Intercede for us with the blessed Virgin, Father, that we might safely come through this time of terrible danger. I swear to you that Adam's welfare, and that of the cause, will become my primary concern.'

She stayed quietly for a while in silent supplication to the Virgin and the Blessed Lord and also to her father's patron saint, St Edwin, that he should not suffer because of his inability to make a dying confession, then rose, outwardly controlled, when the monks came with Adam to carry the bier to its resting place.

The little graveyard in the shadow of the cloister garth was very quiet and secluded. Isabel wept as the bier was lowered. Adam had put a small posy of flowers he had gathered in the cloister garden in her hand and she dropped them upon the shrouded form. She was sad that he could not lie beside her mother in the family plot in Swithland, but here he would lie safe and hallowed. She dried her tears and went with Adam and Brother Eustace to the guest-house. The monk ate supper with them and Isabel learned that he had, indeed, been a former companion of Adam's in the Duke of Gloucester's household at Middleham.

'For some months I was troubled,' he explained, as Isabel looked surprised. 'Perhaps I had always known, in my heart, that the call would come, but my father wished me to become a knight and I had given way to please him. When he understood, Richard willingly released me from service and I took the cowl here.'

'You fought beside him?' Isabel asked, wide-eyed.

'Yes, on the border, repelling Scottish reivers.' His

grey eyes were twinkling at her again. 'So, you see, I understand what drives soldiers and can absolve Adam with a clear conscience.'

She lowered her gaze. Did this man, too, have that strange loyalty to the dead King which Adam and Frank Lovell possessed as well as her own father?

Brother Eustace turned briskly to Adam.

'I have been thinking of the hazards which may face you tomorrow. By now it may well be known that you travel with Edwin Hatfield's daughter. It would be wiser for the pair of you to approach Lynn separately.'

His words brought a chill of pure terror to Isabel. She dared not proceed without Adam.

Brother Eustace noted her fearful gaze and explained.

'King's men will be watching the port and, from what Adam has told me, it may be known that the pedlar was seen in Leicestershire prior to Gilbert Tarvin's death. He should take another guise on this last stage of the journey, which he knows from past experience is always the most dangerous.'

Isabel swallowed nervously and waited for him to reveal his plans for her.

'We have a small convent nearby and I propose to ask one of the nuns to escort you into the port of Lynn. It is often her custom to convey intended novices to the mother house in Bruges and it will not seem unusual for her to be accompanied by a young female.'

'Father, I have no intention of taking the veil; to go so clad would be a grave sin of deliberate deception.'

He shook his head imperatively. 'No, no, I do not intend such a thing. Young women from noble households sometimes travel to the mother houses abroad to see for themselves what life would be like in the convent. Indeed, superiors now advise this course before final acceptance. We should not disguise you as a nun. Merely travelling in Sister Marie Joseph's care would prove sufficient protection. She would convey you to a safe lodging where Adam could join you later.'

Adam reached out and took her hand. 'This would

certainly be a sensible move. If there is need I could lead the chase from you.'

'But what if you—if you fail to join me. . .' Her tears flowed fast again now.

His grasp on her fingers tightened. 'Then I expect you to be brave and proceed without me. The sister Brother Eustace speaks of will take you safely into Burgundy. There, if needs must, you must fend for yourself, either by putting yourself into the hands of the Duchess Margaret, who would receive you graciously for my sake, I feel sure, or by taking sanctuary in some nunnery until you feel secure enough to make a wise decision about your future.'

She appealed to the monk. 'Will this not place Sister Marie Joseph in peril if she knows about me?'

'She will not. She will not ask and you must not tell her.'

'But—'

'Far better for her to know nothing which could incriminate her. That way you will both be safer. She will be informed that a young lady of my acquaintance wishes to travel under her patronage to Bruges. That will be sufficient knowledge for her. Obedience is the rule.'

Again Isabel's troubled hazel eyes sought Adam's and, as he nodded encouragingly, she agreed to the plan.

Later that evening she stood beside Adam in the same chapel where she had watched by her father's body and plighted her troth solemnly before Brother Eustace. Together they knelt before him after exchanging rings. His was considerably too large for her finger and bore his crest—two bars wavy argent on an azure field. Hers, a small gold and ruby ring which had been her mother's, was so small that it could be fitted only upon his little finger. On Brother Eustace's prompting, he bent and kissed her gently upon the mouth. Isabel's heart pounded so strongly that she thought he must hear it.

This ceremony had been so short, and she felt completely untouched by it, yet she was now bound to Adam so strongly that only a Papal dispensation could free her.

She had thought to stand so with John Heyward and then, possibly, with James — and with all her household at Hatfield present. Her lip trembled as she thought how glad her father would have been to have her troth plighted to Adam. She had always dreamed of his nearness on this occasion, his kiss of benediction at this solemn moment of commitment.

As if he read her distress in her eyes, Adam bent and imprisoned her two hands in his.

'You are thinking of your father — of how much you miss him. I'm sure he would have approved this. He thought only of your safety. His first thought after the battle was for you.'

'I know it.'

'You must not regret taking this step. It commits you to nothing inexorably.'

It was as if he had turned a knife in her heart. This meant so little to him, but, to her, everything, yet she must not show how she needed him. The one gift of her love must be his freedom, if he so desired it.

She swallowed her pain and smiled confidently up at him.

'Brother Eustace advised me well, I am sure of it. In Burgundy we will be able to consider our situations — and — and act accordingly.'

His brows drew together as he regarded her steadily, then he gave a quick nod and released her.

As they returned to the guest-house, Adam explained to her what plans had been made for his disguise.

'I shall travel as a seaman returning to my ship. There is an inn near the dock where I have often stayed — The Star. The landlord knows me well and if you tell him you are travelling with me he will provide you with a safe hiding-place until I arrive.'

He stopped outside the door of the cell-like room where she was to sleep and placed two gentle hands cupping her chin.

'I shall see you before you leave. Trust Brother Eustace. He has been instrumental before in covering my escapes.'

'Then he, too, is loyal to the cause?'

Adam smiled wanly. 'How could he be otherwise when he knew the late King as well as I did? Now try to sleep. There are difficulties ahead of us, but, if the Saints are kind, we shall be snug aboard our ship by this time tomorrow and our worries will be over.'

'Does the ship's captain know of your allegiance?'

He grinned, showing white teeth in the darkness of the gloomy corridor. 'You have guessed at the truth of it.'

She sighed. Loving Adam as she did, she could see nothing ahead of her but a world inhabited by people whose sole interest was to wound the English King, a network of agents whose hold on Adam would, doubtless, be stronger than hers could ever be.

She slept better than she had hoped, worn out by grief and anxieties. When she woke the light glinted on the silver and blue enamel of her betrothal ring and she raised it to her lips. Tucked beneath her bodice she had secreted throughout the journey the scrap of white silk in the form of the rose that Adam had given her after their first meeting. She knew such a token could be damning if she should be taken and searched, proclaiming to the world her allegiance to the Yorkist cause, but it meant so much to her that she could not bear the thought of destroying it.

A young female lay servant knocked and entered her cell. Over her arm lay a plain dark gown in homespun wool, a simple linen cap and a wimple.

'Brother Eustace has ordered me to bring these to you, mistress,' the girl said in a soft country burr, and curtsied.

Isabel rose at once and dressed. A pale, strained face shone dimly back at her from the small, scratched iron mirror she had carried with her, for the abbey boasted no mirrors of any kind. Before she breakfasted she hastened down to the cloister garth and sought the newly made mound which covered her father's body. The sky was overcast today, promising rain, a welcome relief from the oppressive heat which had tortured them for much of the journey. She knelt and whispered her prayers, then rose, dusted down her gown, and hurried back to the guest-house.

Adam was there before her. He had put on plain homespun hose and a drab brown frieze jerkin. During the journey he had had little opportunity to shave, and chin and upper lip bore traces of stubble applicable to his new guise as a simple seaman. His skin scratched hers faintly as he greeted her with a loving kiss, and she smiled ruefully at him.

'You look like a demure aspirant,' he commented, grinning, 'now that fiery red hair of yours is well hidden.'

'And you look disreputable enough to deter any respectable female from making your acquaintance,' she rejoined, smiling back at him.

Brother Eustace came to them after matins and outlined the final arrangements.

'I shall see to it that your donkey and cart are returned to Master Skelton's house in Newark after the poor beast has been well fed and rested. There are always merchants and carters who stay here journeying northwards, so there should be no problems. Is there anyone who could ask after you whom I could trust?'

Isabel described her groom, Wat Jessop. 'He is thoroughly trustworthy, and may be anxious about me, but I do not see how he could possibly know I have been here.'

'Since I mentioned to him that I had stayed here on numerous occasions, Wat may well seek information here,' Adam said. 'What do you want him to do — follow you into exile, look for you at Margaret's court?'

Isabel considered. What would Wat wish to do? Matters could become unendurable at the manor, and Wat's loyalty had been given entirely to her.

'Yes, if that is his wish,' she said soberly. 'Life could become intolerable for him if not downright dangerous at Hatfield.'

An elderly monk knocked and entered at Brother Eustace's invitation.

'Sister Marie Joseph is here, Brother, from the Thorney Convent.'

'Ah, yes, I was expecting her. Please ask her to join us here, Brother.'

The nun was pleasantly rounded and younger than Isabel had expected. Her face bore the jovial expression and twinkling eyes which belied the shrewdness Isabel was later to find she possessed.

Brother Eustace greeted her warmly and introduced Isabel as a possible postulant to be conveyed to Lynn. He waited until the door had been firmly closed on all listeners and explained the situation.

'Sister, Mistress Hatfield here is desirous of travelling to Burgundy. There could be dangers for her, should she be found to be in the company of her betrothed. Will you take her safely to the Star Inn? I think you know it well.'

Bright brown eyes peered at Isabel inquisitively and then from her to Adam. The nun dimpled at him delightedly and nodded. 'Brother, I shall be glad to do this favour for you. I have two good horses and we should leave at once if we are to reach Lynn in good time before dark.'

Brother Eustace rose and ushered her from the guest room, leaving Isabel and Adam alone together.

She felt an unaccountable tightening of the throat which appeared to be preventing her from bidding him farewell. He drew her very close and, for the first time, the kiss he gave her was not the gentle, passionless one she had become accustomed to during the days of their journey, but fierce and demanding; then he stood back from her, staring intently, as if he would grave her image upon his very soul.

'Take very great care, sweeting,' he murmured a trifle hoarsely. 'We shall meet again very soon if God wills it.'

Her eyes were bright with gathering tears. 'Surely *you* are in greatest danger. I shall constantly pray the Virgin to hold you safe. You will be at the trysting place before me?'

'Probably not. With Sister Marie Joseph you can ride

fast horses. I must take the road on foot, trusting to a possible lift from some passing cart.'

She was horrified. 'But that might mean you could miss the ship's sailing.'

'No, sweeting, our captain will wait. Have no fear of that, but I do not wish you to wait too long at the inn for me. If I am not with you by tomorrow's late tide you must ask him to sail at once.'

Her mouth was dry at the moment of parting. She managed a smile and went by him to the door.

At the stables near the gatehouse Sister Marie Joseph was chatting volubly to a groom who held her horses' heads. Brother Eustace held out his hand in farewell, then sketched a gesture of blessing over Isabel's bent head.

'God keep you both safe, my child, and grant you the happiness you crave.'

She went past him into the shadowed stable and sought their loyal little donkey. He greeted her with a joyful bray of welcome. She stroked the great ugly ears, her tears coming fast again. He had carried them safely and served them well and conveyed her father's loved form to his burial. She hoped he would reach his home stable safely and be cared for well on his way. She would miss him as she would her own palfrey and dear Cass, together with all the other domestic cats and hounds at Hatfield.

Her few possessions had been packed in a saddle-bag, and Brother Eustace lifted her into the saddle while the groom hoisted the rotund nun into hers. Isabel could not look for Adam in the doorway of the guest-house. She bent to give a last breathless word of gratitude to Brother Eustace and then they were cantering under the gatehouse arch and into the noisy street beyond.

Now she was respectably escorted there seemed no need to take a roundabout route, and they made for the main highway east, passing through the busy quaint market town of Wisbech, where the merchants' houses with their steeply gabled roofs looked distinctly foreign to Isabel. Sister Marie Joseph chattered all the time. She spoke of her favourite food, of her dislike of night prayers which hailed her straight from her warm bed in winter, and of Sister Anne, who always sang off key in choir, so that Isabel needed only to nod and smile and utter no word of her own.

'Wealthy Hansard merchants live here in Wisbech and in Lynn,' the nun explained. 'You will find the port very busy and not entirely salubrious. The Star Inn is a poor place not far from the quay, but the landlord is a good fellow who will find you a clean bed.'

'Are you to proceed to the port of Damme with us?' Isabel ventured at last, when the flow of affable talk was halted for moments.

The shrewd brown eyes flashed in her direction then were quickly veiled. 'Only if your betrothed is prevented from joining you. If the worst happens, I am instructed to convey you to our mother house in Bruges. I have the permission of my superior to be absent for as long as needful.'

Isabel considered, thoughtfully, that Brother Eustace appeared to have a great deal of authority to be so readily obeyed. She had not seen the abbot or the prior. It struck her forcibly that she had accepted very readily Brother Eustace's ability to act in so peremptory a fashion for his superiors. She wondered if he was indeed the unimportant knight of Richard of Gloucester's household that she had been given to believe. She had not questioned his identity. Did the name Brother Eustace cover a far nobler one? If so, that would explain Adam's total trust in the man.

The road proceeded, flat and unchanging in appearance, man-made dikes cut on either side of the highway, until they crossed the Great Ouse River into the port of Lynn and reached their destination. The sky had become very overcast and now it began to drizzle as they entered the narrow streets, bringing dusk early. Isabel was tired and somewhat saddle sore and glad when their mounts' hoofs clattered on the stone-built quay and, for the first time, she saw the great silver expanse of water that Sister Marie Joseph informed her was The Wash.

Isabel gave a great gasp of wonder. She had never seen such a landscape where nothing intruded on her vision but water until she glimpsed the line where sea touched the sky. She shivered and handled the reins clumsily so that her mount sidled nervously. Sister Marie Joseph moved her own horse close in.

'What is it, Mistress Hatfield? You are not feeling ill?'

'No, no, just tired.'

Isabel forced her attention from the terrifying waste of water to the still busy scene on the quay. There were several caravels tied up to the dock, their sails furled, men still scuttling like ants about their decks despite the inclement weather. Men toiled on the quay itself, shifting great bales of wool and other commodities. There was a pungent scent of tar and other, less pleasant smells that Isabel could not identify. From the crowded little houses and taverns on the dockside men continually erupted, roughly dressed seamen and soberly but better clad merchants. She had not imagined such a hive of activity, especially as the hour was now getting late. Sister Marie Joseph put a warning hand on her arm, edging her horse closer still to Isabel's as a small knot of men-at-arms became visible outside the nearest tavern. Passers-by who had previously obstructed the view of the two women had moved on by then.

'You can see how it is,' the nun murmured. 'All outlets to the continent are closely watched and prospective passengers quizzed about their business or asked to produce letters permitting them to travel.'

'Was it always so, even in the late King's time?'

'Oh, indeed. Our kings have found it prudent both to keep a network of spies in their own pay and to watch constantly those they suspect may be in the pay of a foreign court. The French King has always been hostile to British interests and King Henry — the Earl of Richmond, as he was then — had many agents of his own travelling between himself and his mother, the Lady Margaret.'

Isabel knew that formidable lady, wife of Lord

Stanley, newly created Earl of Derby, to be a powerful voice in the counsels of her son.

She shivered again. Adam must soon pass muster when all eyes looked for men of his allegiance. She was grateful for the escort of her voluble companion. One of the men, possibly a sergeant, glanced briefly at Sister Marie Joseph's habit and wimple and as quickly looked away.

The nun urged her gently to move on towards their lodging and Isabel gave one hasty glance back at the sea lapping inexorably against the harbour wall, shuddered again, and followed her guide. How could she confess that the sight of that heaving grey mass terrified her so much that she could not envisage venturing on to one of those frail-looking craft? Clearly Sister Marie Joseph had made the crossing not once but many times and seemed totally unaffected by the sight, but Isabel had never before been to the coast and the prospect of the voyage ahead filled her with utter dread. Yet they must go. To remain in England would be hazardous in the extreme. She swallowed back fearful words and drew up thankfully outside the squat stone-built inn over whose door creaked a sign bearing an indifferently painted star. The picture was much faded from the action of the salt-laden air, but as Sister Marie Joseph called for someone to deal with their horses a man emerged from the doorway, his weather-beaten countenance bearing a grin of welcome. He hastened up to them, his rolling gait proclaiming him to have once been a seaman, bawling for a groom in the broad Norfolk accent Isabel had heard from the men working on the quay. Lifting the portly nun down from her horse did not appear to give him difficulty, for he was not a big man but sturdily-built and stocky. Sister Marie Joseph bent to whisper in his ear. He turned a startled pair of eyes on Isabel then came towards her, arms extended to lift her down.

'Welcome to The Star, mistress. You must be very tired and wetted by this mizzle of rain. Come you in and dry yourself by the fire.'

Soon she was seated in a small private chamber and

hot food placed before her. It had taken but a few moments, while she and the nun dried their cloaks by the cooking fire in the kitchen, for him to have their bags brought from the stable and the chamber prepared for them. They had travelled hard, stopping only once to stretch their legs and eat from a basket of provisions provided by Sister Marie Joseph's convent kitchen. The fare was good and Isabel dipped eagerly into the pottage of bacon, lentils and onions. Already the tiredness was seeping from her, leaving an aching concern for Adam. The rain was still making desolate rivulets down the ox-horn pane of the chamber's small window. Two tallow dips had been kindled and the light was dim in the room, but Isabel knew well that even should the inn boast a supply of expensive wax candles it would be most unwise to proclaim to the world at large that it sheltered anyone of importance. For once Sister Marie Joseph had fallen silent. She was nodding comfortably on her stool and would be soon fast off, unable to rouse to go to the bed which they must share. Tentatively Isabel touched her on the arm and she came to with a faint snort.

'Goodness me, was I falling asleep? That was most remiss of me.'

Isabel laughed. 'Not at all, Sister; I was just anxious to get you into bed where you can rest more comfortably.'

The nun rose and stretched. 'I shall certainly be glad to do so.' She glanced at the streaming wet window. 'Poor Master Westlake will have an unpleasant journey. The main thing to hope for is that the weather will settle again tomorrow. You won't want a stormy crossing, that's for sure.'

'You think he will manage to get here unchallenged?'

The nun frowned thoughtfully at Isabel's frightened expression.

'Bless you, yes, child. He'll need to be cautious as he enters the port, but he'll not manage it before morning now, so you'd best get a good night's sleep while you can. The crossing won't be comfortable. It's a mercy it's a short one.'

She knelt by the bed to perform her night devotions, her rosary beads busily clicking. Isabel sat on for a moment at table. Her thoughts were on Adam trudging through the rain, intent only on the means of escape. She rose and knelt by the nun. Please God he would come early tomorrow and she must not worry him with her foolish fears about the sea crossing. She had given him enough problems over the past days. Now she must pretend that she faced this final part of the journey with eager expectancy. Not for the first time she wondered about her new life in this strange land. Would she feel out of place at the Duchess Margaret's court, and would she find that Adam had other interests there that he had not revealed to her?

CHAPTER ELEVEN

ADAM trudged grimly on as the rain began to fall. He reckoned he had walked about ten or eleven miles without so far encountering a cart or wagon whose driver might be kindly enough to offer him a ride. He had abandoned his familiar pedlar's pack in the abbey. Brother Eustace had smilingly promised to keep it safe.

'I know you, my friend. It is likely you may need it again if you set foot in England, though, Adam, I must remind you that now you have other more pressing responsibilities besides that of your commitment to the Duchess Margaret's burning desire to oust Henry from his throne.'

Adam smiled ruefully at the thought and he glanced down at the tiny band of gold set with rubies and pearls which had been Isabel's betrothal pledge to him. The design was of a true lover's knot and he wondered if it had been given by Edwin to Isabel's mother, Alice, on their betrothal. Dear God, but Eustace had spoken true. Isabel had become the whole meaning of his existence and once he had her safe in Burgundy he must never allow her to risk herself again. She was a treasure beyond price and one which he had expected never to possess. She was beautiful, fiercely courageous and loyal, and practical, to boot. He loved her with every fibre of his being, yet had he the right to insist on the match to her detriment? What had he to offer her?

Margaret would continue to support him at her court, he was sure, and would receive both of them gladly, but there was no fortune to be made there. He would live on as her pensioner, relying on her to produce his means of sustenance, and his pride was galled by the thought. Isabel deserved more. It might be better to plead with Margaret to find a more fitting mate for Isabel and then to leave to seek mercenary employment for himself.

Certainly that way Isabel would be suitably provided for
and his pledge to Edwin amply fulfilled. She had no
dowry, true, but she was lovely enough to attract the
eye of some wealthy Burgundian.

Adam gritted his teeth in helpless fury at the thought.
No, by God, he would not so tamely relinquish his
prize. Isabel was his, pledged to him, bound to him by
ties of shared dangers and loyalties. Come what may, he
would keep her, if the Virgin aided him, and find the
means to give her the safe, comfortable existence Edwin
Hatfield had wanted for her.

He stopped for a while under the dripping eaves of a
dilapidated barn to eat coarse rye bread and cheese. The
kitchens at Croyland would willingly have provided
better, but Adam had insisted on simple fare. Should he
be seen consuming meat and fine manchet white bread
he would come under immediate suspicion. It would go
ill with his guise as a seaman returning to port, and he
was too close to the coast now to risk detection as one of
Margaret's agents. He sighed. The weather was worsening and few labourers would be out. It would be unlikely
that he would see a cart. He certainly would not arrive
in Lynn as soon as he had hoped. Isabel would become
alarmed.

Since there were few people about, he decided to cut
across country and head for the highway. It should be
safe enough, and to take any other route in this flat
fenland where he must be constantly avoiding dikes
would be bound to delay him even longer.

The highway certainly made for easier travelling and
he shouldered his coarse canvas bag almost cheerfully.
To further lift his spirits he heard the distinct sound of
cart wheels and, turning, he saw a covered wagon
lumbering ponderously towards him. The heavy vehicle
moved alongside and a deep voice called to him.

'Be ye wanting a ride into the port, me lad?'

As the vehicle came to a halt beside him Adam
knuckled his forehead and stopped, leaning eagerly up
to view the speaker.

'Aye, good sir. I would be right pleased at that.'

The driver was elderly, could almost be described as an ancient. He was quite small and gnome-like, yet the resonant deep tones which came from so small a body were distinctly unnerving. It was as if the owner spoke so deliberately, in order to deceive.

He leaned down a thin arm to help Adam up and it was strong and wiry and, like his appearance, deceptive. Adam gratefully deposited his bag in the cart and climbed on to the high wooden wheel. He grinned his thanks as his benefactor whipped up his patient cart-horse again. The canvas cover gave welcome protection from the persistent rain, and Adam shook the mist-like drops from his hair.

The old man eyed him curiously. 'Ye've not been at sea long, if I'm any judge.'

Adam looked back at him sharply. 'You're right, old man; I've had but two crossings. I live in Wisbech. But how did you know that?'

'Ye've not the gait of a seaman,' the old man retorted laconically, 'even if ye be dressed as one.'

Adam was silent, looking straight ahead at the road. The old one had a shrewd eye, and, if he had, others were like to follow his example. He must watch his step carefully once in the port.

'You're out late in this bad weather,' he said. 'I was hoping to get a ride so's I could get to the dock before the bridge gate is closed, but I doubt I'll make it now.'

'Ah.' The old man nodded. 'Me daughter lives just outside the port. I'd not be travelling, but she's expecting a wee one, and her man's away from home at present. Lucky for you I chanced by.'

'Aye, I'm glad to be out of this rain.'

'Ye say ye be from Wisbech?'

'Aye.' Adam's fierce black eyes challenged the old man to question him further, and his interrogator chuckled.

'I see ye know ye're own business and mean to keep it to yeself. That be fine with me, lad.'

Adam leaned back tiredly and thought the old man had concluded he'd more than likely lied about his home and had probably walked further than the market town mentioned. He frowned. Men in this neck of the woods must be used to folk wishing to travel abroad for their own reasons, but it was likely the old man would talk of his passenger to officials in the port, and that could spell danger. . .

As if the ancient read his thoughts, he said ruminatively, 'Doubtless ye'll be wanting to get into port as soon as ye can.'

'Aye, but the gates will be closed, I'm thinking, at dusk.'

'Oh, aye, they will.' The old man clucked to his horse and turned again his sharp old eyes on Adam. 'Be ye a good swimmer, lad?'

'Aye, passable,' Adam rejoined cautiously.

'Good enough to swim the Ouse?'

'I think so.'

'She be tidal.'

'Aye.'

'What would ye say if I puts ye off at a safe spot where ye could slip in the water easy and wi'out bein' seen?'

Adam grinned again. He might be reckless to put his trust in a total stranger, but he liked the old man. Doubtless he'd made up his own mind about his passenger's need to enter the port without attracting undue notice and was willing to help him.

The old man cackled his amusement as he read the thoughts which were passing through Adam's mind.

'I've been young meself, lad, though ye'd never think it by the sight of me now. I'd the longing for adventure in me. It's none of me business whether ye be simply running from your master, or keeping tryst wi' some lass, or even more pressin' need than any of them reasons. It's plain enough ye don't want to be questioned overmuch. That be fair enough. My way ye can be in the town wi'out being stopped and ye're credentials scried and, at all events, sooner than before morning when the gates be undone.'

'You have the right of it. If you must know, a lass

does wait for me in the town and we have our own reasons for haste.'

'Right. Well, the tide's out for the next two hours and then 'ull begin to turn, so we've no time to waste. Ye should make it safe enough, provided ye're not fooling yeself, and truly be a strong swimmer. I'd not have ye risk it else.'

The old eyes had taken on a concerned expression now and Adam nodded his understanding.

'Acquit yourself of any blame should ill befall me, old one. I'm used to taking care of my hide.'

His country speech was lost now as acknowledgement of the trust he placed in his counsellor's advice, and the old man gave a little snort of acceptance. He said no more till he drew up the wagon some three miles further on.

'Ye'll have to get down now and follow me, lad.'

Obediently Adam swung his bag from the wagon and jumped down. The old man grunted and cursed at his stiffened limbs, but managed to join him, shaking his head at Adam's proferred arm.

'Nay, nay, time'll come soon when I can't make it, but while I can I will.'

He shuffled off in the gathering dusk down an old cart track and Adam followed, his eyes and ears alert for any signs or sounds that they might be being observed.

The old man waved an arm impatiently. 'Nay, nay, nothing to fear, lad. I knows this way like the back of me 'and, used to both poach and fish 'ere in the old days.' He chuckled again and strode purposefully on then stopped so abruptly that Adam almost knocked into him. He thrust out a stubby finger eastwards.

'Down there, can ye just see the bridge? 'Tis about a mile upstream. Ye'll have to make ye're way down to the bank through the nettles and brambles. There be willow and alder to give cover and the bank slopes easy. Watch yerself, lad, for the men on the bridge keep a fair watch wi' lanterns.'

Adam bent and squeezed the hand of his diminutive partner.

'You don't know how much you've helped, old one.
I'll not forget you.'

The shrewd old eyes, under bushy brows, peered up
at him. 'Me and me like don't care to see some of they
changes come about in our land,' he said meaningly.
'Sign of old age, I reckon, as finds the old ways best.'

Adam's lips split in a wide grin. 'Bless you, old man,
there's many full younger than you who think like that,
praise the Saints. Mind how you go back to your cart.
May your lass give you a fine grandson and God give
you a deal more years to fish and poach near this river.'

The old man chuckled again, lifted a gnarled hand in
salute, and began to make his way back along the cart
track.

Adam watched him out of sight and began to negotiate
the steepness of the overgrown path. It was still light
enough to see his way, though care was needed. He
stopped once as stealthy rustling nearby caused him
concern, but as the sound stopped when he did, then
resumed again, dying down some yards away, he presumed it must be some night creature, and proceeded.
It had stopped raining now, but the grass was wet and
the bank slippery with mud. He cursed once or twice
before reaching the place the old man had indicated
where the riverbank shelved and he could see it would
be simple for a swimmer to slip into the water without
difficulty. He removed his boots and tied them together
with their leather thonging round his neck and lowered
himself into the water, pushing his oiled canvas bag
before him. After the heat of the past days he had
expected the water to be warmer, but it proved icy and
he gave a sharp gasp.

The old man had been right. In spite of the fact that
the tide had not yet turned, the current was strong and
the river's broad expanse seemed a daunting prospect,
but he was a good swimmer, if a steady rather than fast
one, and began to strike out strongly for the far bank.
In the distance he could just make out the dim line of
the bridge with one or two sparks of light along its
length as if already the guard had kindled their lanterns.

The bag helped keep him afloat and, at last, grimacing
with cold and weariness, he managed to scramble out on
the far side. Again he was relieved to discover that the
old man's prediction about this being a fair place to
cross was perfectly true, for there were strong, low-
growing branches on which to cling as he came from the
water. Adam smiled to himself as he got out of his
soaked clothing and rubbed himself down with a piece
of old blanket he had brought with him in case the
crossing proved chilly and Isabel need something to
wrap round her on deck. Brother Eustace had provided
him with a spare jerkin and hose and he wrung out his
wet clothes as well as he could and, wrapping them in
the blanket, thrust them into the bag. He stood up
warily after donning his boots, but this part of the bank
appeared deserted. The old goat had known his territory
well. Adam wondered if he had been used to swimming
the river to meet with some light of love. It would be
like him. Thanking providence for their meeting, he
began to walk briskly in the direction of the port. He
must avoid the bridge, but doubtless he would soon
come across a track which would lead him directly into
the outskirts of Lynn; and his optimism proved correct.
A narrow track led south-east, and Adam followed it
confidently until he saw the low roofs of a barn and
beyond it a house ahead of him.

The house was well shuttered and a dog barked as he
passed, but no one came out. Soon the track widened
and several houses bordered the road and Adam knew
he would soon be in the centre of the busy port. The
Star would be shut up for the night, for it was almost
full dark now, but torches gleamed at street corners and
he could hear the call of the watch as the man made his
rounds. Jack Barstow would admit him. It was simply a
matter of reaching the quay without being stopped. A
man out alone at this hour was always suspect and it
would be as well to avoid the watch. Approaching the
junction of the street with the quay, Adam drew back
into the shadows as he saw light gleam on metal, body
armour or weapon. There were men-at-arms on duty in

the port, then. From here he could not distinguish any
heraldic device. It would be necessary to proceed from
here with the utmost caution.

The houses in the narrow street had overhanging
upper storeys and were facing each other, so closely set
that it would not be too dangerous to jump from one
roof to another. He put down his canvas bag and peered
upwards, orienting himself as to the position of The Star
Inn. It should not be too difficult to make his way across
the roofs to the street where the inn was situated. The
sky was still overcast and there was little starlight. It
was unlikely he would be observed from below.

The problem was the bag. It was not unduly heavy,
but cumbersome, and he needed both hands free for the
climb. He knelt down and rummaged inside. Fortunately there was a length of rope. When packing necess-
ities Brother Eustace had probably thought it might
prove useful. Adam tried its strength and grinned
mirthlessly. Doubtless his former companion had
judged it might be useful as a means of restraint for
some possible attacker if the need should arise. It would
prove a blessing now. Quickly Adam secured the rope
to the metal rings which held the strings used to draw
the opening close. By this means he could draw up his
burden once he had made the roof successfully.

The climb was soon accomplished, though he was
panting once he was positioned safely on the ridge. The
swim had obviously tired him and he would be glad of a
sleep in the inn before venturing into unknown hazards
in the morning. A warm glow swept through his body
as he thought of Isabel asleep now in Barstow's private
chamber. Very soon he would hold her in his arms.

From here he could look down on the buildings which
bordered the quay, for those in front of him were lower
than the roof of the house on which he perched precari-
ously. The quay was unwontedly quiet. Ships lay at
anchor, but there was no sign of life on the decks save
the glimmer of bow and stern lanterns where the ship's
watch dozed comfortably in each vessel. Experience had
taught Adam that this was often the case at night where

no disturbance was expected. There was also an absence of carousel noise from inside the shuttered taverns. The presence of men-at-arms had undoubtedly discouraged such behaviour. A tile moved beneath his foot and slithered down the steep gable. Adam cursed softly as one of the men stationed on the quay turned and looked up, but the chimney-stack hid Adam from view and he gave a sigh of relief as the man resumed his talk with his fellows.

Waiting for no further mishap, Adam drew up his bag and began to make his way along the roof towards the adjoining property. It seemed that this row held only prosperous, well maintained houses, probably belonging to port officials or wealthy merchants. The jump across to the facing house in the street beyond caused his heart to race uncertainly and, again, he dislodged tiles as he took off. The bag he had hurled recklessly down into the street below. The noise of the tiles shattering on the ground below caused him to stay where he was for a while, fearful that the men on guard on the quay would come to investigate, but presumably the noise and resulting damage had been ascribed to some prowling cat. At all events no man appeared in the deserted street and Adam at last considered it safe to descend and shoulder his bag again.

He hammered on the door of the Star until a resonant voice he identified as Barstow's demanded to know his identity.

'It's Westlake, Jack. Come, let me in before those damned men-at-arms on the quay arrive to question my arrival.'

The door was immediately unbarred and he was hastily drawn within.

'Sir Adam,' the landlord said breathlessly, 'I had not expected you until morning. The bridge gate was closed hours ago.'

'I swam the river, Jack,' Adam explained laconically. 'Has Mistress Hatfield arrived safely?'

'That she has, sir, and will be mightily glad to see you in the morning, I'll be bound.' The landlord reached

out to take Adam's possessions and was about to lead
him into the ale-room when a door above was thrown
open and light spilled into the hallway.

Adam turned to glimpse Isabel limned against the
pale light behind her. She had thrown a blanket over
her shift and her feet were bare. Adam caught his breath
at her beauty. He had seen her bright hair without her
hennin several times, but never before streaming unrestrained almost to her waist and touched with pale gold
from the rushlight in her chamber. She was peering
uncertainly down into the dim stair-well, then she gave
a glad cry of welcome, and instantly he sprang up the
narrow stair and caught her close in his arms.

'Adam,' she cried, heartfelt thankfulness bringing a
distinct sob to her voice. 'The Virgin be praised; you
are safe.'

'Softly, softly, my love,' he murmured hungrily. 'Safe
enough, aye, and the happier for seeing you. You
suffered no discourtesy or inconvenience in coming
here?'

'No, none at all, with Sister Marie Joseph to escort
me, but, Adam, there are armed men in the port
and——'

'I know. I glimpsed them.'

'How did you pass unchallenged? It is so late. . .'

He nuzzled his nose against her hair. 'I climbed the
roofs,' he chuckled. 'It seemed the safest way.'

'You might have fallen to your death.' She sniffed
experimentally. 'What is that smell, Adam? I know we
have been on the road some time, but you washed at the
abbey and——'

He grinned widely and kissed her again heartily.
'River water, my sweet. It will prove necessary for me
to wash down thoroughly, I fear, before I can approach
your so sensitive nose again.'

'Swam the river?' Isabel's face paled visibly even in
the faint rushlight. 'The Ouse? But——'

'An old poacher showed me the way and I wasn't
prepared to wait till morning for a sight of you. I can
tell you now, it has proved worth it.'

'That may well be so, Sir Adam,' a stern voice reproved him from behind Isabel, 'but, betrothed or no, this is not seemly for you and Mistress Hatfield to talk so, she undressed and at this late hour.'

Gently Sister Marie Joseph moved Isabel aside and stood protectively in front of her, facing Adam determinedly.

'You should get some sleep, sir. Mistress Hatfield requires her rest.'

His black eyes sparkled as he bowed to her gravely.

'My pardon, Sister, you are quite right. The hour is very late.' He bent and kissed the nun's hand courteously then took both Isabel's and raised them reverently to his lips.

'Go, sleep safe now, my love, knowing all is well. Tomorrow I will tell you everything as we eat.'

Reluctantly he relinquished her hands as she smiled at him gamely, then she allowed Sister Marie Joseph to lead her into the chamber. He waited while the door was barred firmly against him then ran lightly down the stair to join the landlord, who was already setting out provisions for him on the well scrubbed trestle in the ale-room. Wryly he considered that the nun's dismissal was somewhat ill placed after he had not spent a night without sight of Isabel since he had brought her from her uncle's house in Newark. This one would seem unduly long, despite the fact that only a short flight of stair and a barred door kept her from him.

Adam spent the remainder of the night on the settle in the ale-room. He woke somewhat stiff, grimacing as he stretched, attributing his discomfort to the effects of his night swim and scramble over the rooftops.

Isabel looked as demure as she had done on leaving the abbey when she and Sister Marie Joseph joined him for breakfast. His heart raced at thought of that glorious hair now hidden from him under the severe wimple. Their eyes met and held meaningfully as he bowed low when they entered. Her fingers were caught and squeezed slightly. A delicate rose blush suffused her throat and cheeks and she glanced hurriedly at the friendly nun as she brushed by him to reach her place at table. He could think of little now but his longing to have her totally in his charge again and the ceremony in Burgundy which would make her completely his.

They all ate heartily. The rain had stopped and a watery sun pierced the dark horn window and lit up the little room. Jack Barstow and his amiable wife bustled about attending to their needs.

Isabel waited, however, until they were alone before questioning Adam about his plans.

He wiped his mouth after mopping up the last of the bacon fat with his bread trencher.

'Jack, our landlord, will go on board the *Lady Anne* to meet our captain, Job Redmayne. I saw the caravel tied up to the quay from the rooftop when I came in yesterday. I couldn't read the name on her bow, but I know her lines only too well. Job will be conveying a cargo of raw wool to the port of Damme. I haven't consulted with Jack about tides yet, but we should be able to sail later today. Once it's all settled you must go to the quay with Sister Marie Joseph and go on board. I'll follow within the hour. I shall go down to the tavern on the quayside, meet Job there, and board with him as one of the crew returning for duty.' He turned to the listening nun. 'Will you go straight back to Thorney, Sister?'

'I shall wait to see your ship safely out to sea, then I'll leave and report to Brother Eustace that all is well.' She beamed benignly at the two of them. 'I hope, Sir Adam, you will find a way to let us know when you are installed at the Duchess's court and——' she paused archly '—married.'

'We shall contrive it, Sister, never fear.'

The time appeared to pass slowly, though in actual fact it was only just over an hour and still well ·before noon before Master Barstow was able to inform them that everything was prepared for Mistress Hatfield to go on board the *Lady Anne*.

Again Isabel felt a terrible sense of loss at parting. She told herself fiercely that it was for a short time only and soon they would be safely on their way, but Adam obviously felt the same emotion as he held her very tightly to him before releasing her with a little push towards Sister Marie Joseph.

After they had gone, with Jack Barstow as escort, he busied himself sorting through the canvas bag he had brought from the abbey. The clothes he had worn to swim the river still smelt revoltingly of river water and he smiled to himself wryly as he thrust them and the blanket back inside again. The clothing had all been thoroughly dried before Jack's kitchen fire, but Adam would be glad to dispose of them once they reached his lodging at Malines.

He was whistling contentedly, waiting for the time when he also would leave for the quay tavern for his assignation with Job Redmayne, when he heard the ring of iron on the stone passageway outside and knew armed men had entered the inn. He had no time to draw his dagger before the door was unceremoniously jerked open and two of the men-at-arms he had seen on the quay the previous night marched in and took up positions on either side of the door.

Adam's brows rose questioningly, and he was quickly preparing himself to play the part he had assigned himself when another man entered, bending his brown head beneath the low lintel. The words of jovial greeting died on Adam's lips when he recognised the stern, unyielding features of James Tarvin. His eyes flickered to the device of the green chevron between three green dragons prominently displayed on the jacks of the men-at-arms. He had noted with some amusement when he had first encountered the family in Leicestershire that the three dragons vert showed their allegiance to the Welsh usurper. Last night he had not been able to distinguish the men's identity. He had been too far off.

He stood with his back to one wall, facing his rival, the bench he had overturned hurriedly on their sudden entrance lying between them. James Tarvin stood truculently, one gloved hand thrust into his belt, staring contemptuously down at his prisoner.

'So, my instincts were right. I was told a tall, lanky
pedlar had been seen in the district about the time of
my father's murder, and I was sure it was you. Then I
realised you must be one of Lincoln's creatures, treacherously spying out the land. I had enquiries made and
heard you'd sold your wares in Frisby, and I was sure
you'd make for the coast, *this* coast. Where else would
you be heading for on the way east?'

Adam shrugged slightly, but made no move. His eyes
were assessing the worth of the two men on guard.
Despite the fact that Tarvin was armed with sword and
dagger he was convinced that, had he been alone, he
could have handled the man, but three of them made a
much greater challenge, and, for the present, he was
prepared to wait.

Tarvin continued, his tone a distinct sneer. 'The more
I thought about it the more I thought you had come
here originally to draw Edwin Hatfield into your snare.
It was obvious that, when he was found to be absent
from his manor, he had gone to join the Simnel creature,
acting on information from you as agent.'

Adam continued to wait, smiling faintly.

'Oh, I didn't rely only on my instinct that you'd make
for Lynn, though it's well known to be a hotbed of
escaping traitors. I had men stationed at several of the
other ports too, but I proved lucky. It will give me the
greatest pleasure to hand you over to the King's men in
London, and see you drawn and quartered at Tyburn.
They'll, like as not, question you first, and not too
gently. You'll be lucky, you murderous dog, if you'll
manage to walk to the hurdle which will draw your
stinking carcass to the gallows. It will be some satisfaction to me to see you suffer as reparation for the murder
of my father.'

A voice, clear and steady, from the doorway behind
him arrested him in his diatribe and, with an oath, he
swung round to find Isabel, straight and still, facing
him, Sister Marie Joseph dithering nervously behind
her. Isabel advanced further into the ale-room. One of
the guards stepped forward as if to detain her, but she

flashed him an imperative glance and he fell back, discomfited.

'You mistake the matter, James,' she said evenly. 'Sir Adam Westlake did not kill your father. I did.'

Tarvin's brown eyes bulged uncertainly and he tried to speak but could not, completely taken aback by her revelation.

Isabel's eyes were on Adam, who bowed his head slightly. His own dark ones were narrowed and she knew he was silently imploring her not to make any further comments which could enrage James Tarvin and worsen their situation. She inclined her own chin very slightly and turned back to James.

'I saw some of your men on the quay and recognised the device on their jacks. I came back instantly to try to put matters right. I thought you would instantly jump to the conclusion that Adam was guilty of your father's death, and I could not allow you to continue to believe that. It was an accident, James. He attacked my father, who was already wounded, and they fought. I feared for my father, knowing him to be already weakened, and I tried to intervene. We struggled and the dagger fatally wounded your father. I am truly sorry. I shall never feel completely absolved of that act.'

James made a sudden choking sound and snarled, 'You lie to save this fellow? You, my betrothed, Isabel?'

'No, we are not and never were betrothed, James. I solemnly plighted my troth to Sir Adam Westlake at Croyland Abbey the day before yesterday.'

'The wish of that traitorous father of yours, I take it?' Tarvin's face was crimson with suffused blood. He was so furious that he had difficulty in framing his words.

'Sir Edwin Hatfield is dead. He died of wounds taken at Stoke field,' Adam interjected quietly, 'and is beyond any vengeance which could be inflicted by a malicious king. He was buried in the lay cemetery at Croyland.'

'So perish all traitors,' James grated. He turned reddened eyes on Isabel. 'I regret his passing, Isabel, but it is better for him, better for you.'

Again she inclined her head. 'Yes. I have to acknowledge that. And now that you know, what do you intend to do with us, James? Or is it *Sir* James now?'

'Aye, the king graciously knighted me, but that's all of a part. My duty is clear. This man is a self-confessed traitor. He must be conveyed to London with due speed.'

'And I with him.'

James hedged. 'The King will have to be informed. Your part in this sorry affair was doubtless forced upon you. I take it you aided your father in his escape from the field?'

'Of course I did, James. Would you not have done as much for yours?'

He brushed that consideration aside impatiently. 'You are a woman. Obviously you do not consider matters of honour and loyalty as a man does.'

'I consider very well how easily you put aside your professed love for me when you betrayed my father. You did do so, didn't you, James? Without your information there would not have been King's men waiting to arrest him at Hatfield Manor.'

'I suspected that he was heading for the rebels. I had my solemn duty to my King.'

'As Adam had to his.'

James stuttered awkwardly, 'The boy was a pretender, a peasant, even now in his rightful place in the royal kitchens.'

'And your King,' Adam said quietly, 'was a usurper who murdered his rightful King. Does it make it any more honourable because he won that battle at Redmoor by treachery?'

James reddened further. 'The rights and wrongs of that affair cannot come into this. Richard is slain and Henry is now our rightful King. You have plotted against him and must suffer for it. As for you, Isabel, you must keep silent about this shameful business concerning the killing of my father. It will avail you nothing to speak out about that.'

Isabel took her stance by Adam's side. 'I shall go with him and, mark me well, James, I *shall* tell my story.'

Angrily he came close and took her by the shoulder,
pulling her forcibly away from Adam.

'You will do what I say. Foolish woman, don't you
realise that, even knowing what I do, I shall make every
effort to save you?'

'Do not trust him, Isabel.' Adam's tone was urgent.
'If you are indicted, you will burn at the stake. That is
the penalty a woman pays for treason.'

'I swear I will save her,' James shouted. 'She must
keep silent. If I beg him to do so, the King will grant
me her hand.'

Adam gave a grating laugh. 'Give you the hand of a
traitor's daughter? You do not know your king very
well, Sir James. If you have any love left for Isabel, you
will let her go now into exile. You have me in custody.
What will it serve to see Isabel burn?'

James gave a hunted glance from one to the other of
them. He was clearly shaken by the ugly mental picture
Adam had drawn for him.

Isabel said hysterically, 'No, James, I beg of you. Let
Sir Adam go. You have no personal quarrel with him.
He had no hand in your father's death. I swear to you
by the Virgin's sacred name. If. . .' Her voice broke. 'If
you will let him go, I will. . .let you do whatever you
wish with me. I am virgin still. You must believe me.
However long the time before. . .before I must go
before my judges I will strive to please you, but. . .but
you must let Sir Adam go. If you ever loved me, James,
you will do this. . .'

Adam gave a great oath and moved to thrust his way
between them.

'In God's name,' James burst out at last, 'will you tear
my heart to pieces, the pair of you?' He gave Isabel's
arm an angry jerk. 'You love this man? You are prepared
to do anything to save him?'

She was sobbing, but she nodded vehemently. 'Anything, James; please——'

'You tell me you love this man and beg me to save his
life? Do you know what you ask? You would lie in my
arms, kiss me, while your thoughts are with him wher-

ever he goes? Do you think I am made of stone, Isabel?
Yes, I betrayed your father. I thought little of it—a man
does what he thinks he must—but I love you. I have
always loved you. I wanted you to promise yourself to
me back there in the church in Swithland. You would
not. Was it because, even then, you had thoughts of
love for this man?'

'No, James, the love I have for Adam Westlake has
come very slowly. He has protected me, cherished me.
He has placed himself in peril because of me. Had he
not remained to succour my father and me he would
have been long gone. Now I would do anything to
ensure his survival.'

'Aye, give yourself to me, a pretty sacrifice.' James's
tone was ugly. 'You betray our love and expect me to
save your leman. That won't do, Isabel. If there is any
chance of happiness for me it could only come about
knowing he lies in his grave.'

'Not just yet awhile, Master Tarvin.' A voice spoke
coldly from the open window behind him, and he swung
round, startled into sudden fury.

A man was leaning into the room, the casement
pushed wide. He had drawn his bow, and the arrow
pointed straight at James Tarvin's throat.

'Wat,' Isabel breathed. 'Oh, Wat, it can't be. . .'

'It is Mistress Isabel. You,' the groom snarled at one
of the guards who was about to start forward to come to
his master's aid, 'stand still where you are. Master
Tarvin has seen me often perform on a Sunday at the
butts. He knows I won't miss, that he'll be dead before
either of you can move a muscle to save him. Order
them to lay down all arms, Master Tarvin, and take
your hands from my mistress. Do it now.' The final
words were a snarl of fury.

James released Isabel so suddenly that she almost fell,
and lifted a hand to deter any action from either of his
men-at-arms.

'Do what he says. He means it. He's skilful with the
bow. He'll kill me and draw again and get at least one of
you as well before you can deal with him.'

The men sullenly obeyed him and James, keeping his eye steadily on the man framed in the window, slowly undid his own sword belt and let sword and dagger fall to the ground in front of him. He turned cautiously, holding both gloved hands up to reveal the fact that he was completely unarmed.

Wat called abruptly, 'Is all well with you, Sean, my lad?'

'Aye, all is well, Wat. The two men here are disarmed. We're coming into the ale-room now.'

The unmistakable Irish brogue of Adam's erstwhile squire announced his entry from the passage, with the landlord, Jack Barstow, behind him.

Sister Marie Joseph, who had been blessedly silent throughout these exchanges, gave a little low moan, crossed herself, and, murmuring a prayer to the Virgin, subsided on to a nearby bench.

Adam folded his arms, his dark eyes dancing with merriment. 'Well, Sir James, it seems the tables are turned. Now we must decide what we will do with you.'

Isabel had snatched up James's ornamental leather belt with its heavy sword and dagger and conveyed it to Adam, who buckled it on.

He grinned genially at the landlord. 'Have you a strong cellar, Jack?'

'Aye, Sir Adam, what innkeeper has not?'

'Then I suggest we dispose of Sir James's men there while we can consider our next move.'

Isabel moved to his side and placed a hand on his arm.

'What about James, Adam? Will you confine him with his men? You will not do him any harm?'

He shook his head, gently placing an arm round her shoulder.

'Never fear, my sweet. I told you once before I've done too much killing to indulge in it unnecessarily. Sir James, I must ask you to quietly join your men. We would regret to have to use force to compel you.'

James's lips curved in a contemptuous smile. 'I'll give you no trouble. Don't be concerning yourself.'

He walked proudly towards the ale-room door, where the landlord waited for him, brandishing one of the discarded swords. He turned in the doorway.

'You cannot get aboard your ship, you know. The quay is well guarded and so are all of the ports. If you truly love Isabel you'll take her inland and put her in a convent somewhere till she can plead for the King's clemency. As for you, you can go hang, for all I care.' He made a low bow to Isabel. 'God keep you and bring you to safety. I beg you to believe that I truly love you. The King has already granted me your manor. It was not for that that I wanted your hand.'

She gave a little sob. 'I know it, James. If—if times had not been out of joint and I had not met Adam— perhaps we could have dealt well together. God guard you, too, and grant you happiness.'

His brown eyes softened and he gave Adam a mock-salute before Jack Barstow bundled him out of the room and down the passage.

Wat and Sean faced Adam, who stood, brows raised in interrogation, before the window.

'What in God's name brings you two here? I had thought this young fool safe in Ireland before now. Not that you didn't arrive at a God-given moment.'

He hooked an overturned bench forward for Isabel to seat herself and gestured for the two men to sit also.

Wat glanced at Isabel, who nodded for him to explain.

'Well, we'd gone scarcely a dozen miles before this idiot here refuses to go another step. He declares he's determined to join you in exile any way he can and that he means to make for the East coast and work his passage on some merchant vessel. You'd charged me with his safe-keeping, Sir Adam, so I feels I must get him on board before I reports back to Sir Edwin. We had a mort of trouble getting clear of King's men but we managed it and I went to Croyland, since I'd heard you tell how they'd helped you there before.' He cleared his throat and, again, looked anxiously towards Isabel. 'There we hears of Sir Edwin's death and your intention to take Mistress Isabel to safety from Lynn, so we came on here as fast as we could.'

'And in the nick of time.'

'Ah, well, we saw these Tarvin men on the quay as well as King's men on the bridge and I knew we were in for some trouble.'

'You had no problems getting into the port yourself?'

'No, Sir Adam, I had a letter from Brother Eustace informing all and sundry that I was travelling to join my mistress who was bound for a convent in Bruges. He lent us horses or we would never have got here so soon.'

Isabel said, 'You wish to go with us, Wat? Won't you miss Leicestershire?'

'Aye, mistress, that I will, but no more than you will, I dare say. Sir Edwin knew he could always trust you to me, even when you was a small girl, and I reckon nothing has changed now. I managed to catch a glimpse of you with yon landlord chap, then you'd dived in here and we managed to catch up with him. He stops us dashing in 'cos we see these other Tarvin men outside and ——' he shrugged '—— we had to think quick and deal with them.'

Adam's lips curved into a grin of pure delight. 'I shall never forget James Tarvin's face when he saw you at the window and I could see him remembering how well you'd performed at the butts. The man is no coward, I'll grant him that, but he's no fool either, and had no intention of risking his hide pointlessly. The question is, what do we do now? It seems we are all gathered and in a fine trap. It can be but a matter of hours before Barstow's inn is raided again and we are taken.'

Isabel asked diffidently, 'Should we not do as James advised, Adam—try to reach sanctuary?'

He grimaced. 'And suffer as the Staffords did? I'm not likely to choose that route until I have abandoned all others.' He looked up as the landlord walked back into the ale-room. 'All secure, Jack?'

'Aye, sir, for the moment. You'll be excusing me?' He moved to the window and leaned out to examine the street. 'No armed men in sight just yet. We have to get

you all clear, Sir Adam, before they begin to miss Sir
James and his men.'

'How, Jack?'

'I know of a small cove some four miles south of
Lynn. I keep a boat there — for fishing, you understand.
If we could get you out of the port you could be taken
off in the boat and join the *Lady Anne* after she's sailed
some distance out to sea.' He glanced significantly at
Isabel. 'There's some element of risk. There's a fair
swell and getting worse, but I reckon it be your only
chance. Can you handle a boat? If I join you there'll be
too many of us, I'm thinking.'

'How can you warn Captain Redmayne?'

'That's no problem, Sir Adam; I can signal.' He
grinned, showing white, uneven teeth against the
weather-beaten darkness of his skin. 'We've used these
here methods before to bring in illegal cargo and live-
stock, if you're understanding me.'

Adam nodded. 'Certainly I do. Yes, I can row well
enough. It seems our best course, but what of you, Jack,
and your wife? Will you be safe here afterwards?' He
turned to the nun, who was listening quietly to what the
landlord had to say. 'And what of you, Sister? Will you
accompany us, for your own safety's sake?'

She pursed her lips. 'I think not, Sir Adam. If the
landlord can put me on a fair way of getting clear of the
port I can make my way back to Thorney without too
much trouble. I can be far more use to the cause here
than in Bruges.'

Adam hesitated. It seemed that he would try to
overrule her then appeared to think better of the notion
and inclined his chin, frowning. 'If I can be sure Jack
has a chance to avoid retribution, then we'll go at once.'

'We'll have to abandon the Star for a time at least,
but I've kin and friends who'll shelter us till times be
more settled. If I'm caught with you, it'll be the worse
for all of us, so we'd best gather what we need and leave
here quickly.'

It took them all only a short time to make their
preparations for departure. Very little could be taken in

the boat and Isabel's baggage must be left. She took
only a change of clothing packed in Adam's bag and the
remaining gold and her few pieces of jewellery. The
landlord was busied chivvying his wife into packing
what little they would take with them in their flight. He
arrived very soon to inform them he was ready to guide
them.

'We must go on foot. I've made arrangements with a
neighbour to return your men's borrowed horses to the
abbey. Yours, Sister, will be conveyed to Tilney, where
I will lead you after I've seen Sir Adam and his party
off.'

The nun rose briskly to accompany them. 'Don't
concern yourself about me, my man. I'm much hardier
than I look and the walk will do my figure good. I'm
with you.'

Apparently Jack Barstow and his wife had already
made their farewells to their friends and servants, for
the inn appeared deserted but for the men locked in the
cellar when he led them out through the back entrance.

'The cellar has a stout door,' he informed Adam.
'There'll be little chance of any of them getting free
until their company misses them and sends a party to
search all houses and properties in the vicinity. Even
then it'll take time to break down the door. We have
time to get well clear of here.'

He walked ahead with Wat. Isabel and the nun
followed and Adam and Sean brought up the rear. It
was now full afternoon and they had not stopped to eat.
The sky was still overcast and Isabel's heart began to
sink further as she thought of the ordeal ahead — that
small boat the landlord had spoken of. The hazards of
reaching the cove unaccosted disturbed her far less than
the thought of trusting herself to that great waste of
water, not even on one of the caravels she had glimpsed
but some cockleshell of a boat no larger than those used
to fish the Soar in her home county. She forced herself
to look round with interest, occupy her mind, show all
eagerness to fall in with Adam's plans. Once or twice
she turned to steal a glance at him. He smiled encour-

agingly, striding along, one hand close to his hidden dagger. He still wore his seaman's guise and he looked even more disreputable — unshaven, his hair unkempt — yet she could not think any man-at-arms on the look-out for nobly born rebels could fail to notice him.

Jack Barstow led them through the small town, deserted now, the cattle pens unoccupied, the market folk, having finished their trading in butter, cheese and eggs, already departed towards their own villages. One or two solitary folk trudged homewards from work in the fields. Several acknowledged Jack Barstow and did not appear to think it unusual for him to be in company unknown to them. Isabel thought people hereabouts were used to strangers heading for the quay and kept their own counsels.

Now they were leaving the town and were out in open country. Despite yesterday's rain, which had freshened the air, the road was hard-rutted after so many days of intense heat, and Isabel soon began to flag. Sister Marie Joseph was clearly uncomfortable in her voluminous and cumbersome habit. She was sweating profusely and finding it hard to keep up with the men. She walked on gamely until Jack Barstow turned and, noting the women's brave efforts to keep up, drew them off the road and into the shade of a small copse.

'We can rest here. We've plenty of time. The tide does not turn until evening and the rendezvous will not be for hours yet. Better to eat here than on the beach, where we could more easily be seen by search-parties.'

He produced provisions — bread, meat, cheese and a bottle of wine. Everyone was cheered considerably and sat munching contentedly in the green gloom.

Adam had reluctantly refrained from placing his arm round Isabel — not under Sister Marie Joseph's eagle eye. He leaned back against a tree bole and watched his betrothed thoughtfully as she ate. He detected an air of brooding concern in her which puzzled him. Through-out their journey they had constantly been in fear of discovery and arrest, yet now she seemed even more alarmed. Was she regretting the need to leave her beloved land and kin? Did she not, even now, trust him completely? He hoped and prayed she did. It was as well that she had Wat with her now, to reassure her that she had not lost everything dear and familiar. He longed to draw her into his arms, convince her that all would be well, that he would make her happy, but the presence of his companions forbade such conduct. Only when the marriage was celebrated could he bed his bride and finally consummate the match, and his body burned for that complete possession.

As the sun began to wester, Jack Barstow guided them across country, now towards the coast. The wind was freshening from the sea. Isabel could smell the salt tang of it, feel it on her face, tug at her hair, and she shuddered. To the west she could see the grim walls of Castle Rising, but they were too far away to be seen from the ramparts. Now they plunged into deep woodland again and after some half-hour of scrambling over rough brambles, heather stalks and gorse they saw the grey of the sea between the interleaving tree branches. Now they were clear of the trees and struggling over tall dune grass. Below them they could see a small cove and, stretching for miles to the horizon, The Wash itself. Isabel stopped dead in her tracks and Adam, coming up close behind, put a comforting hand on her arm.

'See that, my love. Freedom lies ahead. Only a few more steps over this difficult sand and you can rest.'

She smiled at him gamely, but her heart was pounding with dread which was not lessened when she saw the small boat Jack Barstow was pulling clear of a clump of gorse with the help of Wat and young Sean.

She clung tearfully to the kindly nun on parting.

'I shall see you again, I promise.' Sister Marie Joseph's eyes were misted with tears. In so short a time she had formed a special attachment to Mistress Isabel Hatfield. 'I come often to the mother house. I will send word to Malines and you can come and see me there.'

Isabel kissed her fondly and promised. The men had drawn the boat into the shallows and Adam was waiting to carry her down to it. She thanked Master Barstow for

all his help and the sacrifices he had been forced to make
for them and he shook her hand clumsily, then she
allowed Adam to lift her high into his arms and sit her
gently in the bow. The men were steadying the frail
craft and, as Adam gave the signal, they leaped aboard.
There was no sign as yet of the *Lady Anne*. She must yet
clear the harbour, but Jack Barstow assured them she
would already have cast off.

The die was cast. Adam and Wat, who had had some
experience at rowing on the river in Leicestershire, took
the oars and the boat moved into deeper water. Since
Jack was not to accompany them it must either be pulled
on board the ship or left to drift. Isabel stifled her
feelings of panic as she turned to lift her hand in parting
to the two, Jack and Sister Marie Joseph, left forlornly
waving their goodbyes from the beach.

CHAPTER TWELVE

ISABEL sat huddled between decks, her back against the aft castle of the *Lady Anne*. Before her loomed the gigantic forecastle, or so it seemed to Isabel. Adam was in close talk near the helm with the ship's captain, Job Redmayne, a Yorkshireman, who did not appear to conform in the least to Isabel's expectation of what a sea captain should look like. He was a small, thin, wiry individual, restless in movement and excitable by nature, she surmised. He and Adam appeared to know one another well, and the little party was warmly welcomed on board.

The journey in the small boat had been a nightmare experience. Isabel had cowered in the bows, clinging so tightly to the gunwales that her knuckle bones had gleamed white with the strain. At any moment she had feared the tiny boat would overturn, and she dared not so much as move a muscle. She had kept her eyes firmly from the towering grey waves which threatened to submerge the boat. Indeed, they shipped quite a deal of water, which wet the hem of her gown. Neither Adam nor Wat seemed to think that dangerous or even unusual and she had not wished to ask about it. Her whole attention had been fixed on Adam, who sat facing her, his muscles bunched in the thrust of the oars through the water. Behind him sat Wat, also intent on the unaccustomed hard task of rowing. Sean sat in the stern, hidden from her by the sturdy bodies of the other two, but she wondered if he was as terrified as she was.

It had seemed an age before Adam heartened her by declaring he could see the *Lady Anne*.

'It will be all right now, my love, I can see her rounding the harbour wall. We shall be safe on board very soon.'

Isabel gritted her teeth and managed to smile back at

221

him. The wind tore away any answer she was inclined
to make and she would have found it hard to find the
breath to do so anyway.

All at once the ship's sides towered before them and
shouts came from the main deck to give assistance.
Isabel could not believe that they would ever manage to
bring the bobbing cockleshell alongside safely and
steady enough for its passengers to dare to stand up, let
alone mount the precarious rope-ladder which was flung
overside for them, but it seemed that all that was
required was experience, and at last it was done. Wat
steadied the boat against the side of the larger vessel
while Adam lifted her on to the ladder and climbed up
close behind her.

'Don't look down at the sea,' he cautioned. Her hands
were wet with spray and she clutched desperately at the
swaying rope ladder, but determination not to shame
him forced her to doggedly make the climb, horribly
slowly, hand by hand, until strong arms reached under
her armpits and drew her safely on deck, where her
trembling legs threatened to give way beneath her.

Now she could see Wat and Sean leaning over the
port rail. The wind had got up and the hair of both men
was blowing wildly and they were clutching frantically
at their cloaks, which were billowing up about their
heads. Adam continued his conference with the captain.
Crewmen swarmed about the vessel, bare-footed, competent. No one seemed in the least alarmed that the
waves appeared to be getting so tall that she thought to
see them crash down on to the deck. She had donned
her own cloak and pulled her hood hard down over her
linen cap, but the wind tore through her so that her
teeth chattered. Never had she been so afraid, not even
when the man had borne down on her near the ford at
Fiskerton, nor in her desperate battle with Sir Gilbert
Tarvin for possession of the fatal dagger.

Sean leaned over the side and Wat laughed and patted
him comfortingly on the back. So Sean was being
heartily sick. Isabel was somewhat comforted that she

did not appear to be the only person on this ship totally out of their element.

Adam turned abruptly, nodded to the two near the rail, and came quickly over to where Isabel sat miserably.

'Well, all seems to be well. Job will put us ashore at Damme and our gold will furnish us with the means to hire fresh horses and provide for a night's accommodation on the journey. My darling,' he said hastily, concerned for the first time by her deadly pallor and the trembling of her limbs as she tried to stand, 'what is it? Are you sick, like poor Sean there?'

She shook her head vehemently.

'Are you sure? There is nothing to be ashamed of in confessing to seasickness. I was sick as a dog when I sailed with Duke Richard in King Edward's expedition to France in 1475.'

Again she shook her head, but her eyes filled with tears and her fingers clawed helplessly at his jerkin while her legs seemed about to give way beneath her again.

The captain, stopping briefly near the pair before descending to the hold to ensure the cargo was being kept dry, touched his forelock respectfully towards Isabel.

'Your lady looks very wet and cold, Sir Adam,' he said gruffly. 'Why don't you take her to the port cabin in the forecastle? I made arrangements for you to be accommodated there. No one will disturb you. Out of the wind and cold, she'll perhaps be able to sleep for a while. You've all of you been through much. It's rest you'll be needing. The wind's strong, but we're well on course. There's no real danger. If we hit trouble I'll send for you on deck soon enough.'

He moved off about his business, and Adam put a supporting arm round Isabel's shoulders.

'I think we'll take his advice.' He glanced back wickedly at the two by the rail. 'Wat looks like he has his hands full.'

He half led, half carried her to the companion ladder and down into the dim corridor below. It was growing

dusk on deck and the bow and stern lanterns already
kindled. An overhead lantern swung to the movement
of the vessel. Adam thrust open the door of the cabin
indicated and helped Isabel inside.

It was very small and Adam had to bend his head
constantly. A dim green light filtered through from the
little porthole and the place smelt of wet wool and tar.
Adam placed her on the narrow bunk, fumbled with
tinder and flint put ready on a scarred ship's chest, and
kindled the one lantern. Isabel gazed wonderingly round
the cramped cabin, trying to imagine how the crew
managed to do their work and then eat and sleep in such
insalubrious confinement.

A sudden lurch sent Adam reeling almost on top of
her. He was laughing as her questing fingers tore at his
sodden jerkin again.

'Steady there, nothing to worry about.'

'Adam,' she sobbed, 'Adam, I'm so frightened.'

'What?' He bent to peer anxiously into her fraught
little countenance. 'There's nothing to fear, Isabel.
There's a high swell running and a following wind, but
this is no storm. I assure you I've sailed with Job
Redmayne under far worse conditions and never
doubted him. He'll bring us safe to port.'

Still she clung to him, raising tear-wet eyes to his.
Her whole form was shuddering with fear and he sat
down beside her, drawing her head on to his shoulder,
where she sobbed out her despair.

'That boat—I thought—I thought every moment we
should be dragged down under those—those frightful
waves. Adam, I've never seen so much water. No sign
of any landmark. I'm so sorry—I don't want you to be
ashamed of me, but I can't help it. I——'

'Ashamed of you?' He tilted up her chin with one
gentle finger. 'Isabel Hatfield, you are the bravest
woman I know. Everyone is afraid of something, my
darling, and especially the unknown. I had forgotten
you had probably never even glimpsed the sea before,
born as you were in the heart of the Midlands. This
voyage is literally uncharted territory for you, but I

promise it will soon be over and you may never have to
face such a journey again.'

He bent and disengaged her clinging fingers. 'Your
cloak is wet, and doubtless your gown too. I'll leave you
to change. Ah, I see Job had my bag brought down
here. There's an old horse blanket to rub you down.
Once dry you'll soon feel fine again.'

'No.' Frantically she reached out to detain him as he
made for the door. 'Don't leave me, Adam. Please. . .'

She could not bear the thought of being left alone in
this floating coffin of a cabin. The wooden walls seemed
to be pressing in on her. Outside she could hear the
howl of the wind and beneath her feet she imagined
those broiling, terrible grey waves. No, if she was to
die, she could not face it without Adam. If he was to go
from her, even for moments, she thought she would
break down and pound at the cabin's stout door with
her fists. She needed him desperately, wanted the feel of
his strong, hard body close to her own.

He turned, a slight, puzzled frown creasing his brow,
then he smiled reassuringly and came back to her.

'I—I don't want you to go,' she ground out through
stiffened lips. 'I—I know it's foolish, but I want to see
you—near me.'

His laugh rang out. 'Very well, then. I'll have to play
tiring maid. Sister Marie Joseph would not approve
until the final knot is tied, but we are, after all,
betrothed.'

He undid the strings of her cloak, running his hands
gently through her loosened hair, wet from the salt sea
spray.

His dark eyes were dancing with merriment, then he
sobered suddenly and cupped her chin in his two hands.

'Don't cry, my sweet. You are quite safe with me.'
His lips were gentle on hers, and she gave a little
frightened sob.

'I'm—being very silly.'

'No. Everything is changing for you and the sea is
terrifying. I'll stay; never fear.'

She turned her back to him so he could fumble with

the unfamiliar hooks and lacings of her gown till it fell,
a sodden heap at her feet. She stooped and stepped from
it, retrieving it and throwing it to one side. His pulses
quickened at sight of the soft white skin at the nape of
her neck and the tangled glory of her hair. His breath
came fast as he prompted her hoarsely.

'Off with your shift. You're soaked to the skin. We
must rub you down lest you take cold.'

He towelled her roughly so that her ivory skin
gleamed in the faint candlelight, tinged with a softish
green glow from the one porthole. She resembled a
water nymph, Undine, straight and slim, her shoulders
bowed, her hair disordered, a silky red-gold cloud as he
rubbed it dry.

Her teeth had stopped chattering now and she gave a
little embarrassed laugh as he handed her a creased clean
shift drawn from his seaman's capacious bag. She was
feeling somewhat warmer now from the hard towelling,
and flung back her great mane of hair.

He was watching her intently and she was aware of
the pulse-beat at his throat, heard the sudden rasp of his
breath. Still he did not move to reach a dry blanket from
the bunk behind them.

She bit her lips uncertainly as he continued to stand,
close yet somehow still far apart from her. She was less
frightened now by the storm than the thought of losing
him. She was going into the unknown. Even if they
survived this nightmare voyage, what lay ahead of her
in this strange Burgundian territory? She had promised
herself, after their plighting of troth, that she would
leave him free — out of the great love she had for him —
but now his nearness, the overwhelming longing she felt
to have his arms close round her, proved her undoing.

She moved yet closer, lifted her face to his, reached
up her arms to his shoulders. Now she could feel the
quickened beat of his heart through the thin stuff of her
shift.

'Love me, Adam,' she murmured softly. 'I want you
so very much. I'm cold and frightened and I need
your warmth.'

He responded instantly, drawing her closer, his lips nuzzling her bright hair, breathing in the fresh salt-tanged scent of her.

'My little love,' he whispered, 'of course I love you. How could you doubt me?'

His arms were tightening masterfully round her waist. She gloried in her triumph. Now he would be hers. She would bind him to her with chains of love so that he could not bear to put her aside. She still smelt the river scent faintly on him, heightened by the sea's brine. Her lips tasted salt on the side of his neck where his hair was growing longer again now as she first remembered it, before he had had it clipped for battle.

Now he would lift her up and carry her to the bunk. They would lie snug in the dimness of the rough-hewn cabin and she would not be afraid of anything. She would feel safe, protected, until they docked in harbour. And Adam would be truly her husband.

She gave a soft little cry of surrender.

His body went rigid against hers, then abruptly he withdrew. She felt him gently but firmly put her from him.

'Isabel,' he said gently, 'you are exhausted and cold. You should try to sleep now.'

Her cheeks flooded with shamed colour while her body went icy. She stared up at him incredulously.

He was rejecting her! He could not — must not. She stumbled back from him and his arm came out again to steady her. It took all her resolve not to strike furiously back at him, but that would be to let him know how deeply he had wounded her.

She forced a smile through stiffened lips, though she longed to scream out her frustration and returned sense of terror.

'Come, let me lift you up. The wooden sides will hold you safe. You should try to sleep.'

Without waiting for her consent, he lifted her high and placed her down on the straw palliasse, wrapping the blanket round her shivering form. She tensed under his hold and jerked herself slightly from him. Two slow

tears rolled down her cheeks and she turned her head
away.

'I won't leave you,' he assured her and moved away,
out of sight, while he pulled off his own damp clothes
and changed into the spare set, still smelling abominably
of river water, but at least dry and comforting.

Isabel lay huddled below the musty-smelling blanket.
She had turned her face to the wooden bulwark that
formed the side of the cabin. Dear God, what had she
done? She had offered herself like a soldier's whore and
he had not wanted her. How could she continue to
remain in his company after this, knowing that he had
no more feelings for her than he might have had for
some casual companion? Less — he would have accepted
the rough comfort offered easily by some baggage-train
follower. Yet she must allow him to escort her to
Margaret's Court. It was necessary. How else could she
be assured of the Duchess's protection? But never again
must she reveal her true feelings. Sweet Virgin, she
prayed in anguish, do not let him touch me again, even
by accident or during the normal contacts of the journey
together, for I shall be entirely lost to all pride and beg
him to love me.

Adam stood, his lips held in a hard, pain-filled line.
Dear God, how he wanted her. She had confessed her
love and was willing to surrender herself. Now she must
feel totally rejected. She would never know how hard it
had been to put her from him, but to take her now, to
consummate the match, would deny her any dispensation later.

In time she might come to regret her surrender. Once
she was herself again, and able to realise fully the
meagreness of his fortunes and inability to keep her in
the way her father would have wanted, she might well
consider herself trapped. No, he would take her to
Margaret's Court inviolate. Once safe there, she could
choose freely. He could only hope that he had not hurt
her now so terribly, by his assumed rejection, that she
would not then turn from him in utter disgust.

He sighed, seated himself against the door of the

cabin, leaned his head back tiredly against the rough
wood, and kept his vigil, as he had promised. Eventually
her breathing became even and he knew she had silently
cried herself to sleep.

Isabel was bemused by the splendour of the streets of
Bruges where Adam took accommodation at an inn for
them. They had hired horses at the port of Damme and
rode on so that Adam could ascertain whether the
Duchess Margaret was in residence at the great ducal
palace.

The next morning he took her with him through the
busy, crowded thoroughfares to view the palace itself.
She stared about her entranced, not quite as open-
mouthed as Sean, but almost. Newark and Leicester
had been the only towns she had known and this thriving
metropolis was a revelation to them all, save Adam, who
had been here many times.

'Bruges is the headquarters of the main financial
exchanges,' he explained as they passed over one of the
many bridges over the canals. 'Wealthy merchants deal
here in exotic fruits and spices from the East, pomegran-
ates, oranges, dates, figs and raisins, as well as all the
costly spices.' He pointed to one of the open shop fronts
displaying an astonishing array of silks, velvets and
damasks which quite took Isabel's breath away. 'You
can see there some of the products of Damascus. The
craftsmen here are renowned the world over for fine
crystal vases, reliquaries and books. The Duchess has
one of the finest collections of books in the world.'

'Is she very learned?' Isabel enquired, awed.

'Yes, indeed, and deeply religious. It is a great pity
she bore no child to Duke Charles, but she has dedicated
herself to the welfare of her stepdaughter, Mary, though
now hostile councils have forced her to live away from
Bruges. Mainly she keeps herself to her own private
palace at Malines, which is some twenty kilometres
outside Antwerp. We shall most probably find she is
there, but we will call first at the ducal palace here for
news of her.'

'How long has she been widowed?' Isabel asked. She was anxious to know as much as possible about this great Plantagenet princess who had married Charles of Burgundy and now had the reputation of being one of the most celebrated and glittering figures of the western world.

'Charles was killed at the Siege of Nancy in January 1477, so she has been widowed close on ten years now. She was but thirty-one years old then.' Adam sighed. 'She is still lovely; I think you will agree when you see her. It is hard to remember that she is now forty.'

'Her husband's death must have been a great blow to her.'

'I think so. They were said to be very fond of each other, though she remained, disappointedly, barren. He was killed by a terrible blow to the head during the course of the battle, and his body was hideously disfigured when he fell from his horse. It was two days before any news of him reached Margaret. The body was so hard to recognise. She informed her brother, Duke Richard, that he was identified by his Italian valet, who declared him to be the Duke by the inordinate length of his fingernails. Later, when the body was conveyed to the nearest house, his doctor, a notable Portuguese physician, confirmed the identification by the battle scars on his person. Margaret was plagued afterwards by the neighbouring states and nobles inside Burgundy which fomented war and insurrection for their own purposes. There was the continuing war with France. I think, from her letters to her brothers, she hoped that King Edward would send an army to come to her aid.'

'And he did not?'

'No. He had his own problems by then—constant quarrels with his brother, George of Clarence, and you know what mystery concerns the fate of his son, young Edward. Then, of course, George was finally indicted and executed in the Tower in 1478. Margaret must have been deeply grieved by that. Richard was heard to say once that George had always been her favourite brother. As I said, Margaret was greatly attached to her stepdaughter, Mary, who was only just twenty when her father died. Margaret was even accused of attempting to arrange a marriage between the Duchess Mary and George and was forced to flee to Malines then. Mary, most curiously, also died from a fall from her horse, while falconing, so Margaret was doubly bereaved. She left her two young children in Margaret's care — Philip, who was only four, and Margaret, who was just two. Civil war broke out in Burgundy and in 1483 King Richard, as he then was, sent help to Mary's husband, Maximilian. I was a member of that expedition and met the dowager Duchess Margaret for the first time.'

Isabel speculated on the trust that had been placed in Adam by his sovereign. No wonder Adam had been well received by Margaret when, later, he had been forced to flee from England after Redmoor.

By now they had reached the ducal palace, and all that Isabel had seen before in the streets paled into insignificance beside the glories of this ancient building. They entered the outer of the two courtyards through an arch facing the superb princes' hall, which Adam told her had been built to house the august Order of the Golden Fleece. Later she was to view the magnificent hall, one hundred and forty feet long and seventy feet wide, with two great upper galleries, the large windows all glassed in. Behind the throne dais hung a wonderful tapestry displaying the arms of Burgundy, the colours gleaming splendidly in the light from the great windows, splashes of purple, black and crimson. Isabel stood and marvelled. Surely the whole of her own manor house could have been accommodated within this awe-inspiring building.

Adam left her within one of the antechambers while he made his enquiries, returning very soon after.

'I was right. The Duchess *is* at Malines, so we will start off this very afternoon.'

Despite the delay in meeting this princess who held their very destinies within her hands, Isabel could never be sorry that she had visited this stupendous palace set inside so fascinating a town.

Before leaving Bruges Adam insisted that they buy
Isabel new gowns in which she could be presented, for
certainly her own two now bore the stains of sea-water
besides the dust marks she vainly tried to brush away.
Isabel averted her eyes from the glorious, jewel-like
colours of the silks and damasks, reminding Adam that
she was now in mourning for her father. She chose two
gowns of fine silk, for it was still hot, one in black,
embellished with silver brocade, and another in dove-
grey. Once at Malines she would abandon her linen cap
and wimple for a stylish hennin, which also she would
drape decently in black veiling. Adam forbore to buy
anything, saying he had other garments at his lodging.
Isabel handed over her travelling gown to the inn wench
at Bruges for further cleaning and pressing and then
redonned it for the ride.

On the journey Adam regaled her with tales of the
wonderful ceremony and tournament named, for ever
afterwards, the Tournament of the Golden Tree, performed to honour Margaret when she had first come to
Bruges as a bride.

'Naturally I was not present—it was long before my
acquaintance with Duke Richard—but the stories of
some of the household at Middleham who had been
present kept us entertained for many a long night. It
was such a glittering event that it will always be remembered, I think.'

More and more Isabel was becoming nervous about
meeting so grand a lady as Adam's Duchess was reputed
to be.

The sights and wonders of the journey to some extent
occupied her temporarily, so that she could put aside
from her mind the embarrassing happenings of the night
on the *Lady Anne*.

How could she have behaved so wantonly? Was Adam
so disgusted that he could not bring himself to give an
open display of his avowed affection? Obviously he too
had been embarrassed by the incident, for since they
had landed he treated her with undoubted respect,
almost deference. Fearful of further rebuff, she had

retreated within her own reserve and not again given any hint of her great love for him. Neither had mentioned the affair in the cabin and Isabel had judged it prudent to keep silent. Now the urgency of the ever present fear of arrest was banished, she was growing steadily more alarmed about her own future. Everything in Adam's world in this strange country showed her that he was used to a grander life than she had suspected. Even at the palace in Bruges, dressed as he was in that appalling seaman's disguise, he was treated with courtesy, almost subservience. Apparently he was well known here and a man in whom the Duchess placed much trust.

On arrival in the pleasant town of Malines Adam conveyed Isabel and the two men to his lodging. Here he had two rooms overlooking the River Dyle. Sean and Wat disappeared into a nearby inn where they would stay until Adam could make suitable permanent arrangements for them. Isabel was surprised by the air of prosperity and cleanliness of the paved streets. Adam left her in the bedchamber to change into her black court gown. An elderly woman tapped and, on invitation, entered, ushering in a fresh-faced girl of about fourteen. The two bobbed curtsies.

The girl spoke in hesitating English.

'Madame, my name is Clemence. My mother is — how do you say? — Sair Adam's landlady. He has asked me to come up and — ' she stumbled for the correct words ' — aid — assist you to change, if you will accept me?'

Isabel smiled warmly at the two of them. 'I would be very grateful, Clemence. I'm afraid I speak little French and — '

'*Ma mère*, she speaks hardly any English, but Sair Adam, he speaks some French, so we — how do you say again? — manage.'

'I see. Will you thank your mother for her preparations?'

Clemence spoke rapidly and the woman beamed and went out. Isabel could hear her talking in rapid French to Adam in the next room.

After washing in warmed water scented with mar-
joram she donned the gown with Clemence's assistance
with awkward hooks and sleeve fastenings. The girl
stepped back and clasped her hands in rapture.

'Madame is fortunate that she has the so lovely red
hair. The black is not so dull on her, *hein?*' She deftly
placed the now almost unfamiliar hennin and draped the
sombre black veiling to her satisfaction, then she curtsied and followed her mother.

Isabel stared at her reflection in an old, scratched iron
mirror Adam had fixed to the wall. The girl was right.
Black looked well enough on her, complementing her
fair skin and hazel eyes. She had expected her complex-
ion to have darkened like a gypsy's after she had spent
so many days on the road, but she still managed to look
Sir Edwin Hatfield's daughter. Only a pale band of red-
gold hair showed before the velvet frontal of her hennin,
but it did make a vivid splash of colour against the
darkness of her robe. She put on a simple locket
inherited from her mother's small collection of jewels
and emerged into the outer chamber to find Adam much
changed.

He, too, had made a hasty toilet and put on a doublet
of blue velvet and grey hose. One would have to look
very closely to see that, at collar and sleeve cuff, the
velvet was rubbed, but he had obviously in the past
taken pains to see that his garments were cleaned and
pressed regularly, and he looked every inch a courtier.
To embellish the doublet he wore a heavy gold chain
with a pendant bearing his Westlake arms in gold,
silver, and blue enamel. His dark eyes lit up at sight of
Isabel and he bent and, taking her hand with a courtier's
flourish, kissed the tips of her fingers.

'Well, here we are, after our dubious adventures,
elegantly clad once more. My felicitations, Mistress
Hatfield; you are finely garbed for presentation to Her
Grace.'

The two Burgundian women had made their exits
from his living chamber, and Isabel caught at Adam's
hand convulsively.

'I am so nervous. Couldn't we delay this until the morning?'

He shook his head. 'Alas, no, my love. It would be quite unsuitable for you to stay here with me, or even at the inn without a maid. I must petition the Duchess to lodge you at her palace until we are married. I'm sure she will find a place in one of the dormitories assigned to her younger ladies-in-waiting.'

The idea disturbed Isabel further. She could not imagine being abandoned by Adam in some grand house with strange ladies whose language she could not speak.

The Duchess's palace at Malines proved to be considerably less grandiose than the ducal palace at Bruges and infinitely more comfortable. She was to discover later that the house had been bought by Duchess Margaret from the Bishop of Cambrai and considerably enlarged. It was her favourite residence, bult in red brick with an imposing façade and several large, glassed windows facing the road.

The two were admitted by members of the guard, who acknowledged Adam with smiles of pleasure and conveyed them to an antechamber of the state apartments on the upper floor.

Since there were several people there waiting audience with Her Grace, Isabel was greatly surprised when an elderly man bearing a white wand of office came to summon them to the Duchess's private apartment.

Isabel could not help stopping in the doorway to stare around her in wonder. The walls of this elegant chamber were hung with violet taffeta and, again, she noted the richness of eastern carpets beneath their feet as well as the large, glassed windows and finely carved furniture. At Adam's prompting, she swept a deep curtsy as he bowed low, then he took her hand and drew her forward.

The woman seated in the upholstered chair beside the window to get the best of the light for her embroidery was still exceedingly beautiful. She was dressed in the height of fashion in a gown of purple silk, her butterfly hennin, in the English style, set well back from her finely featured oval face, showing a band of smooth fair hair with no trace of grey to mar it. At her side sat a lady who looked considerably older but was, probably, of an age with the Duchess. At sight of Adam Margaret rose in greeting and Isabel saw that she was tall for a woman and remembered that her brother, Edward, had also been tall and so handsome that men had called him the 'Rose of Rouen'.

Margaret's hand was extended to Adam, who bent and kissed it.

'Thank the Good God, Adam; I feared we had lost you, too. The news I had from England has been all bad — poor John of Lincoln killed and Frank Lovell disappeared without trace, the boy in Henry's hands — and, as the time went on, and no sight of you, I thought the worst.'

Large grey eyes surveyed Isabel. 'And pray, sir, who is this? Have I suffered some anxieties for you only to find you stopped for dalliance along the way?' The words were lightly spoken and there was no trace of disapproval in the voice, which was low and mellow and reminded Isabel of Brother Eustace's mellifluous tones.

Adam turned to Isabel. 'Allow me to present to you, Your Grace, Mistress Isabel Hatfield, the daughter of Sir Edwin Hatfield of Leicestershire, who died of his wounds taken at East Stoke. Mistress Isabel is my betrothed.'

Again Isabel curtsied. Her head was lowered, so she did not see the Duchess's change of expression, but her hand was taken gently and she was raised to meet the Duchess's expressive grey eyes.

'My dear, I am so pleased to have you here at Malines. My condolences on your terrible loss.'

'Thank you, Your Grace.'

Adam said quietly, 'Mistress Isabel was instrumental in helping us escape from the battlefield, and her healing skill ensured my recovery from wounds taken there and later. Unfortunately she could not save her own father. Events became so pressing that it was necessary for her to flee her home. I felt sure you would receive her.'

'Adam, you know I am only too glad to do so. Betrothed, you say? Is this very recent?'

'We plighted our troth at Croyland Abbey before Brother Eustace and wish to marry as soon as possible.'

The Duchess nodded graciously. 'Since you are not yet wed it seems proper that Mistress Hatfield should remain in my household until the ceremony.'

'I was hoping that could be the case, *madame*.'

'Good, then that is settled. Have you a maid, Mistress Isabel? I imagine not, since you two were forced to leave England under hazardous conditions.'

'No, Your Grace; I left my own maid, Bess, with my aunt in Newark.'

'Then we must arrange for some peasant girl to attend you. Perhaps you could see to that, Philippa?'

The maid-in-waiting nodded smilingly, but Adam said quickly, 'I think Clemence Subrous, my landlady's daughter, would be willing to come here and wait on Isabel until we can make permanent arrangements.'

'Excellent. Philippa, I'm sure Mistress Hatfield would prefer a room of her own, however small, rather than be lodged with total strangers, and foreign strangers, to boot. Could you take her to Monsieur Olivier and confer with him about this matter while I talk with Sir Adam about events in England? Return in an hour with Mistress Hatfield so Sir Adam can be acquainted with her lodging before he departs for his own in the town.'

Isabel was anxious not to lose sight of Adam, but the Duchess's voice, though gentle enough, was clearly imperative, and the woman rose, swept a curtsy, and moved to the door to see Isabel out of the chamber.

The Duchess sank back in her chair. 'It is true, then, all is lost? Can we retrieve anything from the débâcle?'

'Not at present, Your Grace. It is my belief that those gentlemen still loyal to our cause would be best advised to remain in hiding until the realm has settled again.'

'You had no news of Frank Lovell?'

'I fear he was drowned in the Trent, *madame*. He was last seen in full armour swimming the river. We may never know the truth about his fate.'

'But, surely, if Henry has not declared him dead, we can hope?'

Her luminous grey eyes were lifted to his pleadingly.

He shrugged slightly. 'He may well have made for Oxfordshire and home, where faithful servants would, doubtless, hide him, but — many men who fled the field discarded their armour and armorial devices. Lord Lovell might have been killed in the retreat and his corpse not identified.'

The Duchess nodded slowly. Only too well, she knew that could be so.

'And now, Adam, this lovely girl? Are you determined to wed her and is she truly willing?'

He hesitated, and her gaze sharpened. 'You offer marriage because you feel she is compromised and helpless in a foreign land?'

'No, Your Grace, I love Isabel Hatfield with all my heart, and her father, I know, would have approved the match, but. . .'

'But?'

'I have so little to offer her.'

'Tush, man, you have security of service in my household. There is much work for you to do; not, however, in England, for a considerable time at least — I would not have you risk yourself again — but in training some of my household men-at-arms and squires, and, later, acting as courier for me overseas. We shall see, but I do not offer charity, my stiff-necked young friend. I value your services highly, and,' she added drily, 'you'd do well to marry your lady swiftly. She will be a brightly plumed bird among my doves and my gentlemen may see her as a prize to be won from you, lack of dowry or no.'

Isabel soon settled into the household at Malines. Clemence Subrous proved a competent and friendly maid and the Duchess's ladies were kind. She saw Adam constantly, for he spent most of his time at the palace, waiting on the Duchess, in training sessions in the courtyards and at the quintain where the young squires,

Sean among them, frequently bit the dust when they rode at the swinging board, endeavouring to hit it full centre and avoid the heavy bag which balanced it striking them from their mounts. Isabel often sat with the other ladies, watching their progress.

Only one among her companions caused her some heart-searching. For the most part the Duchess's ladies were of an age with her, but one, the Countess de la Foix, was considerably younger and radiantly beautiful. Once or twice Isabel had noted the lovely, dark-haired Countess exchange knowing glances with Adam, and realised they had been more than friends during his previous attendances at the Duchess's court. The Countess was lady governess to the late Duchess Mary's children. Isabel burned to question Adam about his relationship with the strikingly handsome and witty woman, but could not find the courage to do so. Fearful of learning more than she wished, she remained miserably silent. Despite his duties, Adam was attentive to her, and their marriage was arranged for the fifth day of August.

The Duchess took a personal interest in the matter of the wedding-gown.

'This will be the last Yorkist wedding I am like to see — for some considerable time, at least — and I insist that you forsake your mourning and wear a gown of my choosing. Your father would wish it, I am sure.'

Isabel agreed, though she was doubtful of the propriety of such conduct, even wondered if it was proper for her to marry at all before her year of mourning was ended. This suggestion, too, the Duchess rejected.

'Nonsense, my dear. In the circumstances you and Adam should wed as soon as possible. You are not having second thoughts about this match? I would not have you coerced.'

'No, no, Your Grace; I love Adam truly, only——'

'Then that is settled.'

It was the Duchess's favourite expression. She was certainly unused to having her opinions disregarded, and Isabel meekly went along with her plans.

'I shall make you a present of the gown. My late brother, Richard, sent me a gift of brocade for the last Christmas of his reign. Somehow I have never fancied to have it made up. It would bring back so many unhappy memories — his death, and his Queen's. . . There.' She brushed aside the thought. 'He too would have been delighted to see such finery worn by the bride of one of his favourite gentlemen, and it will please Adam mightily.'

Isabel felt sure it would, and exclaimed over the beauty of the fabric when the Duchess's dressmaker came to measure her for the elaborate bridal gown.

All seemed to be going well, yet a niggle of doubt often ran through her, especially during the hours of night, when she lay in her cot in the tiny chamber Margaret's master of the household, Monsieur Olivier de la Marche, had provided for her, Clemence sleeping contentedly on the truckle-bed beside her. The Adam she had known and loved seemed very different to her here, where he was accepted as an accomplished courtier, flattering the Duchess's ladies shamelessly, dressed far more flamboyantly than she had ever known him, and very sure of himself in a world where she seemed totally out of water. Only Wat seemed unchanged, reminding her of the quiet, untroubled life at Hatfield. Adam had obtained a place for him in the palace stables, where Isabel was able to see him regularly. When she rode out in the Duchess's train, it was Wat who proudly lifted her into the saddle and rode behind her in attendance.

Her worst fear appeared justified only one week before her appointed wedding day. She was watching Adam play tennis with another of the Duchess's gentlemen of the chamber when a young page presented himself and spoke urgently in Adam's ear. Adam straightened quickly and looked up to where Isabel sat in the gallery, then he donned his discarded doublet and hastened to her side.

'Isabel, something has occurred which makes it

necessary for me to leave Malines for a while. Will you come with me, please, to the garden?'

Isabel rose immediately and accompanied him. The palace gardens were extensive and very well kept. She remembered, fleetingly, that she had once walked in her own humbler gardens at Hatfield Manor with James Tarvin and he, too, had told her he must leave her. A stab of homesickness caught her and she turned to find Clemence falling into step behind them.

Adam stopped in the shade of a small rose arbour and took both Isabel's hands within his own.

'I regret, my dearest, that I must leave you so near to our wedding-day, but I know you will have so much to occupy you that you will hardly have time to notice my absence.'

Isabel looked into his dark eyes searchingly. She had seen that same page who had summoned him so abruptly from the game in attendance upon the Countess de la Foix. Dared she ask him directly what the business was that connected him with the noted beauty?

'I don't understand,' she faltered awkwardly. 'What is this? You told me the Duchess did not intend to send you into danger again, that——'

He avoided her gaze. 'Yes, I know. There is nothing to alarm you. I shall be back very soon.' Then he turned and looked at her intently. 'Isabel, I cannot tell you why I must leave you. As in so many times in the past, I must ask you to trust me without question. Will you do that?'

She bit her lip uncertainly, her eyes misting with sudden tears. 'Yes. . .'

'My little love, I know you must be feeling very strange and lost here, but the Duchess will guard you well and we shall very soon now be married, and cannot then be parted. Kiss me, Isabel, and tell me you will think of me every moment we are apart.'

She laughed shakily. 'I love you, Adam. I am no court lady to hide my true feelings with clever badinage. You know that I shall count the moments until you are by my side again.'

He kissed her hard on the lips, lifting one hand to
smooth the beloved red-gold band of her hair. Her
answering kiss was as hungrily demanding, also revealing to him some measure of her own bewilderment. He
raised her hand to his lips again and then he turned and
left her, walking hurriedly towards the palace entrance.

Isabel stood for a moment, biting her lip to hold back
the sobs she dared not utter, then she nodded to
Clemence and followed more slowly.

Unwilling to rejoin the other ladies, in no mood for
the usual cut and thrust of witticisms between them and
their avowed swains, she retired to her own room. If
excuse was necessary she would declare a need to change
her gown, having caught the hem and snagged it on a
trailing rose stem.

Clemence saw that her mistress was distressed, but
had no words of comfort. She had seen Sir Adam's hasty
departure and wondered if the two had quarrelled.

Isabel moved listlessly to the window and pushed the
casement wide. It was then that she saw Adam about to
mount in the courtyard and caught her breath in a hard
gasp of despair, for beside him, on a prancing palfrey,
was the Countess de la Foix. Behind her, also reining in
a restive mount, was another page whom Isabel had
never seen before. The boy was perhaps fifteen or
sixteen. Even mounted, as he was, she saw that he was
tall and fair and held himself well in the saddle, handling
his mount with consummate skill. Adam turned briefly
to see if the boy was managing and, looking up, saw
Isabel at the window. He raised his hand in salute. The
boy followed his gaze and Isabel saw he was indeed very
handsome, with curling fair hair under his velvet cap,
an oval face and large, light eyes either blue or grey.
The youthful lips curved in a smile and Isabel furiously
closed the window with a bang. How dared the insolent
boy smile so knowingly at her discomfiture? So Adam
had pressing affairs, so pressing that the Countess de la
Foix and her pretty page boy must accompany him?
That excuse was nonsensical. If Adam were on urgent
business, he would be riding alone and in disguise or

accompanied by Sean. She walked hastily to her bed and, sinking down on it, allowed herself the solace of angry tears.

The days following seemed very long to Isabel. Outwardly she appeared happy and eager for the coming wedding ceremony, and preparations for it continued busily. Inside she was seething with resentment and even wondered, bleakly, if all this was for nothing, and Adam would not return to her. Her thoughts turned more and more often now to her home in Leicestershire. How were her faithful servants faring under James Tarvin's rule? She swallowed hard as she thought of James. He must realise now that marriage between them was totally unthinkable, and she hoped and prayed that he would have found the strength to forgive her for his father's death. He had poured no words of bitter fury on her head when she had revealed the truth to him. He had been borne up by his bitter hatred for Adam and his belief in *his* guilt. The knowledge of Isabel's was followed by the need to deal with the rebels and his desire to save her. Her heart ached for him. She knew now that she had never truly loved him, but she would always remember him with warmth. Many times when alone she had sighed for the events of this terrible year, which had cost her her father's life and separated her from all that had been dear and familiar. Yet if the rebellion had not occurred Adam would not have come to Hatfield and she would never have known the bitter ecstasy of love.

On the morning before her wedding she was summoned to the Duchess's library. Here were kept her celebrated collection of illuminated manuscripts behind elaborate wrought-iron grilles specially constructed to guard them by one of the town's many skilled craftsmen.

The Duchess was seated in a comfortable chair, a book of hours in her hand. She pointed to a small padded stool near her feet.

'Ah, Isabel, come and sit down. I wanted to hear an English voice read to me. There are times when only

English will soothe me, and poor Philipa Clare has a severe headache, brought on by heat, I imagine.'

Isabel's French had vastly improved over the last weeks and, as she had a quick ear, she was acquiring a small vocabulary in the Flemish tongue spoken by many of the palace servants and lesser officials. She sympathised with the Duchess's need. Sometimes the babble of foreign tongues outside her door seemed unbearable to Isabel, too.

'Gladly, *madame*.' She sank down on the stool indicated and waited to be informed of the Duchess's choice of literature.

Instead, Margaret remained silent for a moment, then she stooped and lifted Isabel's chin with one slim finger.

'Philipa tells me she discovered you weeping yesterday when you thought you were unobserved. Is it that you miss Adam so terribly? Isabel, he will be home either tonight or tomorrow. Can you not wait for that?' The pleasant voice was gently chiding.

'Yes, *madame*.' Isabel's answer was whispered, and the Duchess's smooth brow creased in a frown.

'There is something more. I asked you once before if you had regrets. We are not hurrying you into this marriage against your will?'

'Oh, no, *madame*, it is just that——'

The Duchess stemmed the eager tide of explanation. 'Just what?'

'I am afraid that—that Adam does not love me.'

'Child, he is head over heels in love with you.'

'But,' Isabel stammered, 'I saw him leave the palace with—with the Countess de la Foix.'

'Ah, Louise de la Foix.' The Duchess made a little sibilant sound, almost a whistle. 'I see.'

'There was a page with them. The boy smiled at me as if. . .as if to mock me, *madame*, and——'

'So you saw the boy,' the Duchess said musingly. 'A fair boy, tall, very like me?'

Her luminous grey eyes were regarding Isabel now with a strange intensity.

Isabel stared back, then her lips parted in a little gasp
of understanding.

The Duchess's mobile lips broke into a smile. 'If he
smiled at you, it was not in mockery, Isabel Hatfield.
He had been told of your father's part in this recent
struggle. He honours both his memory and your courage. There was no mockery in his smile, Isabel; I assure
you of that.'

'He was — is. . .'

'My nephew, Dickon of York, yes. He visits me very
occasionally, when we feel it is safe for him to do so.
But these visits must be brief. There are spies of Henry's
everywhere. It was time for him to return to the care of
the Bishop of Cambrai, where he lodges for a while until
he must move on again. Like you he misses familiar
scenes of home and dear companions. A page
accompanying his mistress is no uncommon sight and I
trust Louise de la Foix with my dearest secrets as much
as I trust her with my beloved Mary's children. I
thought it best for my bravest knight to escort them. I
regret that Adam was forced to keep the truth of the
matter from you. Now it seems I must reveal it. You
can be trusted never to speak of the matter again, at
least to no one but Adam?'

Isabel's thoughts were racing. Yes, she recalled that
Adam had once told her of the younger of the princes.
He had seen him, he'd said, here, then at the Duchess's
court. No wonder this duty came before all other
allegiances. How proudly he had repudiated the slur of
murder on the memory of his late sovereign lord. It was
true Richard of York lived. Where, then, was his
brother, Edward? Had he perished in Henry's hands or
had some other means of survival been found for him?
Both boys were illegitimate, if the Bishop of Bath and
Wells was to be believed, yet, even so, both had stronger
claims than Henry Tudor. Dear God, was she to fear
another deadly plot tearing Adam from her side? Yet
her heart sang at the knowledge that he was true to her.
She had only to wait for his return. Even if her marriage
must be postponed, she would do so now, gladly.

The Duchess touched her hand gently. 'I do not fear any hazards along the way. He will be back in time.'

'Yes, *madame*.' Isabel turned a radiant face back to her.

'Do not fret, child. Richard is over-young yet, and the time is not ripe. We shall not be requiring your betrothed's services in combat for a long time yet.' The Duchess spoke briskly. 'And now I think you should walk in the gardens for a while, put roses in your cheeks. Adam will not wish to claim a bride who looks wan with pining.'

'But I came to read to you, *madame*.'

'Well, yes, but I think I can manage for myself. My eyes are not yet too old.' The words were drily mischievous and also a dismissal. Isabel rose and curtsied, then ran joyfully from the room.

Clemence was waiting, round-eyed with delight, when she reached her own chamber later that afternoon.

'He is back, Mademoiselle Isabel, Sair Adam. Sean has just been with the news. He does but change his clothing and will be with you.'

Isabel flew to her own clothing chest to put off the black gown she had worn all day in favour of the dove-grey one.

He was there to escort her to supper in hall, looking somewhat tired and a little strained around the eyes, but glad to be home and eager to see her. There seemed little opportunity to talk in the crowded, noisy hall, redolent with the smell of roasting meat and spicy sauces. Before the last remove was placed before them he had dragged her out to the scented coolness of the garden.

There he drew her hungrily into his arms. 'You are so beautiful; I can hardly wait till tomorrow.'

Her arms stole round his neck and she burrowed her face in the soft warmth of his velvet doublet, then she withdrew slightly and looked up at him mischievously. 'And did you find travelling with Louise de la Foix exhausting?'

He reddened and she laughed aloud. 'I but tease you,

my love. The Duchess revealed the identity of the Countess's page.'

His eyes widened and she nodded. 'I was, perhaps, just a little jealous. She is very beautiful.'

'Is she?' he asked ingenuously, and she gave him a little push which set them both laughing, then he sobered.

'The prince is safe with friends. He wanted to know all about Stoke and I told him of your father's sacrifice, also the loss of Frank Lovell, whom he knew very well. He was much saddened. He will do well when the time comes.'

Isabel did not wish to speak of that, and she drew him to the rose arbour, where they sat in wondrous silence listening to the sounds of music from the hall, then the coming of the night creatures. She did not want him to go and clung to him a little hysterically when he rose to lead her back to her quarters.

Clemence had almost completed robing Isabel for her wedding the next day when the Duchess swept in with Philippa Clare in attendance. She drew her charge to the window to gaze critically at the gown, then she gave a little sigh of satisfaction.

The overgown was of white samite, overlaying an undergown of white brocade embroidered in gold thread with the Yorkist symbols of rose and sun in splendour. The fashionable deep V collar, which Isabel privately thought came so low as almost to be shameless, but for the cloth of the gold modesty vest, was also of the same rich fabric. The gown, with its tight, long sleeves, cuffed with the same priceless brocade, sheathed her slim young body to perfection, then flared into generous folds and train. So full was it that Isabel had had to practise walking, the fullness bunched high in one hand to reveal the beauty of the undergown, and also kneeling gracefully, under Lady Philippa's tutelage, Isabel's glorious red-gold hair fell free to her waist, signifying maidenhood, crowned with a simple garland of white roses and lilies.

'So,' the Duchess murmured, 'you are the true

Yorkist bride and a credit to Adam.' She slipped a small gold cross on a golden chain round the girl's neck as a final gift, then signalled for her steward of the household, Olivier de la Marche, to enter and lead Isabel to her private chapel.

As she stood beside Adam in the incense-scented gloom before the ornate altar Isabel prayed silently that her father would look down on her from Heaven and grant her his blessing. Adam wore a fine new doublet of tawny velvet which suited superbly his lean darkness. The candlelight gleamed on the ebon smoothness of his black hair and caught the richness of gold and enamelled white roses on the chain which lay across his shoulders. He spoke his responses clearly and proudly and, though her mouth was dry, Isabel responded in the same vein. She was in a daze of mingled awe and delight when they rose from the nuptial mass to be fêted in the great hall.

The Duchess had determined to spare no expense in honouring her loyal agent, and one rich dish followed another in great profusion. From the gallery above, the Duchess's musicians charmed the ears of the company. Isabel hardly knew what she ate, though she shared cup and plate with Adam and drank with him from the loving cup. She dreaded only the final boisterous ceremony of bedding, and took little note of the good-humoured, bawdy encouragement to the groom. At last it was time. The Duchess rose with her ladies to accompany the bride to the door of the bridal chamber. Isabel found her legs were trembling as her eyes caught those of her maid, seated below the salt.

Adam had been granted a small property within the grounds of the palace. There he could accommodate his squire, Sean, Clemence and her mother, who would cook for them when they wished to eat away from the hall, and Wat, who would sleep above the adjoining stable. Isabel was content with this small haven of privacy apart from the court.

Clemence undressed her and left her seated in the half-testered bed, then the Duchess, her chaplain, and those ladies who could crowd into the room entered.

There was a great deal of laughter, gentle teasing and some giggling. The Duchess shooed the ladies from the room while her chaplain blessed the bed and chamber. She bent and kissed Isabel full on the lips.

'I wish you and Adam great happiness, my dear.'

Her eyes were bright with unshed tears as she made her departure, her attendants in her wake.

Isabel sat, dry-mouthed with anticipation, her ears strained for the first sound of Adam's foot on the stair. Through her mind swept the memories of his rejection of her in the cabin on board the *Lady Anne*. How had she upset him? Had she been too forward? She must not make that mistake again. Yet she longed for him so terribly that she could not play the frightened virgin tonight, when she wanted to give him every joy.

There he was at last. He was calling laughing comments to his friends, who had insisted on escorting him to the house. She heard the outer door bang and the sounds of bolts being drawn. He had refused to allow them entry into their chamber, then. Isabel lay back against the pillows, her heart pounding. Outside her door she heard him whisper something to Clemence, then he had pushed it open and paused on the threshold to look across at her.

She leaned forward, straining in the half-darkness to see his features. Was he truly eager for his bride or were his protestations of love in the rose arbour yesterday merely conventional phrases designed to quell her doubts?

'Isabel?' His voice was a trifle hoarse.

She was silent, then she said doubtfully, 'Adam?'

She heard him make some inarticulate sound, then he came to the bed. His eyes glittered in the candlelight as he gazed at her, her wonderful red-gold hair falling on to her proud, taut young breasts.

She felt suddenly very awkward and, sitting forward, linked her hands round her knees to stop them trembling. He was undressing hurriedly. She heard the clink of his ornamental chain and the buckle of his sword belt as he flung them aside on to the clothing chest, then he was beside her, drawing her into his arms, laughing throatily.

'Dear God, Isabel, how I've had the patience to wait so long I shall never know. I thought I would never rid myself of those fools below.' His lips were on her mouth, forcing her own apart so that she felt she would not be able to breathe. She allowed him to lower her gently back on the bed and he leaned close, his breath soft and wine-laden, and she could see the pulse at his throat beating rhythmically. She swallowed hard and immediately he sat up and looked anxiously down at her.

'Do you truly love me, Isabel?'

'Yes, Adam.' Her answer was the merest whisper.

'Do you trust me?'

Her lovely hazel eyes were looking back at him fearlessly now, huge in the soft golden glimmer of the flame.

'I would trust you with all I love, with myself — with my very soul.'

'Then you are not afraid?'

She smiled regretfully. 'Just — just a little.' Then more hurriedly, 'Afraid I shall not be able to please you.'

His laugh rang out in the quiet little room. 'Then we have nothing to fear.'

'But there have been other women — more experienced than I.'

'You are still thinking of Louise de la Foix?'

'Yes, and — and there must have been others, beautiful court ladies. . .'

'And most of them whores,' he commented drily. 'Nor would one be fit to unlace your shoes, Isabel, nor look so breathtakingly lovely.'

'But——'

'But? Do you doubt me, Isabel?'

Her lips trembled. 'No. It is just that. . . On the ship, Adam, what did I do wrong? Didn't you want me?'

'Want you?' He stared at her incredulously. 'God knows it took every ounce of my self-control not to have taken you there and then.'

'Then why. . .? We had plighted our troth. . . I had

feared you did not really love me, that you had wed me
only to please Brother Eustace, or because you had
sworn to my father that you would protect me.'

'I have so little to give you, Isabel — no land, not even
an honourable name which is not tarnished by the slur
of alleged treason. I wanted you to be free to choose.
There are men here at court who would fall under the
spell of your beauty and wed you despite your lack of
dowry. I rely on the Duchess's bounty, little enough
security for the woman I have sworn to protect with my
life. Now Margaret has promised she will keep me
within her household, you will be safe enough, and I
know, if the worst comes to the worst, she will ensure
your well-being.' He gave a wry little twist of the lips.
'In all events, when it came to it I could not give you
up. I need you more than my soul's salvation.'

Her heart sang a paean of joy. Now she was sure he
loved her she could not fear anything.

She opened her arms to him with a little rapturous
cry. Though she was now eager for him and unafraid he
wooed her gently until the very moment of taking. His
lips claimed hers again, hard, demanding, then slid
lower to her throat and the soft roundness of her belly
so that she moaned low in her throat.

There was pain, certainly, and then ecstasy such as
she had never known nor dared to hope for. She
surrendered herself to him completely, so that it seemed
that they fused to a perfect whole, body and soul. She
gave a great shudder of delight, arching back from him,
her lovely white throat, touched with the golden
shadows of light, strained for his kiss.

His fierce black eyes softened and tears touched the
sooty lids. He had not dared to hope that he might
possess her, claim her as his till their lives' end.

'Ah, Isabel,' he murmured haltingly, 'I can never be
truly worthy of you. You are so lovely, brave and loyal;
wife, companion and comrade-in-arms. No man could
expect so much treasure in one lifetime. You have given
up everything for me. Had you chosen James Tarvin,
you could have redeemed Hatfield.'

'I have everything I want,' she said and kissed him fiercely to silence him. 'I thought I loved James, but that seems so very long ago when I was a child and did not understand such things, nor had I met a resourceful, loyal knight who risked his life for a wounded friend and a foolish girl who hadn't the wit to obey him.'

He chuckled low in his throat. 'Had you always obeyed me, lass, I might not have known your true worth.'

Then there was no more talk. His body claimed hers again and she gave herself up to this new wonder of fulfilled love.

She lay in the warm darkness after he slept. Indeed, she had everything she craved. Tonight he had brought her to the very pinnacle of happiness. She loved this loyal, landless knight with all her being and she would go with him even to the fringe of the battlefield itself if fate would have it so. She had thought this hazardous journey had taught her to leave childhood behind and become completely woman, but this had not been so until the moment Adam had made her totally his, and her body glowed with the joy of understanding and commitment.

They had their devoted servants with them. Adam had told her yesterday that he had sent word to Job Redmayne in Antwerp that all was well with them. Brother Eustace, at Croyland, would be first to receive the news and he would contrive to see that her Aunt Cecily was told and dear Sister Marie Joseph. Perhaps eventually James would hear and be glad for her. She had never wanted to hurt him and hoped he would find a woman to love who would be a gentle mistress for her household at Hatfield.

She gave a little yawn, stole a contented glance at the beloved form of her sleeping husband, then snuggled down beside him. His strong, lean body was now as familiar to her as her own. Instinctively, still in sleep, he drew her possessively close, one iron-hard arm tightening around her waist, imprisoning her within the circle of his grasp.

LEGACY *of* LOVE

Coming next month

HIDDEN FLAME
Elizabeth Bailey

England 1797

Miss Theodosia Kyte knew she only had herself to blame for her present dire circumstances, but her only alternative was, she felt, totally closed to her. So as a companion to the old tartar, Lady Merchistan, she made the best of a bad job – until Mr Benedict Beckenham arrived to visit his godmother!

Because of his scandalous background, Benedict's aim was unqualified acceptance by Society, but for that he needed to marry money, and Theda did not qualify, despite his passion for her! Impasse – until that arch manipulator Lady Merchistan put the cat among the pigeons...

ONE LOVE
Valentina Luellen

Atlanta 1864

Shanna de Lancel, though orphaned by the progress of the American Civil War, was more fortunate than most, for she had her faithful servant, her money, and the friendship of Alexander Amberville, who took them to his plantation *Wildwood*. Shanna welcomed the peace, so was all the more unprepared for the arrival of Rafe Amberville – the son and heir, but at odds with his father and brother Wayne! Only slowly did it dawn on Shanna that she was a pawn in intrigue she did not understand, but who was she to trust? Wayne – or Rafe...

LEGACY of LOVE

Coming next month

DEVIL WIND
Catherine Blair

France 1789

High on the cliffs overlooking the sea, Devil Wind castle loomed dark and foreboding. This was Rochella's new home – and she knew instantly that her husband, Lord Devlin, was equally unhappy with their arranged marriage.

At first sight of his enchanting bride, Devlin longed to defy his name and its burdens. For Rochella's safety, he must keep theirs a marriage in name only. Yet, how long could he run from the need to love her as his heart demanded? Spellbound with desire Rochella would soon discover the dark secrets that cast their shadow on a man who had sworn never to love.

ODESSA GOLD
Linda Shaw

USA 1897

Genny Carlyle wasn't sure she trusted Odessa Gold. The man was an ex-convict and a gambler, and who knew what else. It was true – she didn't really have much choice. Yet there was something about Odessa that made her want to follow him, no matter where he led.

Ten years in an Arizona prison had hardened Odessa against the lure of innocent young women. So why, then, did he find himself wanting to take on Genny Carlyle's battles and fight them for her? With Genny, there was a bright future up ahead, but his past was quickly closing in on them, and the time to turn and face the darkness had finally come.

TWO
HISTORICAL ROMANCES
&
TWO FREE GIFTS!